PRAISE FOR *THE SOU[...]*

"I read *The Sound of Rabbits* with a growing sense of recognition and love for Ruby, her family, and the others in her orbit. As in her past and forthcoming work, Janice Deal tenderly nurtures the bonds between reader and character with her great empathy and keen understanding of what it means to be alive. In *The Sound of Rabbits*, Deal offers a moving portrait of one family's hopes, disappointments, and sorrows in a voice that is unflinching, achingly poignant, and unforgettable."

-Katherine Shonk, author of *The Red Passport* and *Happy Now?*

"*The Sound of Rabbits* is a heartfelt novel of fragile love between sisters, estranged through distance and grudges, striving to find their bond, even if they don't have the words to express it. With keen insights and spot-on descriptions, Janice Deal animates her novel with characters from a small town in Wisconsin where parents struggle to make ends meet, children seek their passions, nature is cruel, and the past is never really past. An unflinching, yet loving, portrait of a complicated family."

-Jan English Leary, author of *Thicker Than Blood* and *Skating on the Vertical*

"At the heart of Janice Deal's new novel *The Sound of Rabbits* are two sisters: one who stayed and one who fled. Val, in a sad marriage with two daughters, remained in their small hometown, and Ruby, who got away, hides her disappointments and failures. The two are brought together as their mother approaches death. Re-enacting old conflicts and finding new ones, each woman seeks solace from the other, and refuses it. Deal weaves together the two sisters' stories, present and past, with those of their mother, Val's girls, Val's silent husband, Len, and others they touch in their small town, creating a luminous web in which each interwoven life is a strand that sets the entire web shaking and shimmering. With a lovingly sharp-eyed grasp of the particularities of small town northern Wisconsin, with an uncanny ability to probe the dark and conflicted interiors of her characters, and a poet's way of conjuring layers of emotion with a few perfect words, Deal has written a novel that resonates long after the last lines are read. *The Sound of Rabbits* is a deeply affecting and powerful novel."

-Lynn Sloan, author of *Midstream, Principles of Navigation,* and *This Far Isn't Far Enough*

"Janice Deal's *The Sound of Rabbits* is a lyrical, deeply affecting novel about family, loss, and the ties that bind us to the places we're from, even when we think we've left them behind. After Ruby gets a call notifying her that her chronically ill mother has taken a turn for the worse, she heads to the small Midwestern town where her sister, old flame, and memories of her past live on. Using multiple points of view, Deal immerses us into a vividly rendered town in which the residents share their deepest secrets, while asking us to consider: how to live joyfully, knowing we'll eventually say goodbye to those we've loved, and those who have loved us the most. That question, along with Deal's elegant prose and memorable characters, ensures that *The Sound of Rabbits* resonates long after the final page."

-Marcie Roman, author of *Journey to the Parallels*

"These are small-town people—some sprung but drawn back, some stuck, some contented enough—trying to live their best lives even as so much happens to make them wonder what that is, or even if there's such a thing. Janice Deal writes them into life with such subtle artistry and grace that it's easy to forget that these aren't your own people, hard not to feel firsthand their every pang of love or loss or hard-won recognition. Their frailties and strengths alike, their successes and failures, are the author's triumph: beautiful, moving, and—for all their seeming everydayness—unforgettable."

-Ellen Akins, author of *Home Movie, World Like a Knife,* and others

THE SOUND OF RABBITS

Janice Deal

Regal House Publishing

To Marion Apollo
To David

RUBY

Concert

She was going to be a musician. Slim, accomplished, married
or an approximation thereof. She'd thought, leaving Ladyford
behind all those years ago, that she was close, so close; success
as she saw it was only a matter of taking the step out, and up.
Of cracking life open and sucking out the juice.

But here is George, with his broad laughing cheekbones and
waxy skin. "You are born to HR," he says. Just like that. In
his agency office with the tilted ceiling like a New York City
garret, it puts Ruby in mind of the starving artist and what she's
read about young bright things making do—Patti Smith, for
instance, didn't she sometimes skip supper to buy art supplies
when she was twenty and hungry and living in New York? But
there is really no room for artists here.

"I've done my best," Ruby says, wanting to sound pleased,
half of her already thinking who she might call with the news.
Because she knows what's coming. She's good enough at what
she does. She would have called Drago, before he moved out.
Her mother, who would be happy if she believed Ruby was
happy, can't hear her on the phone, and in any case, Barbara has
been so confused.

"You've done more than that," George says warmly. He is
the agency owner's son; Ruby can never remember his title. Later she will recall it: COO. "The way you handled those layoffs
last quarter...brilliant." When George smiles, Ruby sees his
gums. "The directorship's open."

She'll call her friend Lorna, Ruby decides. "I'm honored,"
she says to George.

~

But on the L ride home she sits by the window and regards her reflection, almost green in the glass. It is November and darkness comes early; this is the time of day when things catch up to her—how her face sags in the black glass, and the way the new executive assistant cozies up to the men on staff and has, so far at least, given Ruby only the most perfunctory attentions—and it is only when she gets home, and sees the Kimball upright, dark walnut, with its figured grain and yellowing keys, that her heart lifts. She dials up Lorna.

"Yes! The concert is tomorrow night," she says. "It'll be like a Paris salon. Just a little bit of Bach, that's right. Cheese. Wine. Uh-huh. Paris in Chicago." Ruby has chosen Bach's *Italian Concerto* because of its energy and joy. Barbara, Ruby's mother, had told her years ago that you have to act the way you want to feel. Well.

Ruby hangs up and can't think why she didn't mention the promotion to Lorna, who would be thrilled for her. She's that kind of person, happy enough herself, and so happy for others. But Ruby's been planning this concert for weeks—just that word, "concert," releases something yielding and optimistic inside herself—and that's what Lorna asked about. That's what they've been talking about, over lunch and on the phone, Ruby excited and messy and exuberant at the thought of reconnecting with her music.

"It used to be a huge part of my life," she'd said to Lorna just yesterday. "The music." They routinely met for lunch at a café in the West Loop.

"Well, it ought to be again. I haven't seen you like this for months," Lorna said approvingly, and Ruby hoped she'd mention that to their friend Jim, too, because Jim works with Drago at the architecture firm; the two men are friendly and it wouldn't hurt Drago to know that she's happy. That she can be happy still.

࿇

Ruby never went home after college. She stayed in Madison for a while, in a two-bedroom ground-floor that she shared with a girl who, like Ruby, had gotten her degree in performance. The girl's name was Kate; she played her harp at wedding receptions. Kate was dating a guy who painted landscapes, and when he moved in it was easier to manage the rent. Ruby waited tables, but then Kate got her a gig playing weddings and she didn't have to be a waitress anymore.

ॐ

"I invited Drago," Ruby had confided to Lorna, at lunch.

"Wow." Perhaps Lorna was thinking about the nights after Drago left, when Ruby ended up at Lorna's place, weeping. The bottles of wine they had killed off, dissecting the relationship and determining that Ruby was better off. The stupid movies they had watched back to back.

"He might not even be in town," Ruby said. "He's been doing a lot of work in San Francisco."

"Didn't you say he's never really been interested in your music, Ru?"

"I just wasn't doing music when we were together, that's all. Maybe I should have been. He likes that DJ."

ॐ

"I'm living the dream," Ruby used to say, and she meant it. That was a happy time. She liked Madison, she liked her roommates, and when the local Chamber Orchestra invited her to play Mozart's Piano Concerto no. 20 in D minor, what she thought was, *This is it.* The wedding gigs were fun at first, and for a long time she really believed that her career job, when it came, would be in an orchestra.

Ruby was patient; she practiced every day. While she waited for the call that would launch her career, she painted the kitchen of the rental. The landlord said she could. Primrose, the color was. She didn't take her time, and the paint went on thick and messy, like Ruby herself, but Kate and the landscape painter professed to be pleased.

∾

"DJs just play other people's music," Lorna said stoutly at lunch. "You're having your own concert now."

"There's no reason why we can't be friends, right? Me and Drago?" Ruby was eating a sub sandwich big enough for two. The flowers on the table were aggressively pink, with crunchy-looking stems. They annoyed her, and she pushed the vase to the side.

Lorna reached out to keep the vase from toppling. "It wouldn't hurt him to see you in your element," she finally said, and then the two friends had looked at each other and laughed, wickedly.

"No," Ruby agreed. "It wouldn't."

"Did you call him?"

"Naw. Email." Ruby didn't mention that sometimes she *has* called Drago in the last few months, or how that went.

And now that she's invited him, Ruby feels anxious. She hasn't heard from Drago; she doesn't know if he plans to come. She made it pretty clear. The DJ with whom he's living right now? She's not welcome. What if he came and brought her anyway? Thinking of this, she stands at her kitchen island and uses chopsticks to scoop up noodles. She had picked up takeout Chinese on the walk from the L and, as usual, ordered too much.

So what? she thinks. *So, I'll have leftovers.* She sucks at the noodles and makes herself plan how she'll set up the living room: four short rows of chairs, enough to accommodate the friends she's invited, and the guests they might bring. The settee, too, for Lorna and Jim, who love each other but don't know it yet. Ruby is jealous of them, of the eager looks they share, but the concert will be about her.

She has been practicing for weeks, and each time she sits at the little upright she is reassured. Uncle Moon got her this piano, secondhand from the Hartmans when Nan, their youngest, left for school; he's the one who cleaned it up. Disassembled it in the barn, labeling all the pieces so he could put them back together later. Moon had an engineer's mind. He used an evil-smelling paint stripper to get down to the veneer; he added coats of gloss tung oil and when he was done the instrument glowed as if lit from within.

Screw Drago, Ruby thinks. He can come or not. She starts unfolding metal chairs and creates neat rows facing the piano. When that's accomplished she takes a seat near the back. She has been saving a pound bag of peanut M&Ms and she holds it against her chest now; when she dips into the bag and surveys the orderly chairs, she feels strong and good. The candy lulls her, but later, when she goes to bed, sleep won't come. Perhaps it is the chocolate. Or the Chinese food. Ruby wants tomorrow night to be a success and she wants Drago to know about it, whether he comes or not. Perhaps from Jim, who is a gossip.

Ruby has invited a lot of people. She has a lot of friends! The cards and texts she gets on her birthday now. The cards she would get after this promotion becomes public. No one would suspect that sometimes she is afraid—of growing old, alone—or that she has made a list. *MIP (my important people)*, it's called, and she keeps it secret on her phone. *MIP*. A list of her connections, and since her split with Drago, if too much time goes by, she calls a person from the list or emails them. She makes plans. Coffee or a movie. A gallery opening. Some people have to be on the list—you have to include family. But then there are people like Lorna, her heart friend. The list, which she draws from when she plans her concert, reassures her and fills the empty places. She has friends! More than she had when she was a girl.

"I heard you had a good turnout," Ruby imagines Drago saying. Or, conversely, "I'm glad I came. You sounded terrific." After the concert, he might be inspired to call Ruby, late and quiet so the DJ he's living with now doesn't hear. When Ruby and Drago's relationship was in its death throes, Drago used to get up in the night and talk on his cell in the kitchen, near the windows where the connection was good and where he imagined Ruby couldn't hear. He was a great slab of a man and his throaty laughter always gave him away; straining in the dark, Ruby could hear him mock her favorite shirt, a frilled moss-green blouse that she loved because she'd gotten it on sale at a store she probably otherwise couldn't afford. "She is not—how you say? Beautician? Good with the clothes?" The next morning Ruby, unloved, made coffee, pretending that she had slept through his betrayals.

But if he called this weekend, after or about the concert, the DJ might hear; she might be sick with jealousy. In the dark heart of night, Ruby smiles. Who knows? Maybe Drago is thinking about her right now. Maybe he'll call her tonight.

And when he does, she'll tell him about the promotion. He is impressed by titles; when he asks her if it comes with a raise, she'll be able to say yes. Ruby flips her pillow over and the other side is cool.

VAL

The C Word

She loves late fall, its stubborn refusal to be beautiful. Outside the great expanse of window glass at the IGA grocery where Val works register, the last of the season's leaves, brown and curled, skid before the wind.

"It's a day, ain't it?" Mousy Pam Robinstadt is making her daily grocery run, loading up on the meat her husband insists upon. Val's husband, Len, works out there at the Robinstadt place—he's been roofing the barn—and he says the man demands three squares a day. "The Mister," Pam calls him, not his given name, which is Bill. Len has told her Robinstadt is a jackass, but he's Len's boss right now, so Val makes an effort to be friendly when she sees the wife. Besides, Pam's nice. Sad. Nice. In her fifties now, she squanders her nurturing on Bill, her kind face marked by sorrow; she mothers her garden, which is beautiful and orderly; she makes her daily trip to the IGA.

"Winter's coming," Val agrees, weighing the little parcel of brussels sprouts, the plastic bag with just two potatoes. The Robinstadts have never been able to bear children, though it's widely known Pam always wanted them.

"How are your girls?" the woman asks. For a split second Val stiffens—has there been talk about Dakota?—but then she registers the woman's shy smile and figures that Len probably mentions their daughters when he's at work.

"Ah, they keep me on my toes," she says.

"And your mom?"

"She loves her candy!" Val says brightly, which is true enough. "I expect that's where my girls got their sweet tooth!"

Pam nods and pays; she takes her time loading the two little bags into a wire cart she brings each day, but after she shuffles out, pushing the cart before her, the store is quiet and filled with gray light. Val likes this time of day, the stillness of it, and she leans against the counter, letting her smile slip. She's tired, wanting nothing more than to get through her shift and head home. Bobby, the youngest of the store managers, and the cockiest, strides by, snapping his fingers. "Look alive!" he says, probably trying to be funny. They aren't supposed to sit on the job. They are supposed to find something to do.

Val, who always has something to do—at home; for Mom; at her other job, the cafeteria at the high school—has been finding herself losing some momentum these past months. She's always been rigorous in her habits, but something has crept over her lately: a dullness of spirit. But she nods to Bobby and moves to the windows, meaning to wipe them of fingerprints; pressing a clean rag to the glass, she watches two girls walk past. Bedraggled, hair unkempt; the little one skips to keep pace with the older. The elementary school has instituted a policy where kids can walk into town for lunch if they have a note from their parents. These girls must be on such a mission; the older holds a carton of chocolate milk, and for a breathless moment Val thinks it's her own daughters, caught unaware. Dakota and Junie are growing so, leggy as colts, with Dakota so pretty, dangerously pretty with her pale heart-shaped face. Val sees a mat in the little one's hair.

"Hey!" she caws at the window glass, but when the girls turn to look, it isn't her daughters at all; in fact, Val cannot imagine how she ever made the mistake. The older girl wears glasses and she moves languidly, with nothing like Dakota's hard, angry step.

Dakota. It was the age, wasn't it? Thirteen going on twenty. Though Dakota has never been like Junie, who is a pleaser, genuinely sweet. Junie clowns to make the adults smile. Dakota has never been sunny; she is dour like her father, who is a musician, or was. A good one too. He traveled as far as Des Moines for gigs; he went over to the Twin Cities. Dakota has Bryan's nutmeg hair, red lights in it; she has his crinkly hazel eyes. She is blessed with her parents' good looks, and Val sometimes thinks Dakota must wonder why only Junie favors Len so.

The hand with the rag drops to her side. She needs to spend more time with the girls. Reading, maybe. Children deprived of stories grow up prisoners of their own boredom. Someone said that to her once. Her mother? Before she got sick? Val stops, thinks, shakes her head. No, not Mom. Carrie, probably, from when they used to hang out.

"We paying you to stare out the window?" It's Bobby again, arms folded across his meaty chest. No attempt to seem funny now. "Why don't you take your break now, since you seem to have started it anyway?"

He's ten years Val's junior. She nods and hurries to the back of the store, past an old woman studying the shelves of cereal and a guy, Sooner, who was in high school with Val's sister. "Val?" Sooner smiles at her. Everyone says he makes meth; he usually looks like hell, and today is no exception.

"Hi, Sooner." The man's face has a queer pallor; it's probably the drugs. His hair is hidden under a dirty knit hat. She nods at him tersely, glancing into his cart and half expecting to see it loaded with decongestants, though there's just a pound of hamburger and some bread. He's a handyman or something, Len's told her, and there is some stupid talk about a worm farm, though the meth lab is likely closest to the truth. Val glances into his sunken eyes; on a better day she might feel bad for him. He's six years older than she is, from a time before, a time Val missed. "I'm going on break. Sorry. Can't talk." She sweeps past and doesn't look back. Three more hours and she'll be done for the day.

It's chilly in the break room. Val pours a cup of coffee and lets herself eat one of the day-old donuts the managers leave out for staff. Val's usually careful about what she eats, but the sugar will give her a lift. When they moved her mother, two years ago, and sold the farm, Len used to buy donuts every Saturday. "To keep us going," he'd said, and though she'd complained that it was bad for the girls, too much of a good thing, the sweets did sometimes cheer her up.

She takes a bite of donut. Jelly, a little stale. She sits down and is still chewing when she hears a cell phone ring. Her purse hangs on a peg by the door, and Val gets up to fumble her phone out of the inside pocket. It might be Mom, or one of the staffers from Cedar Manor. Mom's been having a bad week; something about a rash.

"Sorry, Val, hon." It's the gravelly voice of the school secretary. "Joyce asked me to call up."

Joyce is the principal at the girls' school. At first Val is so relieved that it isn't Mom, calling about red spots in hard-to-reach crevices, that it doesn't register: a call from school, during the day. Not good.

"Is Junie okay?" she asks in a rush. Junie is such a spaz, always wiping out on the playground. Her knees are routinely plastered with Band-Aids. Last spring she broke her arm falling off the monkey bars. Val calls up the image of the little girl skipping past the IGA, hair like a nest of sticks.

"No, sweetie. It's Dakota."

Dakota. Tough Dakota. There is a pause while Val considers this. "Is she okay?" Val asks finally. She doesn't want to examine too closely the second surge of relief: Junie was all right.

"Oh, she's fine, all right. Raising hell, though. Joyce asks that you come get her."

Val throws away the unfinished donut and sits down again with a sigh. This is the second time she's had to get Dakota from school this fall. She closes her eyes. "What happened." It isn't a question, the way Val says it.

"Oh well, honey, I guess Dakota got to cursing on the playground. The C word. For girl," the woman, whose name is Bonnie, Val now remembers, adds helpfully. "Can't have that with the little ones around, you know?" Her Wisconsin accent makes it sound like she says "you nuuuuuu." Bonnie has a beehive hairdo, dyed the yellow of straw, and chapped red hands.

She's not a friend, but she's not a bad person, either; right now Val hates her.

"I'm on my way," Val says. She hangs up and stares at the wall. The principal, for god's sake.

༃

Bobby gives her grief, as she might have expected, but Val isn't about to interrupt Len in the middle of a job. Robinstadt may be a jerk, but he pays well and he's kept Len on, one job leading to the next, because Len's steady. Val lets herself into the Cutlass and decides not to call him. He doesn't know what to make of Dakota these days either. She used to be different, Len will remind her. And when was the change? Between fourth grade and fifth? When *did* Dakota's good cheer wear out, like a—what would Moon have said? A bad gasket? When did she stop drawing her mama pictures of suns with crayoned smiles?

Outside, the air is dank, the day's light muted. There's a cold wind coming from the west, and it breathes the decay of damp leaves, of muck that can only be black, not green. Val wishes she could call her mother, who has seen it all; she has always known what to say to her daughter, to her granddaughter, and Val feels the wish like hunger. *When your kids are happy, you're happy.* Mom knew. *It has always been so.* For all these years she has provided counsel to her younger daughter, good counsel, and understanding, but the Parkinson's has robbed them both of this connection. The disease leaves scraps, platitudes, and on days like today Val misses her mother, and it is almost as if Barbara is already dead.

Val maneuvers the car through the quiet streets. When she had Barbara, she didn't need to trust anyone else with her secrets. Val always had friends when she was younger; she was loved by her friends, but she never relied on any of them. Not really. She was "Bryan's girl," which conferred status, and then she had her mother to talk to. It is hard for her now to open up to anyone else. And when she has, it has sometimes been a mistake.

By the time Val pulls up to the little school, built at the turn of the last century with its brick facing and quaint high windows, she thinks she is calm. She can handle this, just like she's handling everything else—Mom, the bills, her marriage. *In lonely times,* Val reminds herself, *our true natures will show through* (was that Carrie, again?), and she marches into the building with its yellowing floors and wax smell, determined not to lose her cool. The office has a glass wall that looks out over the main hallway, and she sees Dakota before her daughter sees her: pretty, slim as a deer, slumped in her chair with last year's backpack (Hello Kitty, dirty and drawn upon; Dakota has given the kitten devil horns and a crosshatched scar in black Sharpie) mounded on her lap. Her hair hangs over her eyes like a screen. Dakota doesn't straighten when Val walks in. She doesn't meet Val's eye.

"All right, young lady. Let's go," Val says briskly. Dakota doesn't move, but her eyes swing slowly upward, heavy lidded. Val sees that her daughter's blouse is unbuttoned four buttons, two more than the rule at home. Dakota's neck is unblemished, creamy, crossed by a narrow gold chain that Val doesn't recognize. "I said, let's go." Val knows that Bonnie is watching with interest from behind her desk, but she forces herself not to look back at the secretary, not to give her that satisfaction. Only when Dakota drags herself to her feet does Val turn to Bonnie and say, "I'll be in touch."

"Mrs. Clark." Val starts. It is Joyce Miller, the principal, sedate in heels and a boxy blue dress. Her office is adjacent to the main office, and she stands in the doorway, the brass buttons on her dress winking. She gives Val a provisional smile. "Shall we take a moment to talk? Just your mom," she says to Dakota. "Mrs. Clark. This way, please."

Joyce Miller's office looks over the front sidewalk. The principal's desk is crowded with papers and a coffee cup; there is just one chair facing it and Val sits down. STOP THINK CHOOSE, the poster on the wall next to the window says. The principal leaves the door ajar and sits down behind her desk, hands folded on the blotter. "Did Bonnie tell you why we called you in today, Mrs. Clark?"

"Please, call me Val." Val twists around to look at the door, through which she can still see Bonnie and her daughter. The secretary turns away but goes on listening. "Can we shut the door, please?"

"I'm sorry. Of course," Joyce Miller says blandly. "Bonnie?" The secretary reaches from her chair to close the door and Joyce says, "Your daughter has been called in twice for bad language on the playground. It's a concern, Mrs. Clark."

"I'm sorry, Mrs. Miller. I can't imagine what got into her. We don't speak that way at home, I can assure you."

"As I say, she's been called in twice." The principal takes a sip from her cup and nods to herself. "There are young children on that playground. Are there problems at home that we should know about, Mrs. Clark?"

"Everything's fine at home," Val says.

"No trouble between you and Mr. Clark?"

"Why would...As I say, everything's *fine* between Dakota's father and me. Of course."

Something crosses Miller's face. "Dakota's father."

"Len is very involved."

"Dakota's father," she repeats. "That's right, dear."

Bitch. They all know, of course. "We are doing what we can to understand what's going on with Dakota right now," Val says stiffly.

"I know that your mother's been unwell. That must be a stress on the family." The principal pauses delicately, but when Val doesn't respond, she continues. "Well, then. Dakota's language is unprecedented." The principal addresses a spot just past Val's left shoulder. Her lipstick, bleeding at the edges and pink as lemonade, flakes at the corners of her mouth.

"Meaning?"

"Meaning we have to decide what to do about it, Mrs. Clark."

"Maybe you can tell me when you decide." Val stands

abruptly. "I have to get back to work now. I'll bring Dakota home with me."

"That might be best. This has been very upsetting for the other students."

"It's been upsetting for all of us," Val says, striding to the door, which sticks on her way out. "You," she says to Dakota. "Let's go."

Bonnie busies herself at her desk. "You have a good day now," she chirps from behind her computer screen. Val walks ahead of Dakota, brushing past the janitor in the hallway and almost knocking into his broom.

"I'm sorry!" she says; she doesn't turn to look at her daughter until they are outside. "I'm so mad at you I can't even talk right now, little miss."

"You seem to be talking okay," Dakota says. Her face is saucy in the gray lemon light. "Not that I care."

And it's then that Val strikes her, just once, on the cheek, but hard enough to leave a band of red. Joyce Miller probably sees from the front office. The kindergarten room, with its bay window, looks right out over the walk too; Val imagines five-year-olds in Elmo sweatshirts, their little mouths gaping pink Os. STOP THINK CHOOSE.

"Get to the car," Val hisses, tears in her eyes. She's never hit her children, never. "I don't want to hear any more from you," is what she says.

"I hate you," Dakota hisses back. "I do."

Val squints at the sky, its white expanse hiding the sun. It's like dull milk but at least it's not an April sky. She makes herself look past the school to the woods and a clearing; the kids go there to smoke, but sometimes, when Val has dropped the girls off in the morning, she walks there and the sky wraps over that place in a way that calms her. Val wrote a poem about this once, a bad one.

With effort, Val turns her eyes to her daughter. Dakota used to be a child who hugged her mother and made clay pots with pony beads pressed around the rim. She wrote Val notes in oil pastel, the bright, smudgy letters professing undying love: *You are my best friend!* "Mama!" she used to cry when Val picked her up at school. Now Dakota is a beautiful child/woman who will grow into a stunning adult, the gorgeous result of the time when Val and Bryan were together. Exciting, dangerous Bryan. For years, seeing him in Dakota's face has been a comfort. Maybe, Val thinks now, there is too much of Bryan in her daughter; maybe that is what will undo them both.

She watches Dakota slump in the front seat and prepares to get into the car herself. *Don't yell,* she tells herself. *You can still do this right.* She tries to think what her own mother would do, but then her phone rings, and it's the nursing home, and Mom is on her way to the hospital.

"For a rash?" Val says, confused. She looks at the woods and the clearing again. Each tree seems to stand out black, one from another; there is the stillness that comes when you've thought nothing worse can happen but then it does.

Val climbs numbly into the car. "It isn't the rash," she tells Dakota. She lays her head on the steering wheel, missing the look of pity that crosses her older daughter's face.

RUBY

Drive

When the phone rings, it jars her awake. It isn't Drago. It is her only sibling, and Val's voice, across the miles, is frantic. "I need you here," Val says. It is one in the morning. Their mother has had a stroke—maybe—or maybe it's something else. They never know anymore. So many things have gone wrong with Barbara that it's hard to keep it all straight. "The nursing home called this afternoon; she had a bad headache and...I don't know, it's serious."

Ruby's first thought, muddled by sleep, is about lemon squares. She was going to pick them up at Bittersweet Bakery in the morning, before work; they have the best pastries. She was going to serve the lemon squares on a green plate to her friends, very colorful, and if the concert went well, she had planned to allow herself one of the bigger bars, after everyone else went home, washed down with wine, or maybe milk, the powdered sugar lifting in a cloud around her as she ate. Her friends who come to the concert, they might hang out for a while. Ruby would have to be nice, of course, but after that it would be her time to eat something sweet and think about how things had gone with the Bach.

"Maybe it just seems bad tonight," Ruby says, sitting up in bed and rubbing her eyes, which are crusted with gunge. "Should we wait and see?" The last time Mom had a crisis—she'd fallen—Ruby hadn't been able to go up north for a day or two because of work, and when it turned out that Mom was fine, she hadn't gone at all. No broken bones, after all, and Ruby had talked to her on the phone. Maybe this was like that?

She pats the twisted coil of sheets, looking for her reading glasses. The light is still on—she fell asleep with a book, and here is the book. The glasses must be somewhere. Ruby is trying to keep the panic out of her voice, because there is the concert and she's thought of everything. The concerto, then an "encore." And the lemon squares, perfect in their frilled paper cups.

Her friends will see another side of her, Ruby thinks.

"Mom has always been there for us," Val says. This is true, and maybe Val doesn't mean it to sound the way it does, a way that makes Ruby feel trapped.

"I've been up all night," Val says. "I'll get home and the kids will just be waking up."

"Isn't Len with them?" Val is the younger sister, the one who's made the choices she has (not that there is anything wrong with marrying young; if anyone had asked her, that is what Ruby would have said, would have insisted, even). In fact, Len is a nice guy, steady and reliable, and for an eye blink Ruby can see it: her brother-in-law keeping things together for them long enough for Ruby to have her concert, to play her twelve-minute piece, clean and hard, then eat her lemon square and drive through the night.

"He goes to work early, Ruby."

"Dakota's not old enough to watch over Junie before school?"

Val, who's so touchy about her parenting, makes an impatient sound. "I need to get home, Ruby. The kids need me. But someone has to be here with Mom too."

"Val, listen. There's this work thing, a deadline. If I arrived Saturday morning?" Ruby lies because she knows her sister might allow that work is important, as opposed to a concert she'd probably think was indulgent at best. In fact, Ruby hadn't planned to even tell Val about the concert until later, much later. She hadn't wanted Val to know how much it meant to her.

"I'll come if you need me, of course," Ruby adds when Val remains silent. But she's thinking of Bach. The weeks she's spent preparing. The runs in the concerto are a challenge; she's proud of how far she's come. She was so rough at first; it had been a

long time since she'd played. The first time her fingers touched
the keys she'd almost been afraid, but then the happiness had
leaked in. She felt that old uplift. She felt a strengthening inside
herself.

"It might be a stroke," Val says. "Nothing is more important
than this."

Ruby has finally found her glasses in the bedding.

"Okay, fine. I'm coming," Ruby says. "Tomorrow. I mean,
today." Because it is probably already the next day, though the
sky is still black. Her glasses, which were tangled in the sheets
where Drago used to sleep, are bent from when Ruby rolled
onto them in the night. Her breath is sour.

"I am about to have a nervous breakdown, Ruby. You need
to be here."

"Today," Ruby says, something within her going still even
as she hangs up. Maybe if she doesn't move, she can get back
to the way things were before Val's call. She can pretend for
another moment that all she has to worry about is playing well.

God, the drive. How much time has she spent on the road
between here and there?

She burrows under the duvet, and it is only when she looks
at her bedside clock and realizes more than half an hour has
passed that she makes herself sit up again.

Her little bedroom is gray as river stone. She had picked the
color with Drago; he had, has, an elegant taste, and when they
painted the room together, he had instilled in her a vision of
what their home could be: cool, elegant simplicity. A place of
rest. Drago resisted clutter, and entropy, and when he still lived
here he kept those demons at bay. Now books pile on the floor
in every room. There is a pyre before the dresser, and on the
nightstand two stacks tilt, crested with receipts and cards, and
interleaved with Post-its, their penciled reminders forgotten.
Sometimes it worries Ruby that the clutter doesn't bother her;
she wonders if such sloth is a sign of depression. But then she
will take pleasure in one small thing: the Rothko poster, say,
from the Guggenheim, that hangs right over the Kimball. She

has always loved its dim soul. The poster is hers, and hers alone.

ॐ

When she left Madison, she paid to have the Kimball moved along with her books and the POÄNG chair from Ikea, but getting settled in a much bigger city took a lot of energy. For a while she followed the Grant Park Symphony, the Evanston Symphony Orchestra, the Civic Orchestra of Chicago. She made lists. There was an audition for the South Dakota Symphony Orchestra; hell, she would have moved there if she had gotten the job. For a long time, she felt there was room for improvement, that she could do better, though she knew enough not to even consider the Chicago Symphony Orchestra. Eventually the music receded. She had a good job; she got promoted. Years passed and she bought her own condo.

Stacks of books accrued on the Kimball's fallboard. Ruby didn't mean to stop playing, but it was like the last time she'd gone to a playground. She must have been eleven, and she didn't know it was the last time, not then. She only realized it later, when she hadn't been for years.

ॐ

Ruby finds her laptop under the bed; she emails everyone on the list that there will be no concert, struck by the feeling that if she moves carelessly or quickly, clumsily, something within her will shatter. *My mom is sick*, she types. She keeps it short; her friends, many of them aware of Ruby's mother's long decline, will understand. *I am going for Mom*, she writes. Not because Val told her to, she adds to herself, because it seems important that she clarify this.

After Ruby presses "send" she sits motionless, hands in her lap. The faucet in the kitchen drips. She listens. Ruby has been meaning to call the building manager—he's a nice guy and would fix it straightaway—but she hasn't done so yet. Every day she puts it on her list, *Call Andy*, and when the end of the day comes and she hasn't done it, she moves it to the next day. Now the task, resisted so long, has taken on an insurmountable feel and the faucet continues to drip. Ruby sighs, the *Italian Concerto* soft in her ear. Her disappointment about the concert is confusingly shot through with, if she pays attention, tendrils of relief. If she doesn't perform she cannot fail. A part of her wonders if she will ever reschedule, and she hates herself for that.

But first. Packing. Ruby pushes out of bed, starts throwing clothing into a suitcase, trying to remember what fits these days. She has gained weight in the past few months, and there are jeans in her closet that she's never worn, pants two sizes too small that she bought as an "incentive." Tags still on. But she wore these corduroys last week and they were barely tight. Good, and this sweatshirt will work, too, it's always been roomy. Ruby dresses, then mashes another change of clothes into the battered American Tourister she used in college, because Val might have something to say about the newer tan Schlesinger Ruby'd splurged on for her work trips (as Human Resources program manager, she gets to go to conferences occasionally— last time it was Miami—and there had been hope, for a while, that she and Drago would be planning a honeymoon). Better to play it low key.

And Ruby will be there for only a couple of days, tops. Surely Mom will get through this episode—this *stroke*—the way she has before. Sometimes Ruby and Val joke—it is one of the few things they can agree on—that their mother will, improbably, certainly, outlive them both.

"You needed to be here yesterday," Val had said before she hung up.

Ruby kneels on her suitcase to close it (several books and her robe, which is plush and cheerful and patterned with daisies, take up most of the space), then moves slowly to the kitchen. The drive to the town where she grew up—where Val and Barbara still live—is six hours, and Ruby has committed it to memory. For years she has clocked the milestones: the water tower painted with a heart; the gas station with a plaster elephant statue; the Kohl's where Ruby stopped and bought red sweatpants once. They cheered her up; soft and thick, they were studded with childish sparkles. She'd always wanted pants like that. This was at the beginning of this year, when Drago could still be kind; he called them her "candy pants," and he said, then, that she was his sweet.

Drago. For a long time, his wicked humor, his intelligence, sustained her. The way he was making a go of it in a country not his own inspired her in her own attempts to build a life in a place different from where she'd started. A life with meaning. And he loved her; for a while, at least, they shared real affection. Ruby, starting coffee to take with her, looks out the window at the night street and dreads the drive ahead. Thick mist rolls past her window. It is November. The coffee will not be enough. She knows better—*don't call, don't call*—but she picks up the phone then and calls Drago's cell, even though the last time she reached out to him she swore she would never do so again. But he used to be kind. His voice was, once, a consolation. And what if he doesn't check his email? What if he's planned to come to the concert and he doesn't know it's been canceled?

❧

When Kate the harpist got pregnant, she and the landscape painter moved back to Red Wing. At first Kate still played weddings, though eventually she returned to school to get a teaching degree and now she teaches kindergarten. She called Ruby after her son was born; Ruby asked her about the kid, then they both bitched about a classmate, Randi, who had been tapped to play second violin with the Milwaukee Symphony Orchestra. "Dumb luck," Ruby said glumly. There was always room for another violin.

She'd been packing up for the move to Chicago, phone braced against her shoulder and wrapping plates in white paper; at that point she'd endured a succession of fruitless auditions and had pretty much thrown in the towel in Madison. With Kate and the boyfriend gone, it was hard to make rent; the wedding gigs didn't pay that well. She'd decided to move to Chicago for an entry-level job in HR. "I've got a business minor." She shrugged when Kate expressed surprise. Ruby had told her once that she'd never give up. "I'll do HR until I can get something with music," she added. "In Chicago, something's gotta open up eventually."

ॐ

"It's two-thirty in the morning, bitch," the DJ says conversationally when she answers the phone. Ruby, who should be surprised that the woman answers Drago's cell, is not. She suspects the woman likes these confrontations.

"Is he there? I need to tell him something."

"He's asleep." The DJ yawns; she probably just got in from work.

"Tell him my mother is ill." As if Ruby's mother and Drago shared something special. Not true, but the DJ couldn't possibly know that yet. Could she? It was one thing to make fun of Ruby's clothing, but surely Drago wouldn't have brought up Barbara in anything but a respectful manner. He'd been raised to accord mothers—all mothers—an almost religious respect. "The mother, she is the one," Ruby can hear him saying. "Even if she is just the plain and fat. Still, she is the mother."

Ruby hangs up. The coffee is done, and she fills a travel mug three-quarters of the way full, then tops it off with cream. In her head she can hear the DJ's throaty voice; Ruby replays the conversation, hoping she didn't sound the way she felt inside.

She has just taken a first swig of the coffee when her phone rings. There is the brief, irrational hope that maybe it's Drago; maybe he heard the exchange, and when he found out about Barbara he was sorry. But when Ruby glances at her cell screen, it's Lorna.

"Lor?"

"Ru? Oh, honey. Don't cry. I got your email. What's going on?"

"How are you even up right now?" Ruby wipes her nose.

"Insomnia. What else?" Lorna never sleeps through the night. She gets up and reads, or checks her email, though Ruby

has told her light from the computer screen won't help her
sleep any.

"Mom's sick. Val's kind of freaking out."

"Do we know what's wrong with your mom?"

"A stroke? I'm not sure. Lor, this drive..." Without even
thinking about it, Ruby opens the cabinet and takes out the first
thing she lays hand to: a jar of dark chocolate/cookie butter,
dangerous in her cupboard, but Ruby had bought it thinking
she'd make cookies to share. *One spoonful, that's all*, Ruby thinks.
Of course, there's the leftover Chinese food too. She takes the
jar to the window and, looking out at the blackness, digs in.

"Ruby, you can do this."

"I called Drago."

"You what? Forget about him. Just focus on what you have
to do."

"I know." Ruby scrapes the side of the jar with her spoon.
The cookie butter is tussar. It's sendal. Ruby knows these words
because she reads all the time; words rattle around in her head,
and now, again, the music does too.

"Take things one at a time. Just get there. You staying with
Val?"

"Val?" Ruby licks the spoon all around. "I think so. Maybe.
Oh God, remember last time?"

"Don't worry about it. Just get there, hon. Find out what's
going on. Then do what you need to do."

"I have the energy for this, right?"

"You do. Text me when you get there."

"I will."

"You got this, hon."

"Thanks, Lor."

"You got this."

When Ruby hangs up, she puts the cookie butter back in
the cabinet. She wipes her mouth with the back of her hand.
She's glad Lorna called, and she's relieved she didn't get through
to Drago. Drago and Ruby's mother hardly know each other.
What on earth would he even say?

❧

Ruby drives north; the sky is dark but soon enough will secrete its raw pink. Wasn't there a crayon like that? *Flesh*, she thinks. *Fleshy*. The way Mom looked the last time Ruby saw her—two months ago, or maybe three. Too long ago, Val would say, but that was Val, and Ruby was coming now, wasn't she? Their mother, Barbara, always as sinewy and taut as a piece of jerky, had suddenly grown round and malleable at sixty-six, with a noticeable swag of skin below the chin and a potbelly that pushed at her T-shirts like a little fist. "I love my sweets," Mom had said, her mouth and chin trembling the way they do now—defensive about, betrayed by, her body after all these years, and it was true that the little wastebasket in her room was suddenly full of brown-and-green wrappers. Milky Ways, and Ruby had helped eat them, forgoing her diet because…Milky Ways tasted good? Ruby didn't even like caramel, or nougat, but the house was gone, and the farm. Used to be Ruby could talk to her mom, would come away from visits feeling certain about herself and the choices she'd made.

Then Barbara got sick. Really sick, and suddenly it was *stressful* to be home—not *home* home, because Chicago was that, and had been for years—but the place she came from. Ladyford. Pass the Milky Ways, Ma.

That wind, rocking the car. Ruby is used to getting up early for work; she'll drive in instead of taking the L when she's got a deadline, the streets still dark and creeping, but this is different, this pell-mell flight so urgent and strange. Even the Kennedy Expressway was lonely when she first merged on; frail cirrus latticed the sky like frost on a window, and the unfriendly wind knocked her car so that Ruby wished she drove something big, something substantial. All through her childhood, Uncle Moon drove an Impala.

Uncle Moon, who moved into the farmhouse from his bachelor apartment in town after Ruby's father defected; Moon had to be a father to her and Val all those years. He was Mom's brother and he never said anything. He was smart that way, smoking his pipe and staying mute in a house of women, but yeah, he would have had an opinion about the car she drives now. A "crappy little rice-burner," that's what her uncle Moon would have thought.

Sometimes, like now, Ruby misses him. Her uncle loved music and introduced her to classical; it was something they did together, listen to music, and they didn't have to talk, which Moon wasn't any good at and which Ruby tended to do too much of when she was anxious or uncertain. Moon was the one who showed her Bach could be filled with joy. He was the one who helped her see what Beethoven could do. He opened that window.

"Angry." That's what she'd said the first time he played the *Eroica* for her. "He sounds so angry," and he'd nodded, which made her feel proud. She was so little then, and now she's afraid that when they stop making Impalas a certain way—the tail-lights, red wedges, are already so different from what Moon called the "Cheerio lights" on the older models—she'll lose the memory of him and his cars. She'll lose some ground. But this drive, it brings Moon back to her. Ruby would have told him about the concert, she thinks. He would have known the *Italian Concerto*. He probably would have come to hear her play.

Four-thirty a.m. and she's crossing over into Wisconsin. Ruby has turned on the radio for noise, for company—some sort of classic rock station that fades in and out, filling the car. The weather is strange. There is the threat of rain, or snow, maybe—a lid of clouds has moved in and presses low. She senses it more than sees it, this time of day. Ruby glances at herself in the rearview mirror and presses her lips tight. That flat wafer face, round and white as dough, is prettier with make-up—bright blue at the eyes so that they are lit like tropical fish, and a vivid lipstick. Her signature color, something bold and "out there," to make up for the fact that she's not pretty, never been pretty, not like Val. At forty-one, that shouldn't matter anymore, and sometimes she thinks she has outgrown such childish insecurity.

Today, though. Gray lips and hair mashed flat; Val's call has made her afraid.

Ruby turns off the radio because she is thinking about the precision of the first movement she would have played tonight; the other music, fuzzy with static, is a distraction. She cracks her window, and the air, frigid, smells clean and good. Like the forests she'll pass through soon enough, the stands of spruce and heart-leaved birch, soft loaves of moss underfoot. She loves this smell, though she has never loved where she came from. The landscape up north is lonely in a visceral, consuming way; even the filling station she'll stop at, hours from now, is lonesome. She imagines how it must look right now, quiet at this hour as if sleeping, hemmed by trees. Ruby has pulled in there before, for gas and a red cream soda. She knows that inside there is a taxidermied bear in a case, standing on its hind legs and taller than a man. There is always the same woman behind the counter too: sloe-eyed and pock-faced, her dark hair sprayed into a cone. A scar trails like red yarn down her left cheek. Each time she holds out her hand, palm up, for Ruby's cash, Ruby wants to clasp it. She wants to tell the woman that there are other places to live, that no one has to stay here; she wants to offer comfort and thus be comforted.

But all that is hours away. This part of I-39 passes through—not towns, exactly, but signs pointing to towns, and the signs promise restaurants and gas, and from the highway she can see the gas station with the giant apple on a post. The apple must be made of fiberglass and it's huge, shaped to look as if it has a bite taken out. Janesville. Edgerton. Stoughton. She's never stopped at these places, invisible from the highway, though she imagines they have a main street, a movie theater, a place to get coffee. She hopes so. All she sees from the expressway are the strings of houses, just their backs, tan and identical in soldierly rows and separated from the interstate by a trench filled with grass. Eventually she will continue on to 29, and it is about there that her journey never fails to turn from "here" to "there." If Drago were here—or someone like him, but better—that is where Ruby would reach across the seat and take his hand. For comfort, because always there is a sort of passage, that transition from her Chicago self to...whatever she was before. And back again. Trip after trip she flees the north woods and the terrain of her old life, with the expectation that this time— this!—her transformation will become permanent. Complete.

Random droplets smack the windshield and Ruby hits the wipers. They drag across the glass, reluctant. Even when she was a girl, she knew she would leave Ladyford, she knew she would leave Wisconsin. At ten years old she was already thick and bookish, her role set; Barbara would murmur approvingly, "You'll bust the seams of this place, girl." And Ruby clung to this interpretation of who she was, the "smart one," and talented enough on the piano to believe that when she left this place, it would be the music that took her.

You have an artist's name, her peers—Amys and Jennifers and Lisas all—used to tell her when they were girls. You'll be a musician someday. And Ruby privately agreed, picturing an older, sleeker version of herself, wearing a long velvet skirt in a smoky jazz club. At the piano and her thighs no longer rubbing together. Barbara's whimsy—the very thing that attracted the girls' father, though it could not induce him to stay—manifested itself less and less as the girls grew. But it was rooted in their names, which held such promise: Ruby, and Val, which was short for Valentine. And wasn't Val the sweetheart, too, when they were young?

There was that rocky period, when Ruby was in her last year of high school and dating a boy, Tim, who was genuinely nice, and a part of her feared that she might actually stay. Get knocked up and stay, which is what happened to girls who didn't take care. (Like her sister, sweet Valentine—so much prettier and look what had happened to *her*.) One night, the summer after they graduated, Ruby and Tim drove out to the woods to smoke a joint and fuck, and Ruby threw her lit cigarette out of the bed of Tim's truck. To see what would happen. To dare what would happen, because it was then she knew—she *knew*—that she had to leave this place. She flipped the cigarette, laughing. It was a dry summer, the grass caught, and then a blighted jack pine with its drab brown needles. That is how she started a fire. No one save Tim knew she'd done it, though the fire, which burned part of the forest and several working fields before it was extinguished, was referred to as The Burn for years after. They beat at the flames with their jackets, and when it became apparent that the blaze could not be contained, she and Tim drove to town and hunted up the sheriff, who drank beers at the Rusty Nail most nights after eight o'clock. That is where they found him, butt lapping over his special stool, third from the window, and his hand, holding the beer, stayed in the air when he saw the excitement and fear in their faces. They told him a story about driving past, and noticing the sinister orange lick of flames, and since they were both considered "nice kids," they were believed. (Tim loved her then; Ruby understood that. She had never for a moment doubted that he would keep her secret.)

The volunteer firefighters were rounded up, and because the excitement was infectious, because this had not happened in their lifetimes, Tim and Ruby went back to watch them dig the ditches and spray the flames. They knew all the men who fought that fire. Tim ended up helping too, and Ruby brought them water, that line of men, some of them enemies in their day-to-day existence, united, if briefly, by the blaze. She let them think they were heroes, part of something larger than themselves, with their blackened faces and brawny arms. A part of her believed it too.

Ruby presses the accelerator and closes her window. She's passing farm fields and lonely farmhouses lit like ships against the rain. She imagines she can smell the cows, a shit stench that was always worst in the summer, of course, and just before milking, cows gathered like boys in a locker room. Uncle Moon would profess to love the smell, but Ruby always feared it would follow her even after she left Ladyford for good, clinging to her clothing like smoke.

The night of The Burn, the air smelled of char, and also water. The day after, she rode her bike to the site alone, to see the
stinking trees. A haze hung over the burned place, like smog,
and no birds flew there. The forest was like a ruined cityscape,
and Ruby was ashamed to realize that she didn't care. She wondered even then why Tim didn't break up with her—why he
didn't draw away in revulsion at what she had done. He had
always loved these woods.

No, it was Ruby who did the leaving. She stayed with him
until they went off to college: Tim getting his undergrad in
Illinois (he'd eventually go to dental school there), and Ruby
attending the music program in Madison, where she would
find out soon enough that her musical gifts had limits. (She
had already been denied her first choice in schools, but she had
thought that a fluke, a mistake.) But their first Christmas back
home, over mugs of cocoa cozily spiked with rum from Tim's
parents' cupboard, Ruby still felt expansive with possibility. She
told Tim she'd met someone else and that it was serious, which
wasn't true, and that they'd slept together, which was. Tim
had just given her a gold heart on a chain—"Early Christmas
present!" he said—but she told him anyway, watching his face.
He kept smiling, though tears rolled freely down his cheeks. "I
can't be my best self here," she'd said primly. Ruby knew she
should feel worse than she did, but she'd stopped trying to be
good. What she felt was irritation, and the distinct sense that
Tim needed to get on with his life. She understood then that
she had already separated from this place and the people who
lived here.

Well. Tim was fine. He'd gotten his degree and moved back
to Wisconsin. Eventually he'd gotten married. When she has
gone back to see her mother, she has heard this much.

Ruby is hungry. And she has to pee, and there is an exit, and
a lighted place where she can probably get something to eat.
She gives herself permission to stop; she'll be back on the road
in no time. She is thinking about breakfast; staying in bed that
much longer this morning meant she'd left home later than she

intended. She'd skipped breakfast to save time and had eaten only those spoonfuls of cookie butter, a few bites of Chinese, and that was *hours* ago. She hasn't even washed her face. If someone asked her, she would say that she isn't thinking about how Val's clean little house will be cold, because Val keeps the heat to sixty-three. No, she isn't. Her thoughts are like lights on the surface of water; they are seeds in a fire. There are motels in Ladyford, certainly, and Ruby would rather stay in any one of them, but she is smart enough to know how that would look. Not staying with her own sister!

Ruby parks. A cluster of fast-food joints rings together like covered wagons, red and yellow, their color insistent in the flat iron breast of the fields. When Ruby gets to Ladyford, Val will have the house ready, stripes vacuumed rigorously into the rug.

Ruby pulls her coat close. She hopes her mom isn't in any pain. She hopes this is just another blip, another thing for them to get through.

The *Italian Concerto* has a slow inner movement. Heading into the rest stop with head down, Ruby hums that part; remembering the music is almost an act of will. The air is wet, as heavy and gray as gravy. *Water,* Ruby thinks. It smells like water.

RUBY

Rest Stop

The restaurants have a common entrance, and when she steps inside, she is met by the scent of salt and fat and chocolate, all mixed with a stubborn smell of tires, and her heart lifts. This place is familiar to her. There, to the left, is a store that will sell her a magnet in the shape of Wisconsin, or a sweatshirt with a badger on it.

She and Val used to frequent rest stops like this one, when Ruby first got her driver's license. She was giddy with the opportunity then; sixteen, broad shouldered, Ruby wore her new freedom lightly. It made her kind. "Want to go for a ride?" she'd ask Val, who was ten and adored her then. Ruby could propose any trip—to the National Freshwater Fishing Hall of Fame, to the Dickeyville grotto—and Val would acquiesce, eager to spend time, any time, with her big sister. Ruby was already drifting then. She was happy when she was anywhere but Ladyford, and Val seemed to sense it. "You're not home very much," she'd said once, squeezing her favorite stuffed dog. Anxious. "Come with me then," Ruby had said.

Barbara packed them sandwiches and sweaters, and, with Moon, waved them off from the front door. At first Ruby wondered why Barbara let them go so willingly—there was always work to be done, after all, on the farm and with the sewing projects Barbara took in for extra money—and she would ask her mother how Barbara did those days, those weekends, when she and her sister were gone. Barbara was vague at first: "I worked," she would say. "I worked without interruption."

Ruby pressed, and it came out one evening, while Barbara made supper and Ruby did her homework at the kitchen table. "Your uncle and I ate lima beans and ice cream for supper one night," Barbara said. She was at the stove, cooking potpies for the four of them, and her face lit fondly when she told Ruby about the lima bean supper. "It took minutes. Moon brought ice cream bars from town." Barbara opened a can of corn for the pies and looked out the window over the sink, and suddenly Ruby saw how it must have been for Barbara, to accomplish her usual tasks in half the time: no need to cook, no badgering or complaining from Ruby or Val. She felt her stomach drop.

"But you missed us, right?" Ruby asked. "What did you do after supper?"

"Oh, sweetie, of course I did," Barbara said. "We just watched TV." But she smiled to herself when she bent to open the oven, and Ruby understood then how satisfied her mother might have been to finally be alone (because being with Moon was almost like being alone). For years Ruby had believed that she and Val—but mostly she, Ruby—were their mother's world, her only joy, once their father had gone.

The trips became an act of defiance then. She and Val ate chocolate in the car. They rolled their windows down and drove to the silty moraines in Kewaunee County, west to South Dakota and the Mitchell Corn Palace, the Badlands, east to the tony residences of Door County's Fish Creek. It didn't matter where they went. Ruby loved the anonymity, the fact that if someone looked askance—at her sister's dirty face, at the strain of her own pearled blouse buttons—they were going to move on anyway. At those times she didn't actively miss her mother. That was years away yet. She and Val planned nothing, sleeping in the car or staying in cheap motels with money that Moon gave them, coming home only in time for Girl Scout camp, or Ruby's job at the local movie theater, or school, if it was in session. One time they drove through the night, Val sleeping in the back seat; Ruby pulled over and woke her to see the aurora borealis, pulsing and dying, pulsing and dying, in the northern sky.

Barbara showed little curiosity about their trips, but Moon listened to their stories, sometimes packing CDs he'd burned for them to listen to on the road: classical, B.B. King, ZZ Top,

Willie Nelson, and once, improbably, an Icelandic group called
the Sugarcubes. He said he chose the music to go along with
their destination, though the connections he made were never
clear. How did "Hotel California" have anything to do with
Mount Rushmore? But Ruby loved the surprise of it. The rule
was that she or Val would dip their hand into the bag and whatever they pulled out they had to play. The music was—is   a
solace. Even now she can't listen to Lou Reed without feeling
comforted, as though Moon is taking care of her.

She didn't know how to tell him how much it meant to her,
those grocery bags he packed with CDs, but she and Val always
brought a little something back for him, from places like the one
where Ruby stands now. "Thank you, Ladybird," Moon would
say. (He called her that; it was their joke, she always thought, a
play on Ladyford, on flight. He must have guessed how badly
she wanted to leave town. At some point, Val and Barb took it
up, and for a while, before she moved away, even Tim used the
pet name.) Up until his death, Moon kept an ancient freezer,
filled with venison steak, and it was decorated with magnets
from the Midwestern attractions that drew them then.

They were so different, even as girls; Val sat erect in the
passenger seat, alert and silent, watching, and Ruby could not
imagine what she thought about. But Ruby talked for the both
of them, or sang to Moon's music. She prefers noise; she is the
kind of person who leaves her television on. Back then, she
appreciated that her sister, though quiet, was good company.

"Sar-ah!" Ruby, who has been wandering the aisles of the
little mart in the roadside oasis, looking for something—a packaged snack, maybe?—that will fill her up, whirls to see a thin
woman, cheeks and chin raw from the wind, pulling a little girl
by the arm. "Come on, then!" the woman huffs. The child's face
is slick with tears. They are hurrying to the bathroom, and the
girl, who doesn't wear a coat, clutches an ugly plastic doll as if
it were treasure.

Ruby, who remembers what it was like, pities most of the
children she sees.

She doesn't know when things changed between her and Val. No. She does. The last trip they made together was to Duluth, on a chill autumn weekend. Ruby was a senior, she must have been seventeen, and Val hauled a canvas bag of schoolbooks into the front seat, even though it was a school holiday, a long weekend. They left Barbara and Moon picking pumpkins in the fields behind the barn, and Val was loath to say goodbye. "Don't carve jack-o-lanterns without me!" she called, then lingered fretfully at the field's edge, watching her mother and uncle. Ruby, waiting in the car, had to honk the horn to get her sister to come.

Val opened her books as soon as they started driving, then complained she was carsick. They drove to Duluth, where they found the Lake Superior Marine Museum, and Val, who had delighted in the modest, quirky finds of the road for more than a year now, pronounced it boring. Stupid. She left Ruby alone in the museum, standing before a photo of a steel ship from the century before, aslant in a withering storm, and insisted on waiting outside, though it was raw, and almost dark, Lake Superior's bleak breath cutting at her thin canvas coat.

Ruby was lonely in the modest bright museum—there was no one else there save the myopic volunteer who had taken their money—and went outside to find Val standing alone on a pile of jagged rocks that shifted as Ruby clambered up. She hugged Val, which was uncharacteristic of her, and told her sister they'd go eat and after that they'd both feel better. Val replied in a savage flood of words that she hated storms, and pictures of storms, and ships from other places, and that the safest place was home. "Men were jumping off that boat in the picture," Val insisted sullenly, hanging her head so that a fall of hair, smooth and the color of grain shot through with cinnamon, hid her eyes. Ruby hugged her again.

They found a little motel with pine-paneled walls, and Val said it stank of bug spray. Their supper, fish fry, was eaten in silence, for Val had brought one of her schoolbooks, which she propped in front of her, screening Ruby from view. "Lighten

up, sweetie," Ruby had said. "You don't need to do math now."
She was shocked when Val snapped the book shut, eyes shiny
with angry tears.

"Maybe *you* don't! You're so smart you don't even need to
study! But I have to *work*! I'd rather be home! And don't call me
sweetie!" Ruby was stung; a part of her was used to Val liking
everything she proposed.

The next morning Ruby woke early and stepped out into
the chilly morning, coat wrapped around her; frost crunching
under her feet, she walked to the lake a few blocks away. At
first the quiet of the morning and the thin line of blue where
Lake Superior met the sky filled her with hope, but after Val
woke they dragged around Duluth. When Ruby brought her
back to the lake—"Doesn't it seem to stretch on forever?" she
cried, trying to re-create for her sister some of what she'd felt
earlier—Val was unimpressed. "I like the Flambeau River better," she sulked. "I miss Mom and Uncle Moon." Ruby bit her
tongue, not mean enough to say that their mother might not be
missing Val at all. They returned home early.

The next time Ruby took to the road, Val had homework
to do, and the time after that there was a slumber party at the
home of a girl Val hardly knew. Ruby stopped asking after that.
She missed her sister at first, but the human spirit is adaptable,
she came to understand. It became normal to take the trips
alone; then she started dating Tim, and he would join her sometimes too.

Well. That was long ago, wasn't it? Ruby, fingering the ribbed
hem of her sweatshirt, understands that she needs coffee. She
decides against McDonald's, choosing instead a little bakery,
which has red cloth spread on the counter and a grandmotherly
type arranging muffins on a tray. It seems real in the way Mickey
D's does not.

"Good morning, dear," the grannylady says, her smile kind
around brilliant dentures. She has an ample bosom, and Ruby,
suddenly exhausted, wants to lay her head upon it and weep.
There is a part of her, in fact, that has longed to do that her en-

tire life. They weren't sentimental, not in Ruby's family—when she was growing up, emotion was frowned upon, and parceled out sparingly. When Ruby complained that her friends' moms routinely hugged them, Barbara flatly told her daughter that she showed her love in other ways.

"Besides, I *do* hug you," Barbara said, and she did, sometimes. She was a practical woman, and Ruby, who as she grew began to understand what it must have meant to be the only single mother in a small town, held on to those shows of affection with a jealous heart. Ruby got migraines as a teen, during which Barbara was always lavishly attentive. The episodes are splashes of indigo in a landscape plain as newsprint; sometimes, when she is down, Ruby will recall them and they bring her solace.

"Good morning," Ruby says to the grannylady. She bends close to the glass case, and in its reflection she sees the brooch she has pinned to her sweatshirt, winking in the light. It's the pin Barbara wore to her own wedding; the day Ruby left for college, Barbara gave it to her. Ruby reaches up and touches it now, the pearls, like milky teeth, in their uneven ring. The pin is nothing like her style, but she wears it as a medal, for courage. It makes her pretty and strong. There it is now, reflected in the glass bakery case; it flashes fire in the hard overhead light, and Ruby squints her eyes and imagines her own muddled reflection to be slim, and calm, and wise.

Barbara had presented the brooch to her at breakfast, pinned to a scrap of flannel and set against the sugar bowl, and Ruby, afraid to say the wrong thing, had said nothing. It wasn't set in real gold, but they had pretended. She wears the pin every day, fastened to her collar, or to the delicate strap of her brassiere; today it rides the thick, soft weave of her sweatshirt, bobbing just above her collarbone like a tiny ship.

Over grannylady's shoulder there is a window, silver with fingerprints, and Ruby can see the day coming, cold and onerous. She orders coffee, and a blueberry muffin, then takes refuge in a scarred plastic booth where she can eye the clock on the wall. Six-thirty a.m. Someone has left behind a tabloid magazine, and Ruby pages through it. In one article, an A-list actress talks about being a mother and staying fit at forty. "Exercise, exercise, exercise," the actress instructs. Pictures of the actress, who wears short-shorts and has a killer figure, accompany the article. "Any mother can do this, and if they say they can't, they aren't trying." Ruby grunts and wonders what Val would have to say about that. The muffin emerges like a butterfly from its tight wrap of cellophane, and she eats quickly, tearing it with her fingers. She is so hungry, and the muffin tastes good. When she's done, she wads up the cellophane and throws it out with the magazine.

She finds the bathroom, where she can comb her hair and straighten the neck of her sweatshirt. The fluorescent light brings out the signs of her age: wires of gray in the walnut-colored hair she inherited from her mother's side of the family, and a fragile complexion, wearing at the edges like a purse. She's about the same age as the actress in the article, and to Ruby this seems remarkable.

She suddenly wants more food, so she returns to the bakery counter, to grannylady, and grannylady's teeth, blue-white as skim milk. Ruby orders another muffin—"Same as before?"— and another paper cup of coffee.

The woman moves her hands apologetically. They haven't taken enough blueberry muffins out of the freezer this morning; would she like a frozen one?

Ruby thinks of the blank fields that lie between this place and Ladyford.

"Yes," she says, wondering if she should feel ashamed of herself. The muffins are big. "Yes, please." Ruby watches the woman bend to get her coffee, the stiff cant of her hips and the slow, veined hands. "It's cold out," she says, thinking that a woman that age might have arthritis. Arthur, as Moon might have called it. "Bad news to have it so cold so early."

"Oh well," the woman sighs. "We'll see if it's bad." She caps the coffee, tucks it into a bag. When she returns from the freezer, grannylady hands Ruby the bag, smiling again. Ruby notices how crisp the woman's blouse is, the small ways she takes care. "Did you want something else, hon?"

"You're so nice!" Ruby says, and the friendly astonishment on the woman's face is so guileless, so genuine, that Ruby begins to cry.

"Oh, honey," the woman says, coming from around the counter and putting her hand on Ruby's arm.

"My mom is dying," Ruby says, to explain her tears, but in any case it's true: Barbara is dying, slowly and in pieces. Grannylady is a head shorter than Ruby, but her hand is firm and reassuring.

"Oh, sweetheart," the woman says. Ruby squeezes the bag with the muffin and coffee in it. What if this woman invited her home, to a yellow house with two cats as orange as paint, and what if she made Ruby pie, and told her she had always wanted a daughter, a smart, capable daughter, and what if they played Risk well into the night? Ruby could tell the grannylady: My boyfriend left me. My world is shrinking. There is no one left to love me. No. Silly. She will go to Val's house, where she will wear a sweater and her robe and the red sweatpants to bed, provided she can squeeze into them, and she will lie perfectly still under a smooth corduroy blanket in a room as spare and blue as the moon. She will wait for the next day.

"Thank you," Ruby says. "I'll be all right now." She will never see the grannylady again, but for years after, when she passes this oasis, she will think about the woman's kind face.

She plans to let the muffin thaw completely, to eat it at Val's, in fact. Maybe she will even share half with her sister, who has been looking a little thin. But the air is cold when she steps outside, and fear of the day ahead hollows her out. Her mother has Parkinson's-related dementia, which makes her strange, and her sister, Val, has been strange for years. What do they expect of her? Only Moon, closed in on himself the way he could be, had seemed to want or lay no claim. This was before the cancer took him; she pictures the Cheerio lights when he braked the Impala, their rounds a cherry glow.

Ruby lasts until she nears Abbotsford. Still driving, she fumbles in the bag for the muffin, but when she sets to gnawing at
it, the pastry, still frozen, has almost no flavor. The blueberries
are like little stones. She chips away at it with her front teeth until she feels—or maybe just hears—a snap. When she explores
gingerly with her tongue she tastes blood tang. The thin tooth,
the front one, big as a Chiclet and yet fragile as porcelain, feels
serrated, angled, exposing a perfect slice of air where her whole
tooth used to be.

Mother of God, it hurts. The nerve must be exposed.

Ruby swears and yanks the steering wheel so that the car
veers right, swimming in the loose gravel of the shoulder. It
slides forward, then stops, listing toward a ditch thick with tea-
sel. She sucks in her breath; what is left of her tooth throbs, but
Ruby doesn't cry until she hitches herself up to the rearview
mirror and sees the ragged triangle with its nipple of pulpy
red. A matching piece clings to her tongue like a host in the
Eucharist.

She has the presence of mind to peel the sliver from her
tongue and dig through her purse for something to wrap it in.
The only tissue she finds is shredded, stained with lipstick—big
as her purse is, she never has what she really needs—and so she
puts the fragment back in her mouth. The car rocks, buffeted
by wind in this open place, and when she is done with the crying she rubs her eyes with the heels of her hands, which come
away grainy with yesterday's mascara.

"Nothing is more important than this," Val had said. Ruby
thinks of the lemon bars she would have served tonight, dust-
ed with sugar and packed in a paper box tied with string. She
forgot to call the bakery. She forgot to let them know she's not
coming. Someone else will eat them now; they would have been
soft, Ruby thinks.

She breathes in, avoiding the touch of tongue against
tooth. The sky has begun to piss rain again, and the road looks
greased; to either side, trees shake their naked limbs. Out of the
ditch, just ahead of her car, struggles a deer, creeping through

the weather. Ruby sees that its back legs are fused, and as she watches the creature drag its way across the road, she is incredulous that it has not been killed by a hunter, or another beast, or a car. But, no, it hitches inexorably forward, and Ruby stares. The deer's hide, dark in the rain, is the rich butter-brown of caramel; Ruby knows that it is probably full of ticks. Hitch. Drag. Hitch. Drag. There is no other path before it.

VAL

Seemingly Permanent

The girls aren't up yet and Len is gone, having driven the truck to work before it was even full light. It is the quiet hour, when Jellybean (the most affectionate of the cats, and so Val's favorite) rubs against her leg, and there is just the coffee to make, its throaty burble as it passes into the carafe.

God, please don't let me be an asshole today.

That's what she prays every day. Because it's hard lately; she hasn't exactly been the mother—or daughter—she'd like to be. In the hospital last night, Barbara's mouth, strange as a sea creature's, had gaped, and she had stared at the ceiling without seeing. Val hated this latest indignity, the way her mother might have hated it once, but there was something more: Under that feeling was also fear. Revulsion. Her mother's changed face is frightening.

What do you tell yourself so that the changes are manageable? What do you tell others? Val hasn't figured that out yet. Carrie said to her once, "You can spill your guts with me." Val pours herself a cup of coffee and tries to remember how she let down her guard with Carrie. When they used to have drinks together.

She must be strong. Val thinks about Len, who is strong in his way. He has the job at the Robinstadts' farm this week, this month they hope, and Bill Robinstadt rises early. The Robinstadts' farm and outbuildings, spotless, possess the sleek, glossy sheen of toys.

The way her own house used to be. Val peers into the freezer; she needs to go grocery shopping, but look, there is a package of frozen rolls. Eggs and milk in the fridge. Some juice, and the apples seem decent. She will not think about the living room, which is impossibly cluttered now; the towers of paper alone are overwhelming. She'd throw them all away if it weren't for the possibility that something important is buried within the old school papers and ads for sales long past. Just last week, looking for a permission slip from Junie's teacher, she'd come upon a sheaf of Dakota's drawings amidst one of the stacks. Pencil sketches, and good ones too—the best one was a loon—the lines drawn with a hard sharp point. Feathers were scumbled with charcoal sweeps; the loon's eye was the only spot of color. It was shiny, a red bead of paint, and the thought that she might have thrown the pictures away made Val a little breathless; she slipped them into her sock drawer, where she knows they will be safe. Dakota is difficult—she's always been harder than Junie—but she has talents Val can only guess at. Getting along at school? Well, maybe not that.

Hah. Sometimes Val cracks herself up. She surveys the kitchen, which is not so bad. She will stay here, and treat herself to black coffee, in the special mug that Barbara gave her once, painted with vines.

But she must be careful. Too much coffee and she'll get a headache. Her hands will shake. She is past the point of tired—eyes like piss holes in the snow. Isn't that what Moon used to say? Val pushes her mug to one side, touching a ceramic lamb on the table like a talisman before gathering what the girls will need for lunch. She still packs their lunches: peanut butter sandwiches for both; those last apples; wafer cookies, because Junie likes the smiling cookie guy on the package. Dakota probably won't eat any of it.

They'll tell Dakota someday how Len married Val when she was five months pregnant and it was clear that Bryan, wherever he was, wasn't coming back. What a scandal that was, how the locals had wondered about Len, who had always harbored a not-so-secret crush on Val. No one but Val and Len knew for sure that Len wasn't the father. Of course, once Dakota was born, her hair a dark halo, people had their theories. In high school Val hadn't given Len the time of day. She and Bryan had been such a glamorous couple. Wickedly attractive and seemingly permanent. But it was awkward Len, his face red as ham, who emerged victorious.

And which is better, really—passion or respect? Love or liking? He tries, Len does. He is steady and kind, a decent handyman. A good father to both girls. With Bryan it had been feast or famine: five music gigs stacked back to back, during which he'd be intensely happy but unavailable, then nothing. Between jobs, he could be irresponsible—or worse, cruel. By contrast, Len always has some sort of work lined up; no job is beneath him. When money was tight he bagged groceries. Val's two jobs fill in the gaps. They have a little postwar ranch house, painted shell green; they have a black pickup and a Cutlass. They have Junie.

Pastor Tom, in the confiding voice of someone who has stumbled upon irrefutable truth, tells her that God works in mysterious ways, and Val—who has seen Dakota withdraw, who is engaged in the long goodbye with her own mother—has honestly tried to see God in the details. But Uncle Moon is dead, and her own father, Ed: Ruby claims memories of Ed, but Val cannot feature him. There were no pictures of him in the farmhouse, not even hidden, for Val did most of the packing when they closed the house down; she would have found the cache, if such a thing existed. It seems he was another Bryan. Feckless. An asshat, always out of town, claiming to look for work. Ruby tells her that their father's laugh was like copper bells.

Ruby. Well, she got out, didn't she? Though Val remembers feeling sorry for her, ten to Ruby's sixteen, and even Val, a child, understood how her sister didn't fit in. Wearing the Big Girl line from the JCPenney in Rice Lake, while Val could wear anything.

And this: For all those years, after Ruby moved away, Val had Mom to herself. At first this was a good thing, Val set apart as something special, and there was no competing for Barbara's attentions. The hard part was over—Val and Ruby were grown—and Barbara seemed to enjoy her new role, stopping by the green ranch house "just to check in," advising and talking to her younger daughter in a way that Val recognized was new. They both knew Ruby was glad to be gone, and this understanding, rarely voiced, drew them closer.

Dakota and Junie, they brought Val and Barbara close too. Suddenly Barbara and Val were both mothers. Moon would come up with reasons to help around the house; he and Len got on. The two men might be painting the siding, for instance, and Barbara would drink coffee in the kitchen and play with the girls so that Val could get things done. Junie was just a baby then. If Dakota had problems with a girlfriend, or Junie was colicky, Val could talk to her mother. She has inherited Barbara's ferocity when it comes to her children; what she wouldn't give for them both to be happy.

Sometimes Barbara and Moon would stay for supper.

Okay, Ruby helps. She's driving up today; Val made sure of that. Last time, when Mom fell, she didn't break anything, and Ruby, who had some work thing and never made it up north, has made a point of mentioning that. But someone had to go to the hospital with Mom. Someone had to be there, and Barbara so confused, and frightened; she'd grabbed Val's arm and wouldn't let go.

This latest stroke or whatever it is, Val isn't going to face alone. She called Ruby from the hospital parking lot. Woke her, of course, but still. Ruby acted as though her own life was more important than Val's.

When they moved Mom to the nursing home, Len and Val had worked like stevedores. They'd put everything—or almost everything—else aside, to get the job done. It had been a godforsaken time of year, the road to the farmhouse hard to navigate, tortured into icy ruts. They'd already sold, or given away, or thrown out, the bulk of Mom's possessions, Mom "helping" with the great task of it. Never one to snivel, even in her deteriorating state, Barbara made herself shuffle in small steps around the house she had loved.

At first Val had tried to draw Barbara into the process, asking her about this item or that, but this proved to be excruciating. Most of the time, Barbara simply couldn't decide. At one point Val and Len, in desperation, had taken boxes of the Christmas things to the dump. The sight of the old celluloid Santa, perched atop the burning slag, had made Val laugh in terror, and she had to admit, she'd been glad to have Len with her then. He put his arm around her and turned her away from the spectacle, saying in his direct way that the decorations would have disappeared from their lives sooner or later, and that the hard part was seeing it happen. She's always remembered that, just as she won't forget that he stuck by her, doing the work no one else wanted to do. Ruby hadn't helped with any of it, though she'd taken a week off from work and come for the actual move.

The money from the sale of the house pays for Cedar Manor. At least for now. Honestly, Val had thought that with the shock of leaving her home, Mom would be dead within the year. She's still alive, and though people seem to think Ruby, as the elder daughter, manages the finances, it's actually Val. Mom's friend Pearl brought it up just the other day, at the IGA, of all places. Val was ringing up the woman's milk and egg noodles, and Pearl just kept talking, something about her husband learning wood carving, how she knows Len carves, and maybe they might all get together. The woman has a penetrating laugh, and she laughed that day. "I could make us a roast!" she said. Then there was something about Barb, and Cedar Manor, and she mentioned Ruby, how Ruby handled the finances, no doubt.

Val couldn't keep track of what the woman was saying. *None of your business*, she thought, but didn't say. She bagged the woman's groceries deliberately, ducking her head. Barb has made her the executor of the will, and Val swings between pride at that and depthless worry. Cedar Manor was a nice place.

"What the hell?" Ruby had joked about the color of Barbara's room in the nursing home. This was back when Mom first moved in, and Ruby had made fun of the electric blue, not understanding that Len and Val had chosen the paint and done the work. Val had thought (mistakenly) that the new color would be more cheerful than neutral walls. Well. After Mom died, or moved, they'd have to paint it back to beige again. "It's better than the old paint," Val had said. "Sorry you didn't make it up here to see that. Ever." Okay, that was sort of mean; though Val apologized, Ruby's feelings were hurt. She got defensive, the way sisters do. They'd quarreled.

Val hears a call from the girls' room and glances at her watch. That would be Junie; Dakota won't wake without prompting before ten o'clock. Outside, the sky is gray-white, clouds pressed flat and low against the horizon. They look like milk, but with ink stirred in. Milk, ink. The two words go together somehow, as if they might be joined, in a sentence or a poem. Val sits up straighter. She reaches for a pen.

"Mamaaaaaa!" calls Junie. An old soul, she rarely cries, as if guessing that Dakota provides enough drama. But the child's voice is panicky now; pushing the cat from her lap, Val sets her coffee cup down and moves quickly.

"Hey, baby." The girls share a room, painted the same blue as their grandmother's. There had been paint left over, and Dakota helped—she was only eleven then, still capable, at times, of offering to pitch in—sponging fat yellow suns onto the blue. She's since taped posters on her side: angry images from rock groups that Val doesn't recognize. Over Junie's bed hangs a crayon drawing of four cartoonish figures, their heads and hands like balloons. I LOVE MAMA AND DADDY AND SISSY, she has carefully lettered, in red, at the bottom.

"Mama, I had a dream."

"Can everyone shut up?" Dakota, pillow bent around her head, hisses with exasperation. Her pretty face is red and distorted, marked with lines from the bedspread.

"I had a dream, Mama. There were monsters and they had teeth." Junie pronounces it "teef." She'll need speech therapy; the teachers say so.

"Shut *up!*"

"It's okay, baby." Val sits at the edge of Junie's bed and strokes the girl's hair. "Daddy fixed the crack." There used to be a space between the wallboard and the floor, which terrified the child.

"It's seven in the goddamn *morning*," Dakota wails.

"Don't swear," Val says automatically. Sometimes she likes her younger daughter better; is there sin in that? "It's time to get up." She stands and rubs her hands through her hair. In the mirror over the girls' bureau, even in the dim, she can see how the thin skin beneath her eyes is dark as tar.

Junie turns over and searches her face. "What's wrong, Mama?"

"Gram's still sick," Val says. "She'll be okay."

Dakota sighs. "I suppose I won't get to pom squad today, then."

"Aunt Ruby will take you," Val says.

"Aunt Ruby? Yay!" Junie sits up and even Dakota looks pleased.

"She has to see Gram first," Val says.

Dakota kicks her blanket off and stretches. "I hate mornings," she announces.

One of many things the girl hates.

"Just don't swear about it," Val says. She thinks of her coffee, abandoned in the kitchen. Black, and the satisfaction of its bitterness. Such a silly thing, but one more example of how Val can take on what others avoid.

She thinks of her mother. At the hospital, Barbara's eyes had been half-closed, her face loose in a slipping away that Val tells herself is almost like sleep. In this regard, Val is like her mother; she is waiting for something to happen. She is waiting for something to be over.

MOON

Welcome

When his nieces were born, he was pleased. They were perfect, and he professed amazement at their tiny hands, the rubbery smiles that Barbara said were gas. He didn't know what to give them to welcome them to the world, and so he asked Babs's friend Pearl. But she went on and on about her own daughter's habits and preferences, and Moon held the phone away from his ear. When she stopped to take a breath, he said his thanks; still uncertain, he went to Barthel's in town and bought a stuffed animal. One for Ruby, and then one, six years later, for Val.

Babs never made a fuss. It started with a phone call—"Ed's gone again"—and so Moon made himself available. At first it was just picking up Ruby at school. Barbara would make him supper—she said it was the least she could do—and he appreciated it. Before then he'd eaten most of his meals at the diner in town, and so it was a nice change, the dining room bright, the four of them filling out the table. Sometimes Val threw her Cheerios on the floor and they all laughed. He was a part of things, and one night, when he helped Ruby with homework (it might have been a diorama—he had tremendous patience for the folding of paper, the tiny pieces), he just stayed over. The house was big, and Barbara might have said something about feeling afraid.

"Stay, Uncle Moon!" This from the little girls, and the next time he brought a pack of cards. He taught Ruby to play War and Crazy Eights. Eventually he taught Val, though when she got older she didn't want to play anymore. Ruby never tired of the games; sometimes they'd play, barely paying attention, flipping cards while they watched reruns of some crazy British show Ruby liked. He never understood what was so funny, the crude cartoons and repetition, but he laughed when Ruby did.

It wasn't like Babs ever said, "Can you move in?" He did it piece by piece, first keeping some clothes in a drawer. His red toothbrush stayed in the downstairs bath. One day she said, "You don't really need to be paying that rent, do you now?" Since Nam he had worked a series of odd jobs, but now his job became the farm. His family.

He gained weight, living at the house; he didn't get sick as often. They didn't mention Ed after a while, even after the little girls were in bed.

It was good to be needed.

RUBY

Homemade

The rain has let up and the sky looks silver, scraped clean, down to the marrow. And how would a sky sound? It would ring like china, Ruby thinks. She pulls into the graveled drive of Val's house, a two-bedroom ranch the color of mint chocolate chip ice cream. There is the familiar resignation. She is in Ladyford now. *I'm here*, she texts Lorna.

The lawn rises in untidy tufts, which surprises Ruby, and when she drags her bag up the walk she sees a new birdbath, right by the front steps. She stops at the door and rubs her eyes, grainy beneath the lids, as if filled with sand. The birdbath is half up with water that has frozen, and there are leaves embedded in the ice. Since Ruby's last visit, someone—Len, maybe—has painted the door a dark glossy red. Ruby tries the knob—though most people around here leave their doors open, Val's is locked—then knocks, standing on her toes and trying to peer into the round peephole window. Looking through the pebbled glass is like looking through a kaleidoscope. Her whole body is tight from the drive, and she stretches. The tooth fragment is still in her mouth. She kept it there all this time, an awkward communion wafer, and now she spits it into her hand. *Smile*, she reminds herself. All she has to do is get through this next part. Then the part after that.

The door opens suddenly and there is her sister, wearing an old AC/DC T-shirt and a darned cardigan, gray sweatpants pleated around her waist like a skirt. Thin-soled shoes on her feet. Ruby drops to her heels, smiling uncertainly. Val has a way of not smiling and there's no smile now. But she opens her arms and Ruby is enveloped in the sweater as if by wings.

"You took your time getting here," Val says. She is thin. She has always been slender, but now her face has planes and points. Beneath her eyes droop deep purple swags.

"I did my best," Ruby says. "It was a rough drive."

"It was rough here too."

"Well," Ruby says, "I'm here now." Besides their mother, Val is the living person who has been in her life the longest. "Mom. Is she…?"

"She's alive, if that's what you're asking. Oh hell, come on in. There's coffee going." Ruby hugs her sister again, feels the bones of her shoulders, and takes in the living room, which is strangely, almost shockingly, a midden: stacks of paper on the couch and a mess of toys and sports gear littering the floor, the cloudy fishbowl on the television set. No fish.

It is as though she has entered a stranger's home, and the thought that her own house is actually, for once, neater than her sister's flashes across Ruby's mind so that she is satisfied—only for a moment, but still, the satisfaction is there.

Val closes the door against the cold. She does a silly, shambling sort of bow, her hair untidy. It's awkward but she's trying to make light. "The maid didn't come this week."

"Aw, it's fine," Ruby says, holding to herself the secret that she *does* have a housekeeper, a Polish woman named Daria who comes every other Wednesday when Ruby is at work; when she returns home those days, her condo is clean, if still cluttered, and smells like oranges. "You should see my place," is what she says.

The coffee smells good, at least, and Val is baking something, though Ruby doubts she could eat anything with this tooth. Her mouth throbs. She drops her suitcase to the floor with a sigh. "Well. I made it. Broken tooth and all."

"What? Your tooth? Open up." Val leans forward, and Ruby bares her teeth in a smile. "What *happened* to you?"

"Frozen muffin." Ruby shrugs, suddenly embarrassed. "I was hungry! Don't look at me like that. It hurts like hell." The tooth fragment cuts into her palm, and she slips it into her pocket.

"It doesn't look that bad," Val says, and Ruby remembers, suddenly, that her sister has always had a high threshold for pain. The story goes that Val refused an epidural at the births of both her daughters. The way Len told it, the doctor was indifferent but then warmed when Val proved her mettle, remaining stoic through not one but two protracted labors.

"Okay, so it isn't childbirth," Ruby says. "But it does hurt."

Val shrugs and leads the way into her tiny kitchen. This is still spotless, the counters scrubbed white and something, an art project of Junie's maybe, is arranged beside a sugar bowl in the middle of the table. It's a lamb, it looks like, made of clay, and Ruby thinks of the lamb-shaped butter their mother used to buy at Easter. Uncle Moon would slice those thick butter lambs at their holiday dinner, passing out yellow wedges along with the Parker House rolls, and the girls would shriek, "Don't give me the butt! Don't give me the butt!" not because they cared, but because they knew they'd be rewarded with one of Moon's rare smiles. This ceramic lamb—blue daubs for eyes, crusted with sparkles—is an ugly thing.

Val fetches a mug from the shelf over the stove and pours out a cup of coffee for Ruby. "Mom's stable. You'll want to see her sooner rather than later."

"Maybe I will make time in my busy schedule to do just that," Ruby says. She's trying to joke, but it doesn't come out the way she intends; her words sound mean, not funny. Brittle. But then her tooth does hurt like a sonofabitch. Val grabs a sponge from the sink and sets to scrubbing the spotless counter, and Ruby, ashamed, dumps a heaping spoonful of sugar into her cup. There's a carton of creamer on the table and Ruby dumps some of that in too. Val always drinks her coffee black. Ruby told Lorna that once, and her friend just laughed and said this made Ruby's sister bitter. "No matter how pretty she might be," she added, probably meaning to be reassuring, and Ruby ruined it, didn't she, the way she made her friend tell her that she was pretty too.

Ruby lifts the cup to her lips but the hot coffee against the exposed nerve of her tooth is excruciating—a singular, round, and pulsing ache. Christ on a bicycle! She swallows hard and then holds the mug for its warmth alone, hands cupped around the rose-colored ceramic. "The coffee's good," she says. "I'm tired from the drive."

Val turns to study Ruby, who cannot help but notice the way her sister's hipbones protrude through the soft fabric of her pants. "When were you here last?" Val says.

Three months, Ruby thinks. It's not that she doesn't keep track. In the months since, Ruby has thought of one reason, then another, not to make the trip north. But Mom's okay; Ruby is saving up for when Barbara might really need her. The visits here take so much energy, not just because Mom is changing— and she is, but she'll live for a long time, she's tough, she's not even seventy—but because Ruby works so hard to fly under the radar when she's in Ladyford. She doesn't want to run into people she knows. She doesn't want to know what the people she might run into are doing. For years she simply didn't care, but now maybe there is something else. "I took off work to be here," she says, then adds idiotically, "My tooth hurts."

"I can make you an appointment with the girls' dentist."

The sisters stare at one another. "Okay," Ruby finally says. "Yeah."

A buzzer goes off and Val turns to pull a pan of cinnamon rolls from the oven. She places a breadboard made of dark maple on the table and sets the pan on top of that. Ruby remembers Barbara using that breadboard when they were girls. "You can probably eat one of these, at least; they're soft," Val says.

"Thanks," Ruby says. The rolls do smell good. And they're piping hot; if Val has any butter it would just dissolve on top. "Homemade?"

Val doesn't smile, not exactly. "Homemade," she agrees, and Ruby is cheered. Val is a good—no, a great—cook, a maker of comfort foods that stick. Ruby, whose one and only attempt at mashed potatoes resulted in a gluey spackle some Thanksgivings back, genuinely appreciates this about her sister.

"Butter?" Ruby has started moving toward the fridge, but Val shakes her head. "Homemade cinnamon rolls just aren't the same without butter."

"I'm going shopping later."

"Remember those butter lambs we'd get at Easter?"

"I probably took a picture of one," Val says, and Ruby laughs. It's a family joke; for years Val wouldn't go anywhere without a camera. Ruby sits down and tears off a piece of roll. It's good even without butter, melting against her tongue. If not Val's best, still, delicious—the nutty vein of cinnamon lifting her spirits around the pulsing of her tooth. She'd like another, but maybe Val didn't make them for her. "Are the kids at school?"

"It's Friday, Ruby."

"Well, how are they?"

"Great." Val lifts herself up to the counter, where she sits cross-legged, pulling at her roll, licking icing from her fingers. She looks half her age; she looks like a girl. Her nails are blunt, painted in thick, unsteady strokes. Chipped black—Junie's work—and the skin on her hands is papery dry. On the back of her left hand, MILK and INK are written in block letters.

"You should add butter to your list," Ruby says, nodding at Val's hand.

"Oh! Yeah. This was just something..." Val trails off, embarrassed.

"You have beautiful hands," Ruby says. Years ago, when they were children, Ruby resented how people noticed her sister's long fingers and narrow wrists, when Val was already so beautiful. Ruby thinks about her own sturdy hands, large and workmanlike. Good for playing the piano, Barbara used to say. "Do the girls play instruments?" Ruby asks now.

"That's—uh, not in the budget."

"Oh." Ruby tries to think what to say next. She should have known money would be tight. "I just meant, what do they like these days?"

"Junie loves first grade," Val says. "Junie loves everything."

"I'll bet. I can see that." Ruby likes Val's older daughter better but tries not to let on. After a beat she allows herself to ask, "And what's Dakota up to?"

"Dakota." Val sighs and puts her roll down. "Dakota's fine. Dakota's on poms." She looks around the kitchen again, abstractedly pets the cat that has leapt onto the counter, then leans back into the cabinetry. "Dakota thinks a lot about Dakota these days."

Val has always been harder on her firstborn. "That sounds pretty typical," Ruby says. "Teenage stuff." She reaches for another roll.

"I guess." Val looks at Ruby closely. "Can I tell you something?" Her eyelids flick. "Maybe Dakota isn't so fine," she says. "She got picked up for shoplifting at the mall. Did you know that?"

"No," Ruby says. This kind of thing wasn't happening the last time she was here, at least she didn't think so. "What was that all about?"

"I don't know. She won't talk to me." There is a pause, then Val takes a bite of roll and chews vigorously. "She likes you," she says, mouth full. "Maybe you can figure out what's going on. Talk to her, will you?" Val stares at what's left of her roll. "It's hard for me to ask you that," she says softly.

"Sure. Of course. Hell, Val, you know I love Dakota. I just need to get this tooth fixed."

Val looks up, chewing hard again. "Okay," she finally says. "I'll make a call."

Ruby nods. "I could take Dakota out for something to eat. She and I—we can talk then."

"After you see Mom."

"After I see Mom," Ruby says. "And get my tooth fixed."

Something is settled between them, and Val slips off the counter. "Hey, how's Drago?" she asks. "Doing all right?"

"He's fine," Ruby says, which is probably true. She hasn't told her sister that Drago's gone; they'll get to it sometime this visit. But Ruby is surprised—touched, even—that Val brought him up. Her family never really liked Drago; no one ever said it, but Ruby could tell. "Thanks for asking." She looks at her sister, who still has the cardigan draped over her shoulders. "That sweater—I have a friend who designs sweaters. Lexi—have I talked about her before?" Val doesn't say anything, just shakes her head. "No? She's nice, you'd like her. She uses these beautiful linen yarns—gorgeous colors, like ice cream." Val turns and runs water into the sink. "So, my friend?" Ruby says. "She's in Chicago, and she makes these sweaters, but they're not bulky. It's the quality of the yarn. They're expensive but worth it, you know?"

She's talking to Val's back. She's babbling. Val turns to look at her. "I don't care, Ruby. I've got other things on my mind."

Ruby stares. They could be back in Duluth, neither of them wanting the same thing. She pulls the plate closer. The rolls are gone, but she wets her finger and picks up crumbles of icing from the plate. There is nothing left to eat, nothing left to say. "Oh. Okay. So, where do I sleep?"

"We'll figure out something," Val says. She gestures vaguely at the cluttered living room, and Ruby's heart sinks.

The couch there is a merciless tweed; even with sheets tucked in, the cushions scratch like hell. "Maybe there's a quieter place for me to bunk?" Ruby knows there isn't any such place, but surely one of the girls could give up their bed for a night or two. Can't kids sleep just about anywhere?

"I *said* we'd figure something out." Val, moving restlessly around the kitchen, pours the last of the coffee into her own cup. "You know, Mom didn't know me last night," she says.

Ruby fusses with her cup; this is unlike Val, to talk about what is unpleasant, that which can't be changed. "How could Mom not know you?" she finally says. "You're over there pretty much every day."

Val removes the plastic basket from the Mr. Coffee and taps wet grounds into the garbage. She turns and runs her hands through her hair. "I am, Ruby. Sometimes twice a day."

"Maybe she was having a dream?"

Val shakes her head. "She was awake, but she called me Sonny."

"Um...Sonny?" Ruby is suddenly gripped by the inappropriate urge to laugh. She wishes there were just one more cinnamon roll. "Who the hell is Sonny?"

"That's just it; I don't know. And she was pale, and her eyes were all funny. Her...mouth. Not funny ha ha, okay? Funny strange."

"She was tired," Ruby says lamely. But these details are scary, and new; what can she say, since she wasn't there? But maybe that's the point. Ruby sighs. She herself wants nothing more from Val than to have her old sidekick back, that younger, sweeter sibling, someone to affirm her, Mutt to her Jeff. The thought surprises her, but it's true. Val used to idolize her and it's nice, Ruby thinks, to be adored.

"You know how it is. Up and down. She'll be better this afternoon," Ruby says, and then tries to think when *she* knew that things were going wrong with their mother. And she wonders when Val understood. For sure. There were those cloudy middle years, before what Mom carried within her had a name, when their get-togethers were strange, but not marked by loss in the way they are now. "Anyhow, this isn't new. She's been this way for a while."

"You *always* say that," Val says.

"Well, it's hard to see the big picture when you're with her all the time."

"Exactly. I. Am. With. Mom. All the *time*."

"I know, Val."

"It gets harder every day."

"I get that," Ruby says. It used to be she would come away from a weekend with Barbara feeling impatient but not afraid. Mom hadn't been as attentive, perhaps. Or there might be a lapse that they'd laugh about later, like the time they made popcorn in the new microwave oven Ruby had brought Barbara. They were having a little party. Ruby was home; she'd brought gifts. She was staying at the house with Mom, and Val, pregnant with Junie, had come over with supper. Barbara probably was starting to have trouble cooking, though Ruby didn't know it yet. She's ashamed of that now, the not-knowing, though she'd had the grace to thank Val for the good meal. Meatloaf, Ruby still remembers.

Sometimes those suppers—there could be tension. Ruby would see how Val and Barbara connected over parenting. Though she tried to hide her jealousy, sometimes it showed; it probably showed that night. She ate too much for starters. She might have been abrupt with her niece. To compensate, Ruby made a point of inviting Val and Dakota to stay after for popcorn and a movie, but Val refused, suddenly prickly herself. She'd swept Dakota before her out the door, Dakota protesting that she *was* done with her homework (and what kind of homework did a first grader have, anyway?) and that she wanted popcorn too.

It ended up being Barbara and Ruby alone in the house (where was Moon? Ruby can't remember), and Ruby had stood at the big front window, watching Val pack her daughter into the truck. Dakota carried a stuffed animal back then, though she held it carelessly by one leg, as if, even at six, she didn't want anyone to know she cared. Ruby stayed at the window, waving until the truck drove out of sight.

Ruby didn't see her mom use the green metal bowl. She heard the sparking, though, and when she ran into the kitchen she saw the white light arcing through the cloudy microwave window. There wasn't a fire, thank God, but the fine new microwave door was spoiled with a burn. Barbara stood in the middle of the kitchen, hands to face and her head swinging back and forth on her neck like a tree in the wind. Ruby told her mother she'd pay to get the microwave fixed, but Barbara, perhaps embarrassed at her lapse—"I don't know *what* I was thinking!"—never took it in. When they sold the house, the microwave went with it, a brown scorch still marking the door. Dakota said she saw a grizzly bear in it.

Ruby and Barbara laughed about the popcorn ("Mom! You're supposed to be a *better* cook than me!"). Har har; a couple glasses of wine, and the incident almost became a joke. Later, there was nothing funny about the listing walk, and the dementia, creeping so subtly that some visits Ruby thought it was her own imagination at play. She wanted to believe that things could be the way they always had, with Barbara bouncing back from every adversity. Hell, she'd lost her husband to the world. She'd lost her father to cancer, and she'd held on to her farm for years.

Val probably caught on months before Ruby that something was going—had already gone—terribly wrong, but they never talked about it until Barbara's deterioration became impossible to ignore. Ruby finally made herself ask Val if she'd noticed Barbara's behavior getting stranger and stranger, and her sister said yes, maybe she had, and they left it at that until the diagnosis. Then Moon died, and although it took a while, finally it was Len who suggested they move Barbara to a nursing home. For her own safety.

"We've been through hard times with Mom before," Ruby says now.

"Well," Val says abruptly, "now that you're here, I need to take a shower. I feel like I haven't washed my hair in days." She pulls a plastic garbage bin from under the sink and sets it next to the door that opens out to the garage. "There's a lot to do around here."

Ruby rubs at her mouth. "You'll get me into the dentist, right?"

"Absolutely," Val says. She picks up the garbage bin again, hugging it to her chest. "I'll make that my top priority." She turns and stalks into the garage. She doesn't shut the door and cold air reaches in.

Don't be that way, Ruby means to say. *I know how shitty this is.* Even leaned back in her chair, her stomach is a soft roll, lapping over her waistband. "This coffee is good," she calls, and leans down to pet the cat, a black-and-white Junie brought home last year, named Jellybean. Jellybean is soft-looking, as loose around the middle as Ruby, and Ruby croons to her. She and Val argued about coffee the last time Ruby was here. Ridiculous, really. You'd think they were twelve. But being back here in Ladyford together seems to make them both act in ways she would like to think they've outgrown. That time, Ruby had criticized a latte from the little café in town; she called it cloying, and Val had called her pretentious. It wasn't as if *Val* had served the coffee, but maybe she knew the owners. In any case, the latte was horrible: a weak, miasmic hazelnut that, like a smell, stayed with Ruby long after she drank it.

Ruby left early that time. She told Val's girls that something had come up at work, and she told herself it was because she was sick of sleeping poorly. Val had put her on the couch that time too.

Val returns to the kitchen, tucking her cell phone into a pocket and swiping her palms together briskly. "Well, I got you in. He'll see you at eleven-thirty." She takes a swig of coffee and goes back to scrubbing the counter.

"The dentist? Eleven-thirty?" Ruby glances at the wall clock; it's past ten. "Doc Braden?" That's the dentist they went to as girls; he was old as Methuselah then, so God knows what he looks like now. She imagines the old man's face, darkened with age. He had a cleft in his chin that could hide an olive.

"Same old office, but it's Tim now. Actually."

"Tim who?" Ruby stands, crumbs cascading from her lap.

"Tim Baxter."

"Ha ha." Her old flame. Wouldn't that be rich? "C'mon, it's with Braden, right? The old guy?"

"'The old guy,' as you put it, has been dead for years. If you paid attention to anything Mom or I said—" Val pauses in her scrubbing. "I know it might be a little awkward." She shrugs. "But Tim's the only game in town."

"Shit."

Val turns to her and leans against the counter. "And they can see you now. I talked to Carrie. His wife," she says. "I called her;

that's how you got in so fast. He's usually booked. Seriously, he's good."

"Great," Ruby says.

"For god's sake, grow up," Val says. "How many years has it been? I mean, c'mon. The guy's really happy. He and Carrie, they're even expecting."

Something drops in Ruby's stomach. She looks outside at the weird sterling sky. "A kid?"

"No, a kitten." Val's laugh is almost but not quite mean. "Yes, a kid, you dope! Be sure to congratulate him when you see him."

"How do you even know all this?"

"Ruby. It's a small town. Carrie's my friend. Carrie and me—"

"I can't do this," Ruby says. She looks down at her belly; frosting smears her sweatshirt, which pulls a little tighter across her breasts than she remembered. "No way." She fumbles in her purse and pulls out her phone.

"What are you doing?" Val puts her hands on her hips.

"I'm calling my dentist. I have to go home and take care of this."

Val's face darkens, but Ruby moves to the sink, where she can look out the window at her sister's yard. She is disconnected once before she gets a phone tree; it takes several more minutes before she reaches a human being.

"This is Lynne," the woman says. Her voice sounds clipped, almost angry, but when Ruby asks for an appointment tomorrow she laughs. "We can get you in in two weeks, Rudy. If you can come in at seven a.m."

"This is an emergency. I'm driving down from Wisconsin."

"Rudy, I'll do my best, but if I were you, I'd have it taken care of there."

"My name is Ruby."

"I'd still have it taken care of there."

Ruby squeezes her eyes shut.

"I have another call coming in, ma'am. Shall I put you down

for seven o'clock? That's in two weeks," the woman reminds her in a helpful voice.

"Never mind," Ruby says. She opens her eyes and when she turns around Val is waiting.

"I got you in today," Val says. Ruby stares at her sister's folded arms, at the skull ring Val has worn since she was a teenager.

"I know," Ruby says. "Because you're besties with my ex's wife."

"We're friends." Beneath the pride in Val's voice is something else.

"Even if Tim could do something temporary to stabilize my tooth, I better go home tonight. I'll get in somewhere."

"Ruby, that doesn't even make sense. Carrie said you have to put the tooth piece in, what? Milk or something? You'll have a long drive back. At night. And you said you'd talk to Dakota."

"I'd rather drive through the night than sleep on that couch again."

"Well, then take my bed! Ruby, you are not doing this to me again. You are not leaving me here alone with Mom."

"I can't help what's happening," Ruby says.

"Yes, you can help. It's always something!" Val's voice is rising; she stops, takes a breath. "What was it last time? Work?"

"Don't yell at me." Ruby is suddenly calm. Of course she can't leave. Mom is probably okay, but what if she isn't? "I'll stay." Ruby stands and looks hard, not at the spotless kitchen but at the living room beyond, its strata of toys and tennis shoes.

"I can't help it," Val says, following her eyes, and in that moment Ruby is sorry.

"Val, listen." But before she can say anything to make it right, to make it different, Val's cell rings, and Ruby jumps.

"Len," Val says, glancing at her phone. She moves into the living room. "Hi," Ruby hears her say. "Yeah, she just got in." There is a murmur of unintelligible conversation, and then Val yells, "You should get going, Ruby!" She pokes her head into the kitchen. "Here, do you have the tooth? Give it here." Ruby fishes the sliver of tooth out of her pocket and hands it to Val, who fills a sippy cup with milk from the fridge and drops the piece in. "You have time to go see Mom before your appointment if you hustle," she says, screwing the lid on the sippy cup and handing it to Ruby. "Carrie said they were squeezing you in." Val returns to the living room without waiting for a reply.

Squeezing me in so I can feel like a stupid ass. A baby! God. Ruby crumples up her napkin and flips the lid on the trash. The box on top, flattened into the coffee grounds and banana peels, is for cinnamon rolls: *Just Like Homemade,* it carols in blocky red letters. "Homemade my ass," Ruby murmurs. She spies the creamer, still sitting in its paper carton on the counter, and stows it in the fridge. There's not much on the wire shelves, but several sticks of good, pale butter are stacked in the door. Homemade cinnamon rolls just aren't the same without butter. Ruby grabs a stick, peels back the foil, and takes a bite. "Mmpf," she says.

Her fingers are greasy when she turns back to the counter. Someone has left a stuffed animal there; it's probably Junie's, a bear. It still wears a tag. Val told her once that the kids keep the tags on, to make the toys more collectible, and this one—blue and soft—looks relatively clean. Ruby examines the toy, then abruptly stuffs it into her sweatshirt pocket. Hey, she'll have a baby gift for Tim and what's-her-name, won't she?

Congratulations, she thinks.

Her sister is still talking to Len when Ruby passes through the living room on her way out, but Val cups her hand over the receiver and says, "Be sure to visit Mom first."

Got it. Ruby gives her sister the thumbs-up and bares her wrecked teeth, hand on the open door.

"Don't let the cat out!" Val is shouting now, pointing. "The cat, the cat!" Ruby looks down and sure enough, there is Jelly-bean, humming and twining around her legs. "The last thing I need is worms, or feline leukemia—can you please close the door so she doesn't get out? *Thank* you!"

"You're welcome," Ruby says, shutting the door with its tiny peephole window of pebbled glass behind her. The bear in her pocket is dense and warm. She never knows what anyone wants from her.

Ruby pulls her phone from her back pocket and there's a text from Lorna: *Glad u arrived safe. Hang tough. Don't worry about concert. Next time, honey. Jim and I must content ourselves with a movie tonight, but it def won't be the same. We miss you!*

Ruby stares at the screen for a moment. Lorna writes texts that are like emails; her emails are like letters. She lives in a walkup, the lobby lined with small silver mailboxes and smelling of incense. Curry. Ruby loves visiting there. Lorna has strewn throw pillows on the floor of her living room and maintains a terrific library of movies. Motherly, she takes care of the people in her life.

She could call Lorna back. *Next time,* she texts instead. Ruby longs to call Drago. He was her best friend, until he wasn't.

Val

Berryman

The door closes behind Ruby. "Goodbye!" Val yells at no one. Her heart clatters painfully; there must be a physical explanation for how she feels, the sweep of maroon behind her eyes, the pressure in her head, in her veins. If you asked Ruby, Val supposes, her sister would say she has a temper. But that's not how Val sees herself.

"You still there?" she says into the phone. She and Len had been talking about Barbara. These days it seems they are always talking about Barbara. "My sister's here," she says, as if Len didn't know, as if he hadn't heard their exchange. "God, all she thinks about is herself."

"You two going to fight?" In high school, people said Len was slow. But he's direct and doesn't talk unless he has something to say; that's something Val likes about her husband.

"No," Val says. "But she waltzes in from her life in Chicago—I mean, thanks for making the *time*." Val hitches her voice up, meaning to sound like Ruby: "I just loooove Chicago! You should meet my friend Lexi, she's a designer? She makes these wonderful sweaters? You have to get one of her sweaters! You have to spend five hundred *dollars* on one of her sweaters!" Val pauses, breathing hard. She hadn't meant to shout. "Mom's probably going to die and she shows up talking about *sweaters*." Val's mouth gets dry when she is upset, and then it is hard to talk.

"Now we have a little more help," Len says.

"She doesn't want to be here."

"But she's here."

"Yeah," Val mutters. "The house. It's such a mess."

"What, Valley? Say that again?" He must have the phone up to his bad ear.

"Did you want something?" she asks then. It doesn't come out the way she means it to. "I'm just tired," she says. "I'm sorry, Len."

"Do you know someone named Berryman?" Len asks.

"Berryman?" Val takes a breath. "Berryman," she says. "Wait, Len. Someone else is trying to call. Can I call you back?"

"'S okay. It doesn't matter. I'll be home late, though. Don't wait supper for me." He hangs up before Val can reply, and she thinks that at least the Robinstadt job must be going okay, if he's working late.

Val switches over calls without checking to see who it is. It might be the hospital, a thought that twists her gut. "Hel-lo? Hello?" She stands and dumps her sister's full coffee cup into the sink.

But it's a computerized sales call, and she hangs up, almost in tears. She feels so rushed. She feels afraid.

Ruby will be at the hospital soon enough. Would she call to say how Mom is doing? Probably not, not after the way they left things, but Val suddenly wishes she would.

Val thinks about Ruby's tooth—it did look painful—and for the space of a moment she feels bad about the dentist. No getting around the fact that it'll be awkward for Ruby, seeing Tim. It would have been better for her sister to go somewhere else, though it was the truth: Tim is a decent dentist, and the only one in town.

RUBY

The Rules of Engagement

Ruby means to see her mother first. She promised Val, and so she drives to Cedar Manor, the senior village where Mom lives. That's what it's called—a village—and it is perched on the near side of the river, its low-slung buildings paved in brick and chocolate wood, with the usual flags out front: United States, Wisconsin, and something else, Ruby has never been sure what. The front entrance is covered with an awning like a fancy resort, and carriage lamps—wrought from twining black metal, straight from the 1970s and comfortingly so, being reminiscent, for Ruby, of childhood—flank the doors. Ruby goes so far as to park, a good enough spot because the lot is half empty. She stares at the entry doors, at the stout woman in a pale smock who cleans them with a twist of newspaper. *They try here*, Ruby thinks. The nursing wing is to the left and behind.

That's where Mom is now. The days of small lapses are gone, and there are new rules at play. New ways to be together. Val says it's like tending to her girls when they were smaller. The patience, the redirecting. Most of the time she's better at that than Ruby is. Ruby doesn't know how to handle the sudden dark moods, what almost amounts to tantrums.

When Barbara becomes petulant, Ruby defaults to a cheery obliviousness that she hates. Like the mother of a girlhood friend, Charlene Stepnor, Ruby chirps and clucks, holding on to the fraught rictus of a grin. Mrs. Stepnor had been uptight. She wore the clothing of a nursery-school teacher—long denim skirts and holiday sweaters—and she smiled anxiously at whatever Charlene and Ruby might come up with: the tight jeans, the slasher movies, the music by Skid Row. She hated when things were messy, or ugly, or sad; Ruby always suspected that she herself wasn't quite *nice* enough for Mrs. Stepnor's tastes, even though Charlene's teen years became a horror show of drug abuse far beyond Ruby's own modest dabbling in pot.

Throughout it all—the failing grades, the pregnancy at fifteen—Charlene's mother maintained a false cheer that Ruby mocked. Now she feels for Mrs. Stepnor, wherever she is. Charlene and her family moved away in Ruby's sophomore year, to a farm community in Missouri—Mrs. Stepnor's birthplace— where Stepnor kin could close ranks around the new baby. Val, who seems to know these things, told Ruby once that the child has been raised as Charlene's much-younger sister.

Poor Mrs. Stepnor, Ruby thinks now. Now she sees the dignity in smiling—even blankly, doggedly—under circumstances you could never have imagined. Barbara can be painfully blunt and impatient now, her old strict code of reticence forsaken. She raises her voice, at restaurants and even at church when Barbara is well enough for Ruby to take her there, and through it all, Ruby has smiled and smiled. "Mom, be nice," she might say in a mawkish voice that isn't her own, to which Barbara will retort, "Bullshit!" Barbara used to be a careful dresser. She used to take care. Barbara doesn't smell the same anymore, and Ruby knows she can't help it.

Ruby touches her tooth with a forefinger, probing to convince herself that the pain, needling, extending to her sinuses and maybe even her ear, is as bad as she thought. She'll go see Tim first, she decides. Her mom is probably sleeping anyway, probably needs her sleep. It's started sleeting, and Ruby sets the wipers going as she pulls from the senior village lot like, her mother might once have said, a bat out of hell. Barbara used to write her letters, beautiful letters. *Bat out of hell. The whole dog and pony show.* The letters, written in a strong angular hand, stopped some time ago but Ruby has kept them all.

The wiper blades pull across the glass, screeching when they swipe to the left. She'll need to get them fixed. Ruby tries to remember where an auto body shop might be. There was a tornado here, around the time Dakota was born, a bad one that tore through downtown. When Ladyford rebuilt, everything changed; Ruby doesn't know where anything is anymore.

The rules have changed, she thinks. *The rules of engagement.*

VAL

April

Val makes another pot of coffee; she has to go into the IGA at lunchtime to make up some hours. From yesterday, leaving early, and Bobby so pissed off. It'll be a long day. Caffeine will help. She looks into the living room and thinks that she should really clean off the couch at least, with Ruby here, but what she does is pull on a long-sleeved shirt—its colorful tie-dye cheers her—pour herself a fresh cup of coffee, and look out the window. It's so gray out, everyone saying how they hate November and the slush already piled high. But Val, what she hates is April.

Here's how it happens: It is April, and you are driving to Marshfield, to the doctor. Although it's still cold at night, during the day the sun warms the earth and the sky is a clear seamless blue. Blue as an egg. A mist of green has appeared on the trees. Beautiful, yes?

It was another in a long series of appointments, but this time they were seeking a specialist. Mom's GP at home—Dr. Gordon, with his seamed face and homely manner—had conceded that Barbara's needs had finally outstripped what he could do for her. And though the sun sifted like pollen into the car on the drive to Marshfield, and the trees lifted in their light coats of green, and the coffee in her travel mug smelled good (hazelnut, from the little shop in town), Val knew on some level that what this new doctor would say would be bad. Barbara was quiet beside her, and she was quiet on the drive home, too, after the doctor gave a name and a life to the changes they had all tried not to see. So silly, that once the disease was named it became real.

(A disease like that doesn't happen overnight, of course, but even though the Parkinson's had been slowly building for years, Val still thinks of time in terms of Before the diagnosis, when Barbara didn't *officially* have Parkinson's, and then everything that came After.)

While Val and her mother waited in the doctor's waiting room, Val gazed outside at the trees, which were shy and yet resplendent in their celery coats. The weather was soft and so it made people gentler: the receptionist, who joked about her husband; even the truculent kid, Brianna, whose parents owned the coffee shop where Val got her coffee to go that morning, had been uncharacteristically sweet. The world Val saw outside the waiting room window—lemon sun and crisp damp earth—did not match what was about to happen. It did not match the world she and Barbara—and Len and the girls too—were about to enter.

The diagnosis seemed like a mistake then. It still does, and Val carries within herself a certain wonder, or disbelief, that her family is not, in fact, immune to the misfortunes that you read about and shake your head over with a shudder. You think these things will never happen to you, but then they do happen, in the same order they happen to everyone else. Illness, death. Val keeps waiting to hear that Barbara's condition can be reversed. But Parkinson's can't be undone; it can only get worse.

After the diagnosis, after the silent drive home, they found Moon waiting for them at the farmhouse with the girls. Junie was little then, and he stood on the porch as they drove up, holding her in his arms. Dakota came running out to the car to greet them, and Val remembers catching Moon's eye. Just barely, she shook her head. For the first time she thought: *It is my responsibility to be happy. For the children.*

She went home that night and after the kids were in bed told Len what she had learned. They held each other, understanding what lay ahead and what it meant: up until now, Barbara and Moon had sustained them.

The next day, at breakfast, Barbara called and announced

that they were going to do something special. It was a Saturday—no school for Dakota. Len was working, but Val drove over to the farmhouse with the girls. When Val came in, Junie balanced on her hip and Dakota swinging, always swinging, from her hand, her mother was already making sandwiches in the kitchen, slicing the crusts off the way Dakota liked, and labeling sandwich bags the way she used to when Val and Ruby were kids.

Val came up to her mother at the counter and put her arms around her. "We're going to have a picnic today," Barbara said. Moon was sitting at the kitchen table, the way he did weekend mornings, reading the paper, legs crossed, and drinking cup after cup of black coffee. A patch of bare leg showed between trouser cuff and boot top; he looked over his reading glasses and nodded. Moon had always been there when they needed him. It never occurred to Val that they might lose him first.

"We'll take the tractor," he said, and Val could see it out the window, how Moon had already brought Horehound out (he'd named the John Deere that, after a kind of candy) and hitched up the trailer. The trailer was something Moon had refurbished, replacing worn slats and painting the whole thing with green gloss. The rims of the wheels were red. Cancer had probably already started its slow burn through Moon's body, but no one knew this yet. He'd lined the bed of the trailer with pillows, and an old blanket.

Moon drove the tractor, with Dakota sitting before him on the seat. Barbara and Val and Junie rode in the trailer, even though Val knew the ride was probably hard on her mother, the way they jumbled over the ruts in the fields. They drove to where the little man-made lake on their property started. Moon used to put sand at the edge, so the girls could play, and they picnicked there. "Them there are mermaid swords," Moon said of the water iris that grew along the shoreline. He smiled at the girls. The sun was flint on the water, and Barbara laughed and pretended to chase Dakota, and Val felt loss like physical pain, because it was clear to her—it was clear to all the adults—that they were making memories while they still could, while Barbara's body and mind would allow it. There was still a little time to get to know each other that much better.

Afterward, at the farmhouse, Moon put records on and pulled a face, marching to the music with a broom. Dakota laughed and laughed, though when Val asks her about it now, she claims not to remember anything about that day. Junie, of course, was so little that she doesn't remember a thing.

Val wishes she had written down every detail, the way Moon waxed Horehound's hood and Barbara lifted her knees high, clowning uncharacteristically to the music. "Look at Grandma dance!" Val had sung out, whirling little Dakota to the music. In the weeks following the diagnosis, well-meaning friends had urged her to keep a diary for the girls, so that they could keep these memories intact. Val still might do it. But every time she picks up a pen and tries to find the first words—*Grandma danced to the 45s, the song about the tuba*—she cannot think how to explain the way she and her mother came together almost fiercely that day, creating a day out of love for Val's daughters. Barbara's granddaughters.

Driving home from Marshfield, at the beginning of After, the trees were a lime fizz, and Val and Barbara said exactly nothing to each other. Val was just trying to keep her mind still. She knew she needed to be brave, but she couldn't guess how April would be spoiled for her now, how new-greening trees would become connected to disaster. And she didn't yet know—not until the picnic, and the little party afterward—the forms that bravery can take. Years later, when she is a very old woman, she will not remember the specifics of the picnic, and the drive from Marshfield will have become conflated with other hospital journeys. Sharp light on water, new buds. These things will, with time, lose their edge. But Val will always remember, and it will bring her comfort, how being cheerful is its own form of courage.

She is impatient when people like her mother's friend Pearl drop by, asking about Barbara. Val will say: "Oh, we filled

Mom's birdfeeder today, and she was so happy! We got out to the IGA and bought M&Ms, Mom's favorite." She's not lying, these things are true, and there is grace to them. But Pearl, who fancies herself a realist and has always been free with her opinions, hears her and screws up her eyes, not understanding how Val has made a choice about what to focus on—the positive—and how crucial this is for herself, for the girls.

The phone rings, pulling Val back to the morning, to November, to her mother in the hospital, Val's clean kitchen and the coffee, steaming black and starless. It's the school.

People don't understand the energy it takes. What it means to be brave.

LEN

Little Minx

Len is in the habit of listening to the radio on his drives to the Robinstadts'. He favors a call-in station hosted by a sarcastic host named Jeff, whom Len imagines to be in his late middle age. Jeff keeps the show relatively clean, but he seems bitter; he makes fun of his callers, sometimes while they're still on the line, more often after they hang up. Len, who has made a lifetime of being nice, who is prey to melancholy but does not let it show, will slap the steering wheel with the heel of his hand and laugh out loud at the characters who call in.

This morning the caller is a dim young woman who dates a married man twice her age. The man won't leave his wife for the young mistress, though she has promised to get breast implants. The mistress has a tremulous voice that quavers when she opines, "I kin get them any size he wants."

Jesus. Ignorant. Not like my Val, Len thinks. Val is his sweetheart, with that cinnamon hair. Smart, smarter than he is. Val is the one pays the bills and keeps track of the expenses, not only for them but now for her mother too, and she has a way with words, don't she? "You're so smart, and I'm so dumb." He told her that, all those years ago in high-school math, for Chrissake. That still embarrasses him, thinking of the gang of them that sat in the back, cracking up and getting away with it because the teacher liked them; it might have been that Val was sitting on Bryan's lap when Len spoke to her—those two were together then. He sometimes wonders if she remembers that day too. Her eyes were painted with a brown shadow that sparkled, like the Flambeau.

The road to the Robinstadts' winds through second-growth

forest, and the windshield this morning is iced like cake. The property is remote but beautiful, like a model of what a farm should be. Len admires it; the place he grew up on was nothing like this.

Len struggled in high school; his folks hadn't lost the farm yet, but they were poor, everyone knew it. He'd go to school, and then to the diner, working the early supper rush—he was a decent fry cook, and it's maybe there that he felt his best, flirting with the waitresses, who were all older and called him hon, and there was Mr. John, the boss, who treated him with respect. (Len is still a good cook. On the weekends he makes the girls pancakes, and they're light and thick, they hold the butter.) Then it was home, and chores. God, he and his folks, they could barely stay on top of everything. There was a sister, Lenore, but she's always been sickly and never quite right in the head; she couldn't do much then, still can't. Not her fault. He'd start his homework at ten o'clock at night. It showed.

Sometimes he thinks back to how he must have looked to Val: always half-grown out of his clothes, and the way his face would turn red as soup when he tried to talk to her. Just because she was out of his league didn't mean he couldn't try. She's always been something special, Val has; she doesn't give herself credit, her sister Ruby being how she is. No one's as smart as Ruby. Don't mean you're dumb.

Val's a good daughter. Barbara getting worse like she is, in the hospital again, though she's pulled through before. They all miss Moon. They've just got to get through it, this latest thing, though Len sees how it's hard on his wife, trying to do all she does. Val loves them two girls, and damn she worries. Especially about Junie, that she'll lose the sweetness and hope she has in her. *It's not too late for her*, that's what Val has told him. *I can still make a difference for her.*

That makes Len sad. It's true Dakota has hit a rough patch—there was that trouble at school yesterday, again—but she will be all right in the end; Len wishes that to be true. Hell, look how he turned out, and no one in his court, not ever! Dakota has people who love her and all that love has got to count for something. Years ago he told Val he would love her baby, and he meant it, but when he made the promise it was only because he loved Val. Len knew he could pretend caring about a child if he had to; before the wedding, he and Moon worked in Moon's shop together, making a crib for the baby. After Dakota was born, it turned out that he didn't have to sham after all.

This morning Len is almost all the way to work when he glances at the clock on the dash and sees that he has a little time. He pulls over to the roadbed, keeping the heat cranked, and turns on the overhead light. He reaches into the glove box and removes a piece of dirty chamois. Inside is rolled a pocketknife and a stick of wood; he has started whittling, and he's good at it. Len finds chunks of wood and lets them tell him what they are. This one in the glove box, now. It is a deer. He holds up the wood, eyeing it: birch. He'd chosen hardwood because even though it's harder to work, the white wood is beautiful and holds detail well. He's making this piece for Dakota; she is hard and beautiful too.

Len turns off the radio so he can think. To either side of the road is a green mat of pine. No cars on the road at this hour; he is alone. He loves this time of day. The wood has a pleasing weight; he's already roughed out the deer lying down. Today Len uses the knife like a plane and starts shaving bits away. The trick is to keep the knife, which is sharp and fat-handled, loose in his hand. The trick is to keep it slow. He shaves and hums; he is warm in the car, even though outside the day is bitter. Len thinks Dakota will like this deer, even if she won't let on. He sees deer every day, and they remind him of his daughter: the alert steps, the watchful nature.

The whittling settles his mind. Len's fingers are thick but agile. He'd give up anything for Val, those girls. His girls. His mystery. They're enough to get up in the morning for, enough to keep him humping at the jobs he does. That thing he's doing now: Robinstadt is a jerkhole, looks down on him, but Len can put up with any amount of grief if it means food on the table.

No one else has stood the man half so long—Robinstadt's handymen usually quit, or are let go, within days—and one project after another keeps coming. Now it's the roof. Okay. The wife isn't so bad; she asks about the girls every time, and she gave Junie a doll. God knows why she had it, grown woman that she is. When he brought it home for Junie, some plastic baby wrapped in a blue knit blanket that Mrs. R. must have made herself—all fringed around the edges, it was. The smile on Junie's face! Like he'd given her the moon. He wishes he could make Dakota smile like that—he hopes maybe the deer will do it. He's all awkwardness around that girl; she doesn't like to be hugged, but he loves her like his own.

And he's kept another promise to Val; Dakota will never hear it from him.

Len takes a breath and carefully makes a deep cut in the wood with the point of his knife. He digs a cut almost parallel, but slanting into the first one, then picks out the sliver of wood, leaving a channel. It is the start of a face, the deer's gentle face. Wind rocks the car and joy cuts through him. Sometimes he'll wake up and Val's gone to the girls' room; there's a chair there and she'll sleep in it, because she says he snores. It's okay. He'll go in and watch the three girls before they wake; hell, he's always up before they are, he has to rise before dawn. Morning. His best time. It's then he can tell them in his head the things that are too hard to say, how he can't believe his luck. No one who knew Val in high school would have thought he'd have her as his own, least of all his parents, who said that he shouldn't be taking on another man's child when he had enough on his plate. "A little minx"—that's what his mother had called Val. But they'd lost the farm by then, and it broke them, Len thinks. They came to the wedding, at least, Mom in a plain dark dress she'd worn to her own mother's funeral. They've never taken any pleasure in his wife or either of his children, the way he might have hoped, but he don't hold it against them. They live out by Mom's sister now, near Oelwein in Iowa.

After Len works at the wood for a few minutes, he wraps it

carefully and puts it away. He wants to finish the deer; he looks forward to leaving it at Dakota's bedside one morning, before he goes to work. She is the kind of girl who won't want him watching her find it—audiences make her put up her guard, he's seen that at Christmas and her birthday—but it pleases him to imagine her face when she does see what he's made. She will know. She will know that she is loved.

He pulls on stiff tan work gloves, clapping his hands to warm them, then shifts the truck into gear. No use getting to work even a minute late; Robinstadt would have his liver.

He drives fast the rest of the way, but still he notices, the way he always does, the soft blur of trees and hawks, tipping on the wind above them. It is getting light. Clear delicate yellows and pinks leaking into the sky. Robinstadt is waiting for him at the barn, wearing the padded Eddie Bauer coat that he keeps spotless, and breath hangs like fog around his long fleshy face. Len rolls his window down.

"I've been waiting here," the man says.

"And I appreciate it," Len replies, parking the truck and unpacking his tools. He doesn't hurry; he is on time, same as always.

"Just because a man has children, doesn't give him an excuse to be late," Robinstadt says. Len nods. The man repeats the warning daily, for lack of anything to complain about. Len has learned it's best just to go along.

Robinstadt shuffles his feet, following Len into the barn. When Len bends to strap on the pads he wears on his knees to protect them, Robinstadt stands close, hands in his pockets, then smiles. Robinstadt smiles seldom and when he does it is sudden and nasty. "I hear your daughter is consorting with that war vet, you know," he says. "You best watch that."

"My daughter?"

"The older one. With that crazyman Berryman. He's trouble, boy. A man needs to keep an eye on his children. He needs to mind his house. I'm just telling you what I hear."

"I think you are mistaken about Dakota." Len stands straight and gazes at Robinstadt, his voice firm; the man looks away. They walk to the raft of ladders then, Len selecting one and carrying it out of the barn.

"Well. Look out for that vet, that's all. He's off." Robinstadt, keeping step, pauses, screwing up his face and looking off toward the woods. "And the bears are in my garbage again. Don't go leaving your trash in my barn."

"No, sir," Len says. He sets the ladder and starts climbing, eager to escape the man. "Bears are a trouble," he says over his shoulder. "The only one I like is my girl's. Dakota's. She has a blue stuffed bear; she loves it, even though I reckon she's getting too old for them stuffies. She has that sweetness in her."

Robinstadt grunts, and Len keeps climbing. The man is a bag of wind. Len doesn't care that Robinstadt doesn't know his family, or care for them; it is enough for Len that he has one. And the talk about Berryman? Len will call Val after a decent interval, after he gets some work done. She will settle his mind.

He'd die for Val, he thinks. He'd die for them all, his three girls. They're his kin now.

RUBY

Plaque

She's on the town's main drag and drives slowly, scanning the shops she passes: the plain wood facade of the bakery, closed after twenty-one years—*Thanks for Your Business! We're Moving On!*—and a dress shop, the jewelry store, each narrow window display shrouded in orange gel meant to cut the sun. The tornado in '02 tore out much of the downtown, but some of the shops are still familiar. Barthel's General, for instance. Ruby went to school with the daughter, who must run the business by now. Someone has taken pains with the displays. The mannequins are backed by a cardboard castle, painted in tempera, meant to set off clothing, cheap Goth T-shirts and designer knockoffs in black, geared to the teens. The mannequins are stick-thin and faceless but for cartoonish red lips, the clothing hanging on them like signal flags.

Ruby slows down, studying the display. One of the shirts is roomy, draped, decorated with sequin lips and ragged black stripes. RENEGADE, it says across the top. Ruby accelerates, driving too fast through the green and the dark of the day.

చ

Finally: Tim's office, nestled into a dip in the earth just past the feed store, in a small aluminum-sided house. The same office where she and Val went as girls; they both got braces here. A sign reading Timothy Baxter, DDS, in raised wooden letters, hangs to the left of the entry, which is a screen over a heavy wooden door painted brown, the way it always has been. Ruby pulls the car beneath it, her head snapping forward when she hits the curb. What the hell was she going to say to a guy who had fumbled with her breasts in the back of his truck? Ruby checks her face in the rearview mirror. When they were young, when they were together, Ruby used to sing to Tim after sex; she'd lie naked in the truck's bed and sing him the only song to which she knew all the words: "Sugar Mountain."

Well. Her tooth throbs with each beat of her heart. *You can do this.* Ruby crams the sippy cup and the stuffed animal she took from Val's into her purse and takes a deep breath. Then another. When she finally hurries through sleet to the door and into the waiting room, she tells herself she is calm. The waiting area is small and generic, painted a bright yellow that makes the space cheerier than she remembers. Three padded chairs line one wall, and at the far end, a woman in a raincoat clamps one arm around a wriggling toddler and rifles through her purse at a cut-out window. The window frames the top of a woman's head: brassy hair centered around dark roots, like a sunflower, and when the head jerks up Ruby sees the eye shadow first.

"You must be Val's sister!" The blond looks crabby and sleepy but then she smiles, revealing a set of uneven teeth. "Just go on in. Dr. Tim's waiting."

Is this the wife? Carly? Ruby smiles back, relieved to see the woman's beige teeth and large bosom; *okay, then.* Pressing a hand against her mouth, she steps into the hallway leading to the examining rooms, the receptionist bobbing her head encouragingly. "Val's sister," she repeats. "I've heard about you!"

The examining room is clean and small and the dentist chair looks new. Tim waits by the door; he is still thin, his waist-length hair pulled back with elastic, but his white dentist's tunic confers a tidy maturity that makes Ruby, who remembers him naked, feel shy. His lean face is gaunt now, but Tim's eyes, behind wire-rims, crinkle reassuringly. The cross on a cord around his neck is made of painted clay.

"Hey!" His voice is the same: reedy, lonely notes in it like the cry of a hawk. "Ruby! We meet again, and all because of a broken tooth." He extends his arms and Ruby takes one of his hands in both of hers, avoiding a hug.

"Long time," she agrees.

"Sit, sit. Open. Let's take a look." Ruby slides into the chair and the slick plastic cover on the chair squeaks beneath her, like a fart.

"That was the chair," she says.

"Sure it was," Tim laughs, winking at her as he reaches for a pair of thin plastic gloves. His hands are clean and blunt-nailed, unadorned save for a plain thick wedding band that refracts yellow points of light. "You have a good trip?" he asks, pulling on the gloves. "Highways clear?"

"Sure," Ruby says. He adjusts the chair and she opens her mouth obediently. On the wall opposite is a Hopper print—the one with the gas pumps—expensively framed and matted. Beneath it hangs a macramé owl with blue beads for eyes.

"Oh boy," Tim says, his hands gentle in her mouth. Where to look now? Into the mirror of his glasses? At the ceiling? Ruby decides to close her eyes but then she must smell him: soap and tobacco, an undercurrent of pot. So familiar, but there is a man smell now, too, different from when he was in high school and in some ways, still new.

"I have the other piece," she murmurs. "I can't stay long." Her lip brushes his knuckle and she is mortified. "Excuse me," she mouths, and lip and hand touch again. She resolves to be still then, hunching her shoulders and settling into the seat, but when Tim tells her that the tooth can be bonded together today as a temporary fix, she sits up straight. "How long does that take?"

She's suddenly thinking of her mom, certain Val has discovered that she never made it past the parking lot of Cedar Manor. Ruby reaches awkwardly for her purse, which she set on a stool near the window. "Let me get the...fragment. The piece." When she leans over to dig out the sippy cup, she can feel her sweatshirt hike up, exposing the way her hips lap over her pants. *Muffin thick*, she and Lorna always joke when they start new diets, meaning muffin top. "Here," she says, thrusting the cup at Tim. He fishes out the jagged piece, and Ruby looks away as he carefully begins to clean it.

"This'll be an hour, tops. Ruby, you've got to do something. You're in town for a couple days, right?" He puts his hand on her arm. "Hey, I heard about your mom. I'm so sorry, Ladybird."

"My ear hurts," Ruby says, looking past his right shoulder. If she meets his eyes she might start to cry. "Because of the tooth, I think."

"That happens," Tim says. He is already readying a tray. "It's all connected."

"Unfortunately," Ruby says.

&

He works with joy, a man in love with his tools: the bonding material, which has the consistency of toothpaste; the narrow brushes with which he applies it. Ruby is surprised. She has assumed, she realizes, that he has settled for something in his life. But he whistles between his teeth, tunelessly. Once he actually sings, and his breath smells sweet.

"You're looking good," he remarks at one point, and for a second Ruby thinks he might be making fun of her. But his face betrays nothing cruel, or unkind. She straightens her sweatshirt beneath the paper bib laced around her neck.

"Hnnh." She grunts her thanks. Saliva pools in her mouth as in a well.

"What are you doing now? Music, I bet. Am I right?"

"HR," Ruby says. If his hands weren't in her mouth, she could tell him that she has a gift for managing people to whom she is not related. She could tell him she's won awards.

"You like it?"

Ruby maneuvers her face away from his hands. "Oh, sure! I work at an ad agency. The offices are really cool."

"Well, I'm doing this. As you see." Tim chuckles. "Mouth open, okay?" He takes her chin firmly and arranges her face back under the light. "I got married three years ago." He pokes at her gums with a wicked-looking instrument, nodding as though something has been confirmed for him. "We're saving for a house. We're doing good." He pauses. The instrument pokes again. "You got a place?"

"A condo," she says. "It's on the thirty-third floor."

"That must be some view!"

"It is," Ruby says. In fact, sometimes after work she will stand in her bedroom for long stretches, just looking at the city, its lights that blur and wink.

"I met your wife," she says when he takes his hands away. She tries to sound nonchalant; her mouth is full of blood. She hopes he won't ask if she is married too.

"Carrie?" Tim voice betrays his confusion. "Where—the diner?"

"No, out front. She greeted me."

"Oh! You met Shana! Our receptionist. Isn't she a sweetie?"

Damn. "Oh, I just thought. Val set up the appointment with Carly."

"Carrie," Tim says pleasantly.

"Yeah, she set up the appointment with Carrie, and I just assumed—"

"I think it's just that my wife and your sister are friends. Val called Carrie, and Carrie called me, and we worked it out."

"Right." Carrie might still have long hair in a mullet; she might be a TV watcher, the veins in her legs bulging like snakes. And Ruby had almost forgotten him, after all. Tim. She could tell him she had a good life. Her life *was* good.

Wicked, wicked dental tools; they scrape at her teeth like little files. And there is that conduit—a nerve?—that burns from tooth to ear. "You have plaque," Tim comments. "You gotta brush, missy."

Sometimes Ruby goes to bed in her clothes; she doesn't always brush her teeth before she sleeps. "Nice owl," she says, breaking free from his hands when she twists her head to look at the macramé, to spit blood into a tiny ceramic sink sluiced with water.

"Oh, Carrie's mom," Tim says, glancing back at the hanging. "She makes things." He shrugs. "You know, nobody really ap-

preciates how much love and work go into something like that."
He adjusts his glasses. "Carrie's an artist, you know."

Crafts, surely. Decoupage and the like. Ruby brightens.
"An artist! Will I get to see her work sometime?"

"She has a show coming up in Ashland. She does some nice
stuff." Tim beams at her, peeling off his gloves. "Listen," he
says. "I'd love for you to meet her. Carrie."

Ruby, lying back in the chair, touches the tooth with her
tongue. It feels whole, and numb, and she thinks to herself that
in all the years to come, she will carry with her this reminder of
Tim and the work he does. It is fused to her so that she might
never, completely, dismiss him again.

"I know you want to get back to your mom. But you should
eat something anyway." Tim pulls a chair over and sits down,
extending his legs. "You can use that tooth in about forty-five
minutes. Come on over to our place. We'll get you a sandwich,
put some meat on your bones. You look exhausted," he says.
"Seriously. Come for lunch."

Ruby glances at her watch. It's past twelve-thirty now. She
thinks about what it would be like in the nursing wing, drinking
coffee out of coated plastic cups. Val might be there, having
changed from the AC/DC shirt to something pressed, something that shines like chromium. The girls won't be out of
school for a few hours yet. "Okay," she says. "But let me make
a call?"

She stands unsteadily and pokes in her purse again, extract-
ing her cell phone, which is pink, bejeweled, flat as balsa. Her
mom's number, in her room, is programmed into the phone,
of course, and Ruby tells herself, when it rings and rings, that
she's tried, that this counts as trying. The rings continue, hollow,
unabated. "No answer! I even let it ring!" she will say cheerily
to Tim, to the sunflower receptionist in the yellow lobby, to
Val, even—ignoring the flicker of reprieve that licks at her,
persistent as a tiny flame.

TIM

Chubby

She's still chubby, Ruby. Round as a pudding, though her face lifts when she smiles. And those yellow corduroys! All these years, he's imagined her differently. Or maybe he's just misremembered the look on her face when she told him, at his parents' house, that she was setting him free.

He wants Ruby to meet Carrie. He's proud of his pretty wife. He did all right, didn't he? And maybe the two women will hit it off: Really! They're both smart, and Carrie can be kind, and one look at Ruby tells you she needs some of that. That tooth. *God.*

He was never a standout at anything, but then he went to dental school. He works well with his hands. He works well with others. In the months after his breakup with Ruby, he threw himself into his studies. He excelled.

Tim knows everyone says what a nice guy he is. The way he's always thinking about other people. Poor Ruby, for instance. Tim washes his hands, whistling. He grabs his jacket from the rack in the hall and tells Shana he'll be back after lunch.

Ruby's waiting in the lobby, hand to her face. Woman looks like ten miles of bad road.

"Ready?" he asks her, smiling.

PEARL

Everyone

Nights are hardest. Bob goes to bed early, and Pearl herself, never a good sleeper, stays up past eleven so that she can sleep through the night. Or most of it, leastways.

When she was younger it hadn't occurred to her that her friends might die off before she did. Or move away. She hadn't figured on being lonely. She knows she's lucky she still has Bob, and it's a good marriage, but ever since their only daughter moved down to Florida the days are long. Ginny! When she was in high school the house was full of kids. "Better we know where they are; better they like to come here," Pearl always said. Bob ignored them. He might grunt when they came through, but Pearl put out snacks.

Since he retired from the insurance agency, he's happiest puttering in his shop. Pearl wipes her hands on a dish towel patterned with cherries. She's made tuna noodle casserole, so there will be leftovers.

"Bob!" she calls. She's careful going down the steps into the basement, holding to the wooden railing, which is just a two-by-four nailed to the wall. She has to be vigilant; you break your hip and that's the beginning of the end. Sometimes she thinks of her bones having a sheen like glass. Inching down the stairs now, she imagines them, shifting inside her skin.

The basement is unfinished, and cold; Bob always wears a thick U of W sweatshirt when he works down here. He ties a shop apron over that. He's bent over the workbench, and there is the smell of paint.

"Dinner already?" He looks up, eyes bleary. When she calls him to meals he's always surprised, as if he's just woken up.

"Ten minutes," she says. Pearl used to meet up with Barbara, with Louise. The Three Amigas, they called themselves, and they'd drive all the way to Hayward for dinner. They'd gossip a little, but it never hurt anybody. They all went to the same church; they did the Coat Drive for years.

"I'm almost done here," Bob says. He gestures to the wooden numbers spread out on the bench and pats his jigsaw; Pearl, who has learned to pretend an interest, knows the name of every tool down here.

"The postman won't miss our address now." It's a joke; they've had the same postman, Jim, for decades. Jimmy. He goes to their church.

Bob nods at another pile of wood. Blocks for carving his next project, she guesses. Basswood, cottonwood, butternut. Tupelo, pine. Pearl recites the names in her head.

Louise retired south, the way so many seem to do these days. Pearl, though, she'll never leave Wisconsin. This is her home. She goes to visit Barbara at Cedar Manor and her old friend's smile is still sweet. Pearl brings chocolate; her friend's teeth are terrible, but the doctor said it doesn't really matter at this point, if it makes Barbara happy. For a while Pearl tried to time her visit so that she'd run into the daughter, Val. Val has her mother's strong features and Pearl still thinks maybe they could be friends.

It's important to have friends of all ages.

But when she ran into Val last time, on the street it was, the girl was this side of rude. She rushed by, phone at her ear. She didn't have time to talk, that much was clear; Pearl didn't even get to ask if they might have a cup of coffee together sometime.

"Come on to the table after you wash up," Pearl says, starting the slow climb up the basement stairs. Bob will be mostly quiet at dinner; there's no news since they talked at breakfast. Some days, Pearl goes most of the day without hearing anything but her own voice. "I'm taking care," she'll tell the good silver and the framed photos. She polishes. She dusts.

Pearl uses cloth napkins at mealtimes; they each have their

own for the day, cozy in its ring. She rolls the napkins tightly: blue for Bob, gold for her. The rings look like shells. "This is good," Bob will say, laying the napkin flat across his knees. He won't have taken a bite yet. "I hope you're hungry," she'll say.

Sometimes she sees Val working at the IGA. Pearl still might say something. She just wants to talk about the Old Times. She could tell Val a thing or two about how it was. Barbara was a good dancer; when Pearl had a problem, Barb was the one she went to.

"You need a dog," Ginny said when Pearl called her last week. Ginny had been cross; the children were sick.

Everyone needs someone to talk to. Everyone needs something.

DAKOTA

Quilt

"Fuck the IGA," Dakota says.

She's sitting at the kitchen table, pretending to eat lunch. She'd wanted to warm up the can of SpaghettiOs she found in the pantry when she came in, but Mom, who is seriously pissed off, said Dakota has to eat the lunch she took to school. "We are not wasting food. That lunch was good enough for school when I packed it this morning, it's good enough for now. That's where you should be right now. At school, eating your lunch." Mom stands with her arms folded over her chest, frowning.

Dakota makes a face at her sandwich. Mom's all freaked out because when Dakota went into school today, she was told she's on suspension until further notice. That hadn't been clear yesterday—to Dakota or to Mom—and Mom had to come get Dakota and now she's going to be late to work at that stupid grocery store. The way they treat their employees, those stuck-up managers that think they're so cool—and what have they got to be proud about? Little Hitlers, every last one of them; they talk down to Mom like she's trash and she just takes it. "Fuck school. Fuck those idiots at your job."

"You're happy enough I have this job when it pays for your poms," Mom says.

"Take me off the team, then, see if I care!" Dakota says, angry enough to cry almost. She pushes her plate away. What has Mom guessed about poms? Nothing. She can't even begin to imagine how the girls whisper, how they act like Dakota is garbage, though they smile to her face. And don't think she hasn't heard what they say, about Dad not being her real dad. They make fun of him, too, the pom girls do: his awkward walk and dull face. He's embarrassing, sometimes, but Dakota feels sorry for him. He loves Mom and she doesn't love him as much back; Dakota understands that. Gram used to say, *People love you as much as they can.* Well.

She only got on the team because she's pretty.

"Are you going to tell me what happened yesterday?" Mom says. They never did talk; Mom picked her up, there was the call about Grandma, and that was that. Mom actually sounds more tired than mad, suddenly old, and Dakota thinks about how it might make a good painting, the lines in Mom's cheeks like African scars Dakota has seen in books. Dakota's art teacher, Ms. Cress, says that damaged things are more interesting to draw than the things that are perfect. Dakota likes Ms. Cress, maybe because she is the one teacher who seems to like her. And Dakota likes the class—once Dakota started doing assignments in her sketchpad it was like she was able to find something that had always been there, hiding, and Ms. Cress gives grades based on Dakota's work, not on who she thinks Dakota is as a person. It's the only class Dakota's getting an A in.

"A lot of the teachers don't like me," Dakota says. "They judge me without knowing me. I'm just giving them what they expect."

"I don't care what anyone else does," Val says. "I expect you to treat people with respect."

"Is that what you're doing at that stupid job, being respectful? You let everyone walk all over you," Dakota says. "I won't make the same mistake, believe me. Sorry that embarrasses you." When she came to get Dakota at school, Mom's face had been bright with shame. She apologized to everyone, it seemed like: the principal, that secretary with the gross hands, even the janitor. "At least I have some pride."

"That's it! Go to your room!" Mom turns away and ties on her red work smock; she swipes her coat and keys from the table and stalks to the door leading to the garage. "Your father and I will talk about poms. If I have anything to say, you're off the team!"

There will probably be a fight; Dakota has noticed that when she gets in trouble, it causes tension between Mom and Dad. Usually Dad takes her side, and that makes Mom crazy. Mom used to be pretty and light. She used to cook, and when Dakota was bitchy in the morning, she wouldn't get bitchy back.

The only reason Mom cared about what happened at school was because people like that secretary were there, looking down on them both.

Dakota stomps to her room and slams the door. "I'm not hungry anyway!" she yells, though she has taken the sandwich with her. She throws herself on her bed, hands folded behind her head, feigning that she doesn't care about any of it. Maybe when she was little Dakota just didn't know any better, but it seemed like Mom and Dad liked each other more then. Jesus. Wasn't it the job of parents to be happy, to be happy together? Like loons. Years ago Gram told her they mated for life and so Dakota sketched a picture of a loon for one of Ms. Cress's assignments, coloring in only its scarlet eye. She balances the sandwich on her stomach. So okay, she's off the team. Mom really does think this is punishment.

Dakota sighs and looks around the room. Junie has pretty much taken over; her stuffed animals and toys are all over the place, her drawings taped to any available surface. Junie's into drawing ladybugs right now, and they're everywhere, in every conceivable color. Right by Dakota's bed, Junie has taped a crayoned rainbow. Although Dakota finds many things about the room irritating—its small size, the chilly blue paint that she's never liked—Junie's presence is not one of them. Dakota actually finds her little sister's vibe comforting. She would never admit it to anyone, but she likes being surrounded by the smiling plush toys, the baby doll Len brought Junie from one of his jobs, its plastic face smudged with jam.

The toys are sweet and make the room more cheerful and comfortable than the rooms of Dakota's friends. One of the boys who likes Dakota, Kevin, has papered his walls with ugly Slayer posters (he gave one to Dakota and she doesn't really like it, but she put it up anyway); Kevin boasts that the only color he likes is black, because black is the color of darkness. (*Duh!* Dakota thought but didn't say.) Under the Slayer posters his bedroom walls are painted black; he did that himself, without asking his parents, and now he's grounded. Then there is Maddie, one of the girls on poms. She has a room so perfect it's like from a magazine, but it's not comfortable either. Maddie's mom won't let her daughter hang out there with her friends. "No soda or snacks in your room," Mrs. Fletcher always warns. One time a group of girls did gather there to listen to music and read one another's texts, but as soon as they got up to leave, there was Mrs. Fletcher, smoothing the flowered bedspread and straightening the books on the shelf over Maddie's desk. It was weird. Maddie's house, while beautiful, has never been a place Dakota likes to hang out.

And for all the posturing—the Slayer boy likes to speak ominously about capitalists and rebellion and the evils of democracy—the lives of her classmates seem so sheltered, their concerns so foolish (Will I pass math? Does that boy like me?), that Dakota has to work to fit in. She pretends to find the same things funny or interesting, but next to them she feels ancient. She goes to school; every day, afterward, she feels like crying.

Listen: the garage door. Mom leaving, without saying goodbye. Whatever.

Dakota's wanted to quit poms for weeks, the girls are so mean. She sits up; her shoes have left marks on the quilt. Gram made it from clothes Dakota used to wear when she was a little girl: red flowered fabric from a dress Gram bought her, at Field's in Chicago; a duck print that was one of those jumper things, the ducks green and yellow and smiling. Dakota still loves the ducks and thinks they are cute. One time she told Maddie that, and Maddie admitted that she has a special teddy bear *her* grandma gave her. It was just the two of them here in Dakota's room, and for a little bit, Dakota thought she and Maddie might be friends.

But the next day Maddie went like a little lap dog and told

Shannon and Kylie about the duck fabric. They laughed at her. "I hear you like baby things," Kylie said. She's the pom girl who almost bests Dakota in looks. Then the three of them—Kylie, Shannon, Maddie—talked about their plans for the weekend: the mall in Rice Lake, a movie, lots of posts on Instagram so everyone would know how much fun they were having. They talked about it in front of Dakota, and then they didn't invite her. Dakota just sat, pretending not to care, but inside, her hate was incandescent. She could have lit the room with it.

Now she kicks off her shoes and draws the quilt around her. One square is denim from jeans Dakota wore through at the knees, and another nubbed flannel the color of snow. Gram used to make beautiful things; she used to hold Dakota close. Now she stares and her eyes are empty; sometimes she's angry.

Dakota loves the quilt.

She puts the sandwich on the floor. Outside, the car spins gravel. It makes a chuffing sound pulling out, though Dad works on it when he can. He works on it even when it's cold and dark out, sticking his arms into the car's insides like a doctor might. When she was little, Dakota would bring him coffee and sit with him. She hasn't done that, not for a long time, but she can't hate Dad, the same way she can't hate Junie. Neither one of them gets mad very often. They both seem to need her, a little.

Mom has a short fuse. Even if it's her idea to pull Dakota from poms, she'll be mad that Dakota is no longer part of the group; being in poms is supposed to be an honor, and even Dad seems proud that his daughter made the team. Dad with his sandy hair, and her own long hair so dark. Kylie brought that up, too, her face set with contempt. "Recessive genes," Dakota spat. She read about that once, about the monk and his peas; when she was younger she used to love science. That was before her grades started slipping. That was before someone started the rumor that she's a whore.

Dakota's phone beeps and she pulls it from her pocket. Kevin has texted her—*MEET L8TER?*—even though he's grounded, and Dakota pulls the quilt tighter. It's a crazy quilt, the way the patches are arranged. That's what Gram told her when she made it. "For my crazy girl," Gram whispered, but the way Gram said it, it was a good thing.

She hasn't slept with anyone, though no one—not even some of the teachers—seems to believe that. She tries to say it, but it's like it comes out Glurgamugger. Like nonsense.

The sandwich looks dry. It *is* dry. In a little bit, maybe she'll go get some milk. Dakota stares at the ceiling, the cloudy light fixture speckled with flies. She's waited so long for childhood to be over, but she might never be done being angry.

Was she not the kind of daughter her mother wanted to have?

She can't be like Junie, who thinks the world is a friendly place. Junie has Len's round, pink face, Dakota thinks, but she, Dakota, has his eyes. She has his sad eyes.

RUBY

Silhouette

After promising he will bring her back to her car by three o'clock, Tim drives them to his house, in an ancient Ford with rusting panels. Ruby doesn't say much, just listens to him talk and leans against the passenger door, which rattles. The road is slippery. Tim drives maddeningly slowly, past the red-painted King Burger and then right on Highway 27, Ruby staring out the window at ranch homes and split levels, the satellite dishes that attend to them like lovers.

"How's your family?" she asks. Tim's parents, who would be elderly now, have always lived in the area. They are country people, kind and resourceful; Ruby remembers liking them.

"Oh! God! They're great!" Tim reserves a special enthusiasm for the people he loves, and Ruby was once in that circle, a wide warm place that was bland but also safe. "Slowing down, but doing okay."

"I'm glad," Ruby says, and means it. Tim's mom made her a scarf once, of raspberry wool, freakishly long and beloved because of that. She still has that thing, Ruby could tell Tim. It is soft and funny, different from the things she has acquired in the years since. Maybe that's why she liked the red sweatpants, their cheerful winking sequins. Maybe they reminded her of Tim's mom.

"They moved into town. Val tell you that?"

"No," Ruby says.

"They're right on the Flambeau."

"Your dad always liked the water." Ruby gazes out the window again. It must have been a drought summer. The lawns they pass are close-cropped and balding, the grass as crisp as burnt hair. She remembers Tim saying once—it must have been that first semester in college—that he liked going home because he enjoyed his parents' company, which had struck her as extraordinary. She wonders now what he thinks of a woman who could leave her sick mother to have lunch with an ex. But then, he'd *invited* her. She glances at him. The skin at the corners of his eyes is crinkled like fabric. From smiling, no doubt; he was always a smiler. She remembers that small dark mole on his right cheek. Eyes on the road, Tim says that he and Carrie live at the Best Western El Rancho—or near it, anyway—rent free because they take care of the motel.

"You live in a motel?" Ruby says. "I thought dentists made a ton of money."

"Not here they don't," Tim says. "Besides, it's a good deal. I cut the grass and deal with the plumbing when there's a problem; Carrie plants flowers and takes reservations; we both keep the rooms clean. And Carrie does the waitressing downtown too. Good tips." They are saving money this way, he says, what they can put aside from his practice. But there are expenses, always: his new dental chair, for instance. Ruby nods. She has forgotten that in Ladyford most people have two or three jobs, just to get by.

The motel isn't far, and Ruby remembers it, a one-story affair circa 1950, with a portico like the one at the senior center, and rooms facing the parking lot. The adjacent El Rancho restaurant is one of the fancier joints in town, at least it used to be. Ruby remembers coming back from college for wedding receptions there. All her high-school friends were getting married, fast, at nineteen, and then having kids, sometimes nine months later, sometimes sooner. It has been years since she's even driven this way. The Dairy Queen across the road is closed for winter. It used to be open all year long.

"Damn," she says, pointing. "I thought you could buy me a Dilly bar."

THE SOUND OF RABBITS

"Ha, yes! Come back in a few months and I will!" Tim parks the car and turns to her, his face eager. "Okay. Let me show you the place."

Ruby's heart sinks. Suddenly she wants to leave, the way she wanted to leave the endless sleepovers in fifth grade, when the girls seemed so foolish and tiresome, but she is hungry, and the alternative is to go to the nursing home now and see about her mother. Which she should do. Which she will do. After she eats. She'll feel better then; she usually does.

They make a circuit of the motel on foot because the sleet has stopped. Tim skirts a garden neatly bordered with rocks, the husks of summer flowers trimmed back to stubble. The buildings are dark wood on top, reddish-brown fieldstone on the bottom. Heavy avocado curtains, lined with plastic, hang in the clean square windows. "Hey!" he says as they approach the front entrance. "You got a place to stay? Carrie and I, we've got a great setup here, we can give you a deal!"

"I pretty much have to stay with Val. She wouldn't understand if I didn't."

"Sure, that's cool," Tim says. He kneels and rolls an errant rock back to its place beside the path. The hollow it fits into is grass and earth made smooth; it has been there, she sees, for a very long time.

For a moment she imagines the comfort of being in one of these rooms, alone, and how it would feel. God, she's tired. The rooms here are probably cramped and dark; she imagines a heater that wheezes, and mice claiming a network of paths between the walls. Surely even Val's couch is preferable, and she will see the nieces, who love her. But this would be the one plausible place in town she could stay without Val instantly taking offense. She would not have to wake early when Len passed through the living room on his way to work, trying to be quiet but bumbling even so, the gurgle of the coffeemaker and the whine of his jacket zipper loud in the darkness, though she would assure him she was getting up anyway, smile as she is smiling now, for and about things that she does not care for: the macramé owl, the cost of a dentist's chair, the toy she has brought for Tim's baby, still snugged in her purse.

"The front office!" Tim declares. Ruby sees herself reflected in the glass door. How does she look to Tim? Is there a shadow of the girl she once was, hidden in that reflection? She stops, just for a moment, staring at her silhouette reflected in the glass, the gray day showing through. She stands straighter; how tiresome to labor at holding to the best possible vision of oneself. The other, lesser views keep leaking in. Ruby misses her mother, again, because Barbara always had faith in her. Barbara wasn't sentimental, but she had faith. She promoted, and nurtured, Ruby's best self.

Tim pushes through the door, smiling proudly. The walls of the office are paneled with gleaming fake wood and hung with photos of lakes surrounded by birch trees. Birch trees surrounded by lakes. A countertop, orange laminate, is topped by a little gold bell and a plastic stand supporting two tidy blocks of business cards. One says:

TIM BAXTER, manager

The card is graphic and interesting, simple, printed in fresh colors: tangerine and blue. And there are similar business cards for his practice, and next to them stands a funky plastic dog with jointed legs, like the one Ruby used to play with when she was three.

So what if it's funky? So what if in Chicago these very touches would be retro, would be cool? The high-school girl behind the front desk turns down the volume on a little television long enough to give Ruby the fisheye. The girl wears a name tag—Brianna—and multiple facial piercings that make Ruby feel certain she hates working here, as she, Ruby, would hate it. But Tim is blithe. "How was the concert?" he asks, and Brianna laughs, showing her teeth, and tells him that she got stoned and the concert was good.

"Any business?" Tim rubs the nose of the plastic dog.

"Not yet. I got my algebra done." When the girl smiles again,

Ruby can see how her teeth are all crowded up in the front of her mouth.

She's smart, though, if she's doing algebra. And the girl clearly likes Tim, the way everyone likes Tim. Ruby can see that he would be a good employer. Cool and funny. He'd overlook the pot if she did her job. She smiles at Brianna, introduces herself, because she sees herself in that bitter thrust of lip, and she doesn't mind, not really, when the girl stares but won't return her smile. She wouldn't have either, would she, at sixteen? And when Tim leads her through a back door, into a damp quadrangle, or courtyard, filled with garden statues and, probably in the summer, flowers, Ruby is certain this Brianna recognized her, too, as smart, a kindred spirit with sophisticated tastes (perhaps she saw the green glass ring Ruby wears, from a little gallery in the River North district). This cheers Ruby enough that she bends over a concrete garden gnome and clowns for Tim, the way she did when they were friends. "Monsieur gnome!" she chirps. "Mon ami!"

Tim laughs. "Idiot," he says fondly, and she allows herself shy pleasure at this. Why not? When he doesn't, after all, really matter? "That Brianna, she's a funny kid," he says. "Good worker, though." He winks at Ruby conspiratorially. "Don't tell my mother, but I'm still smoking pot. She'd kill me. But hey, it's not the pot around here that's the trouble." He lowers his voice. "They say Sooner's got a meth lab. I can't believe he's gotten into that shit."

Ruby feels the little surge of interest, a quickening; Tim's always been something of a gossip. "Sooner. Meth? *Really*? Val told me he raised—I don't know, worms or something."

"Worms, meth. Whatever. He's holed up back at his mom's old place, so who knows? I steer clear. You can do that here," he says. "Steer clear. It's a good place to live." He points to a house. It stands behind the motel in a great square of parched lawn, next to a swimming pool covered with tarp. "There you go," he says. "That's where we live now."

"Huh." Ruby pulls her hood close. The sky has started spitting rain again, and a windbreak of poplars behind the motel moans. She thinks about her mother, no doubt sleeping in her twilight room, but Ruby doesn't want to check her watch. She is afraid to check her watch, and by the time they circle the pool, of which Tim is very proud, and reach the house, which is well kept, the bleached bones of driftwood fanned like rumpled jeans across the side, she has decided to believe that it is not yet even one o'clock. The house is a split level, painted lemon, and except for the driftwood it is like every house of every student in her high school, every student who didn't grow up on a farm. She stops, taking in the wood-paneled sides, the skim of brick dashed with river stones. What did it say about her that she has rejected this life? Ruby tries to imagine herself waitressing, the way Carrie apparently does. Would she in fact be happy, doing that? The fact that she even wonders this bothers her.

"Ru, look." Tim is pointing out the driftwood, a sculpture Carrie has put together, he says. Ruby nods. She reaches out and strokes the wood with one finger. Why not have lunch with someone who tries to be an artist up here?

"I'm glad you'll get to meet Carrie," Tim says, smiling, and even though the rain is picking up he lingers to point out details in the sculpture; he talks about where the wood came from, and there's a long story about a trip to Oostburg. "We would walk the beach and take the wood we found," he says.

"Uh-huh," Ruby says. Water runs in rivulets into the neck of her sweatshirt. She's cold, and wet, and glad when he finally takes her arm and steers her to a side door, and inside.

"We'll get you something to eat and send you on your way, okay?" The house is dim and still, rain sounds muted to a dull thrum. A pretty rag rug lies over floor tiles worn shiny.

Light flicks on in the hallway and a woman peers at them from the top of a few carpeted steps. She has a coat over her shoulders and her hair is wet. "Carrie! Babe!" Tim says. He moves to greet her, and she smiles when he hugs her. Carrie is small, with delicate features, and her blue-black hair gleams like the cheek of a crow. It tapers to points on either side of her face and is cut so well, Ruby can't imagine she's gotten it done anywhere around here. The woman's belly rounds importantly beneath a man's shirt; Ruby figures she must be at least six months pregnant.

Ruby shakes her head like a dog, water spraying out everywhere.

Carrie is pretty, she sees. Well, then. Surely she is a bitch.

BRIANNA

Biggie

After Tim and the fat lady leave, Brianna turns the television back up and fishes around in the little fridge under the front counter; she's starving. She got stoned before work but it doesn't matter; Tim's cool, if a little clueless. He doesn't care. Half the time he's stoned himself. Take that lady who came in today; Brianna would bet Tim doesn't even know Biggie has the hots for him. Written all over her face, which has pits in it, like an orange.

Brianna climbs back up on the stool behind the counter. "Wanted to jump his bones," she confides to Suki, her cell phone cupped in her palm. Suki's the best; just one year older, and that much closer to leaving this place. They talk every day; they have their plans. Rooming together at U of W, for one thing, and the things they'll do after that. "Kill me if I ever get that fat, okay?" Brianna listens to her friend's reply, her head cocked, nodding and picking at a salad she brought from home, in the Tupperware with the sort of gross lid. Grayish, no matter how much she washes it. And not a salad, exactly. More like a head of iceberg, filched from the crisper. It's damp, and hard and white in the middle, but it fills her up, keeps her out of the mayonnaise jar of M&Ms Tim keeps in the cash drawer. No problem with *his* metabolism; it's not a stretch Biggie would think he was hot. "She was old, though. Decrepit. Happens. I mean, look at my *mom!*" She laughs then, because her mom is working on a second chin, which Brianna swears will never happen to her. Then Suki tells about what went down in math, which Brianna had ditched, and how their friend Cody scored some beer, because Cody has an older brother. Brianna and Cody have what Suki calls a friendship with benefits. Wink.

Brianna knows he got the beer so that he can talk about it later, in front of Brianna and Suki. She knows all this is for her, and to a lesser extent for Suki, and this pleases her.

"Count me in," Brianna says, her teeth flashing white. "It's all good. Wait, I gotta go. Carrie's here."

Brianna hops off her stool and palms the phone as Carrie steps into the lobby. Her boss's face shines with rain, but she's scowling. "You didn't close the drapes in 12," Carrie says sternly.

"Oh. Sorry."

"We close the drapes to minimize sun damage. Try to remember, please. I know it doesn't come out of your pocket, but it comes out of mine if we have to buy new bedspreads because the old ones are all faded."

"Yes, ma'am." Carrie looks at her narrowly, as if she thinks Brianna is being sarcastic, then turns on her heel. "Have a good day!" Brianna calls, but Carrie has already slammed the door.

Sometimes Brianna helps with the cleaning, now that Carrie's pregnant. Something about the cleaning supplies being bad for the baby. The cleaning can be a bitch—people are pigs—but Tim pays her extra when she works beyond the front desk, and sometimes people leave tips. Brianna is fast; she does the rooms in half the time Carrie used to, and sometimes Brianna thinks Carrie resents that. Room 12 looked good when she was done with it; she'd sprayed air freshener and put the paper strip on the toilet. So what if she left the drapes open? It's fucking raining out today, anyway.

She dials Suki back immediately. "How's the queen?" her friend asks.

"Jesus. She was stuck-up before, but now that she's pregnant—*damn*, she's bitchy AF." Brianna pushes the Tupperware away, leaving threads of water on the orange counter. She leans back in a stretch. "Anyway, so that lady that came in today?" She relates to Suki, a parting gift, that the lonesome Biggie wore a weird sweatshirt, "like something from the *men's* section," Brianna titters, and yellow corduroys. "Banana pants," Brianna proclaims solemnly, before dissolving again into laughter.

"What's her name?" Suki asks.

"Something weird. Reuben or something."

"What kind of name is Reuben?"

"Who cares? She's basic." Brianna laughs. She's dying for a cigarette but she'll have to wait until she gets off work.

"Where's she from, anyway?"

"With pants like those? Probably here."

"That Carrie, she's got competition, then!" Suki predicts, the last word before they hang up, and it's so absurd, this *warning*, that they text each other about it later, so indispensable are their observations, their witticisms, to one another. Pearls, really, the things they come up with, and there is in their exchange a complete absence of remorse. They're both so young, and cruel, though they don't know it, not yet.

RUBY

Baby on Board

"Ruby, Carrie. Carrie, Ruby." Tim gestures extravagantly, like a clown, Ruby thinks. He takes Carrie's hand and Ruby follows behind them, up the few steps, through a short hallway and into the living room. The room is plain: no drapes, wood floor instead of carpeting, no tchotchkes, and in this way it is already different from the local houses Ruby visited when she was a girl. And the books! Piles on the floor, and bookshelves crammed full, jumbled teeth in a mouth. A few books lie splay-backed on the couch, which is red velvet worn to lavender in the creases. Ruby reaches down to a coffee-table–sized volume. *The Odyssey.* Homer. She puts her hand to it, touching it lightly, as if it is a small and friendly animal, and she is comforted.

Tim puts his arm around Carrie's shoulders and squeezes. "Ruby's a friend from way back. You know, she grew up here too. Remember me telling you about her? She's Barb Kopecky's girl."

"Barb's girl. Sure." Carrie studies Ruby for a moment, then sticks out her hand. "Your sister called me about you today."

"My tooth. Yeah." Ruby clasps Carrie's hand, which is small-fingered and dry. "Thanks for getting me in." She nods at Tim. "Your husband here fixed me up." Ruby smiles, and Carrie smiles back, but her eyes are assessing. Even pregnant, the woman's thighs and hips are narrower than Ruby's own. Ruby licks her lips. Her tooth throbs.

"Hey, I thought you and me and Ruby could have lunch together," Tim says. "Use up that Colby." He slips Carrie's coat off her shoulders and disappears around the corner, into what must be the kitchen, still gesturing broadly, and Ruby wonders,

Are they nervous? Do I make them nervous? But then she glances at Carrie; up close, the woman's eyes are shrewd as a cat's. Not nervous. The opposite of nervous. Crackled green and gold, they flick up and down, taking in Ruby's corduroys and her sweatshirt. Everything Ruby is wearing is wet.

"Sure," Carrie says neutrally. "I gotta leave for work in a little bit though, okay?" Ruby sees that she wears a pink polo under the unbuttoned striped Oxford, lettered on the left breast to read *Minnie's*, and Ruby wonders if Carrie is a good waitress, if her customers like her.

They can hear Tim knocking around the kitchen, the sound of the fridge opening, and Ruby pulls free from Carrie to touch *The Odyssey* again. "So you know Val, huh?" She smiles, still trying, though it's coming back to her, as it does at every office party, ever: small talk is exhausting. She didn't think Carrie would be so pretty, with the birdwing hair and those kohl-ringed eyes. Like an Egyptian queen. Ruby sighs and tugs at the front of her sweatshirt; the waistband of her pants cuts into the flesh of her hips. She will start eating better tomorrow.

Carrie isn't smiling; she stopped smiling when Tim left the room. Has she guessed how her husband once touched Ruby's breasts? That Ruby, with her sturdy legs and dimpled chin, once broke his heart? For a moment, Ruby doesn't know if she is sorry or proud. Bending awkwardly, she opens the Homer. Carrie hasn't yet invited her to sit down.

"You like to read! I haven't thought about Homer since freshman year of college." Ruby has opened the book to a picture. Odysseus stares out at her, weighted with impossible armor, his expression that of a blind man.

"I do read," Carrie says. "Believe it or not."

"I meant—"

"I've talked about *The Odyssey* with Val, in fact. The Hero's Journey."

"Hero's Journey," Ruby echoes, turning to another page. She stares at a picture of the sirens.

"Val comes into the diner where I work," Carrie says, reaching over and taking the book out of Ruby's hands. Her voice is naturally husky, as though she smokes, or drinks, though probably neither, now. Clean living because of the baby. "We talk about books. She likes poetry—well, you know that." Carrie sets *The Odyssey* on the overloaded shelf behind her and then remains standing, hands linked under her belly; later Ruby will remember that, how it seemed odd. Or maybe not. Maybe she was already ushering Ruby out the door.

"Yeah. Poetry, I know," Ruby agrees, though she knows nothing of the sort. Val? Poems? "What has she been reading again? I forget," and she almost laughs, because she used to do this when she was a girl, circling 'round something until Val or Barbara gave it up, whatever thing it was she needed to know. "You are like a first grader," her mother sometimes admonished her. "Fishing, always fishing for the information."

"I lent her my Bukowski." Carrie shrugs. "Maybe that? I think she was writing something and wanted to see how he did it." She glances back at the wall, covered with a woven blanket, orange and brown and coarsely pretty, that separates them from Tim. "Timmy? You need help in there?"

"A-okay in here!" comes Tim's reedy voice, and Ruby thinks how it is muffled, as though he is under a blanket himself, or caught in the fridge.

Ruby giggles. God, it's her who's nervous.

"What?" Carrie's eyebrows pinch together. "Oh, Val's poetry, the stuff she writes? It's not very good, is it?"

"Some of her stuff is okay," Ruby says.

"We're all entitled to our opinions." Carrie shrugs. "She got mad at me the last time I took a look at her work, though. I told her what I thought! Oh well." Her hair droops over one cat eye, and Ruby understands with sudden lonesome certainty that Carrie doesn't care about Val, or whatever poetry she's apparently writing. She doesn't care about Ruby.

I know you, Ruby thinks. Carrie is the kind of person who wants you to feel that while her opinion matters, what you think of her matters not at all. *I knew a dozen girls just like you in high school.* "Maybe she's written more since then," Carrie says. She smiles at Ruby, poisonously, and in this moment Ruby misses her mother absolutely. Barbara would know what to do. The old Barbara. The real Barbara. Her mother would see what Carrie is and would maintain the upper hand, even as she managed to say something kind, or at least fair.

"She has," Ruby says, but at least she knows the next part is true. "And our mom's been sick, and she's a mom too." Next to the couch is a wicker chair, and Ruby sits down in it. She stares at the fireplace, layered with ash.

Carrie arches one eyebrow. "What a good sister you are."

"Damn straight," Ruby mutters, but then Tim's head bobs around the corner.

"Okay, then!" he says, eyes moving between the two women. Too cheerfully, he adds, "Let's eat, you two. Ruby, your tooth okay?"

"It's fine," Ruby says, which is true enough. She's hardly even thought about it, not since she stepped in this house.

"I think you can eat something now. Just be careful," Tim says, and he takes Carrie's arm. "All right, hon, let's get some lunch in you too."

Ruby stands and follows them into the little kitchen, which is the flat color of mustard. She brings her purse with her; it will be something to fuss with, and she'll give them the stupid bear at some point, won't she? There's a rusted starburst clock hanging on the wall, the time frozen at eight thirty-five, but there are also beautiful red cotton mats on the table and the food looks colorful and good: cheeses and meats fanned on a metal platter, bread that looks to be homemade, and applesauce in a blue pottery bowl. A basket of apples, shining like mirrors. A round frosted cake with a piece cut out. Tim has troubled himself to make things nice, the way Ruby's mother used to do. Ruby realizes how hungry she is, almost hungry enough to weep.

"Okay, now," Tim says. "It's okay, you just sit." It's unclear who he's consoling—her, or Carrie, or the pale sandy cat who has crept into this yellow room—but they all sit then, in unison, even the cat, who leaps with grace onto Tim's lap, rubbing its jaw against his arm. Everyone, *everything* loves him. He's Midwestern nice, nicer than Drago probably ever was, and Ruby wonders where the men like that are, the single ones her age. With the population in Chicago, there should be plenty of them, a lot more than here in Ladyford.

They all bend to the food. Sleet ticks against the window. "So I'm riding my bike again," Tim says into the silence.

"Good," Ruby says politely. "Where to?" though she doesn't care. She reaches for an apple, then pulls her hand back. Her mouth is still numb; with her tongue, she gently touches where the needle went in. What if she bit into that glossy fruit and her tooth broke off again? The thought makes her a little sick, and she spoons applesauce onto her plate instead.

"All the way over to Minneapolis, took a few days. Carrie had a show there, and we met up."

Ruby knows this is her cue: a show? Clearly she's supposed to ask about it, but stubbornly, she does not.

"Carrie had some pottery," Tim says. "Some jewelry. Babe, you should show her your stuff."

"No one expects much from me, living here," Carrie says, looking straight at Ruby. "That's taken a lot of pressure off. It's like, 'Oh, Carrie, she's off in bumfuck, what's she been doing?' But I'm here, living my life, doing my work. I like making jewelry." She pats her belly, ripe as a seed. "And I'm good at it, you know. That's my secret weapon. People underestimate me."

"I don't," Tim says proudly.

"You know, some people underestimate Val," Ruby says. "I'd like to see most people try writing." She takes a bite of her sandwich, and her tooth is thick and numb, as if it is wadded in cotton.

"Some people *try* it," Carrie says to the cat.

"Ah, dessert! I almost forgot about dessert!" Tim says. Poor

Tim. He never could keep up with the girls in high school, either, their razored, unerring cruelties, unleashed one upon the other. He leaps up and pulls a cookie tin from off the top of the fridge. When he pries up the lid Ruby can see a baggie of pot inside, and the twisted blackened ends of roaches. "See?" he says, appealing to them both. "Yum." He spills a little pot out onto his napkin and shakes it, separating out the seeds.

Carrie rolls her eyes, but she says, "You know I can't do that. I sure miss smoking." Patting her belly, showing herself off, she nods at the cookie tin, its endless gilt round of evergreens and sleighs.

She's not really sorry, though, and that man's shirt—it has to be Tim's. It looks good on her, too, funky and cool, just the kind of shirt an artist should wear. Not like Ruby's friends from around here, who used to slop around in big pastel T-shirts when they were pregnant, shirts from Walmart with sayings— *Baby on Board!*—which had allowed Ruby to look down on them. But Carrie lives here anyway, even though she would never, not in a million years, wear a Baby on Board shirt. Around her neck is a delicate choker, silver lace tipped with turquoise.

"Did you make your necklace?" Ruby asks. It really is pretty, but what she says is, "It looks homemade."

"I did," Carrie says. "That's funny. Your sister likes this necklace too. She comes into the restaurant sometimes." She regards Ruby across the table, clicking her glass with her rings, which gleam and gleam.

"So you said."

"Nice kid," Tim interjects. He slathers a piece of bread with mustard, then another. "Sorry," he nods at the bread. "I can't resist. Carrie made it."

"We've had a few heart-to-hearts," Carrie says. "Me and Val."

"I imagine she could use a friend." Ruby touches her tooth with her tongue.

"Who couldn't?" Carrie says. "But in the end, you know? She's a little young."

"Excuse me?" Ruby sets her sandwich down.

"Oh well," Carrie says. "It's just, one moment you think someone's going to be your friend and then you wake up one day and realize no, they're not."

"Well, Val's pretty busy," Ruby says. "Like I said. She's kind of at that stage of life where—it's not like she can just go to the tavern and hang out."

"I don't go to the tavern and hang out," Carrie says.

"You go to the library and hang out," Tim says, getting up and retrieving a bowl of pudding from the fridge. He mounds a little on his plate, then sets the bowl in the middle of the table.

"I can't see Val doing that either," Ruby says.

"The one thing Carrie doesn't like about Ladyford," Tim says, "is she hasn't found it easy to make women friends."

"You don't say." Ruby reaches for the pudding and sets it beside her plate.

"The women here have their alliances," Carrie says. She cuts herself a mingy piece of the cake and takes a tiny bite.

"Like in a family," Ruby says.

"Have some cake," Carrie says.

"No, thanks. I've got my sandwich here." Ruby has made it sparingly: a piece of bread, the thin slice of cheese.

"I think they might be jealous of her," Tim says. "There's some nice women in town, though. I keep telling her, think of them as potential sisters."

"You must just love having a sister," Carrie says. "I don't have a sister, myself—three brothers, can you believe it?" She smirks. "Val and I, we *were* close for a while. She said to me once, she said, 'We're almost like sisters.'" Carrie pauses, studying Ruby. "No offense meant."

"None taken."

Tim looks hard at his sandwich, then gazes out the window. Perhaps he really is clueless. Perhaps he just pretends to be.

"But then it comes down to, friends are friends, and family is family. Right? Family is so important." Carrie rubs her belly, slowly. "But maybe I'm just thinking that way for the obvious reasons." She reaches over and punches Tim lightly, proprietari-

ly, in the arm. "Boring old me." She laughs. "Baby on the brain!
But you have to admit—Ruby, right?" She turns to Tim. "This
is the life."

Tim grins. "This is the life."

Ruby squints at Tim's wife. She seems flush with secrets.
There is the fact of the baby, of course, mysterious and swimming, but there is also Carrie herself.

"What can I say?" Tim says sheepishly, and he is smiling,
there is pride in his voice. He puts his arm around Carrie, and
Ruby watches them watch each other. She bites into her sandwich, dry as a paddle. This room is too small, too yellow, too
warm, its walls closing in. Or maybe it's her that's too big.

"Excuse me," Ruby says. "The bathroom?"

Tim points toward a small hall behind him. "Through the
archway," he says. "To your right."

Ruby stands, touches her back pants pocket, and her phone
is there. "Excuse me," she says, nodding to Tim, and when she
gets to the bathroom, she closes the door and sits on the closed
toilet. The bathroom is painted dark green. Black-and-white
photos hang on the walls in red frames. Val's bathroom, with its
pink walls and mismatched towels, is nothing like this, and Ruby
pulls out her phone and sends Val a text. *Hi!* she says. *Mom was
okay*, she types, hoping that this is true. She thinks, deletes that
line, and types instead, *We are all hanging tough! Thanks for setting
up the dentist appointment.*

She waits to feel better, then texts Lorna: *I feel dowdy, help!*
Ruby moves to the mirror and tries to smooth her hair behind
her ears. *My important people*, she thinks. Her face is a white moon.

When she returns to the kitchen, Tim and Carrie are leaning
together, as if in consultation. But then Tim swivels toward her,
his face friendly. "So tell us about you, huh? How do you like
Chicago? HR, huh?"

Not a mean bone in his body, Ruby thinks. "Great. It's great,"
she says. "I'm in charge of the employee stock-purchase plan."

"Sounds important," Tim says encouragingly. He puts his
arm around Carrie and squeezes.

"Oh," Ruby says. "It is. They offered me a promotion." She sits down, waiting to feel satisfied; it occurs to her that it isn't enough for him, *them*, to know what she's made of herself. It doesn't mean as much unless it makes them a little jealous too. Ruby starts scooping pudding from the yellow bowl onto her plate. Spoonful after spoonful, she can feel Carrie watching. It's chocolate, and she imagines the smooth comfort of that. It will make her feel better; Ruby read once, somewhere, how chocolate can have a positive effect on the brain.

She almost says something about that, chocolate and brains and about how she's taking care, good buddy, but Tim unwraps himself from Carrie and seals a joint with his tongue. "Shame about the music, though. You still play, you know, for fun?"

"Sure," Ruby says, because there was the thing with the concert, and she'd meant to see it through. "Sometimes. I've been working on some Bach." Ruby stops; she sounds so lame. "That was a long time ago," she says. "The music." Something flashes across Tim's face, and Ruby, afraid it might be pity, adds, "I just...you know, I got this promotion."

"So you said," Carrie says.

"And I minored in business."

"I remember the jazz concert you were in. In high school? I don't think half the school had heard jazz before then." Tim smiles at her. "Chicago's nice," he says. "Bet you've got jazz clubs there. Good places to eat."

"Yeah, there are some good restaurants—"

"Are you seeing anyone?" Carrie interrupts. "Val said you were seeing someone from..." Here she taps her teeth, pretending to think. "Russia?"

Ruby spoons up more pudding because it's true, the chocolate *is* a comfort. "Croatia," she says. "We broke up. Just." Carrie looks surprised and for just that moment Ruby feels like she might have the upper hand; later she'll look back and wish she had enjoyed it more.

"I thought you two were almost married or something. I mean, that's the way Val made it sound."

"Well. I'm not really into getting locked into a relationship." For years what she had was enough, or almost—late nights with books and booze and the sex, which was usually great, and outside the window Chicago, buoyant, its skyscrapers slatted with light.

It is a beautiful city.

"No interest in a family then, huh?" Carrie's voice is all politeness.

Who are you, Norman Fucking Rockwell? Ruby thinks, though what she says is, "I love the city!"

"Pardon me?" Carrie says.

Ruby pushes away the bowl of pudding. It would look bad if she took any more. And if she eats another serving she'll feel bad later, the pudding gut-heavy and rounding her out. "Where are you from, anyway?" she asks Carrie, praying it's not New York City, though it could be.

Carrie glances at Tim. "I'm from Iowa City," she says. She takes a sip of iced tea, staring at Ruby over the rim of her glass.

And Ruby is relieved, because being from Iowa City isn't much different from being from here—Ladyford. Carrie with all her pretensions, and she must see something in Ruby's face because she continues, "So…no family, huh? Well. I hear that you've always been…*independent.*"

"Proudly so."

"I don't think—" Tim begins.

"Anyway, there's Val, isn't there?" Carrie talks over her husband. She sips and sips. "Your mother got her grandkids. And your mother…" Here she pauses delicately, lips pursed. "It sounds like she took a turn for the worse?"

Small towns, Ruby thinks. "Where'd you hear that?"

"Probably someone at the café," Carrie says. "Maybe one of the ambulance drivers?"

"The Parkinson's was bad enough," Tim says.

Ruby studies her hands. "My mother has had some challenges," she says. The sandwich and pudding swarm in her gut but her voice is calm.

"How's she doing now?" Carrie says. "Okay?"

"I don't know," Ruby says. "Val called me early this morning. It sounds pretty bad." She stops herself, understanding that any troubles she might have would be entertainment for someone like Carrie. "But she's rebounded before. She will again." Ruby makes herself sound sure, though she is nothing like it.

"And you're here visiting *us*," Carrie says. "How *nice*."

"Ruby had the bad tooth. She just got in. But she's heading to her mom's after lunch. Aren't you?" Tim says. Ruby knows he's trying to be helpful. He balances the joint in his fingers, twirling it.

Long pause, the sleet outside, the sandy cat yawning and stretching. "Yeah, I love the city," Ruby finally says. She is very tired, and if she were at home she might lie on her shiny quilt, which is brand new, the way things from her childhood were not. "The yard work here must be a bitch." Ruby turns to Tim, who has paused in lighting the joint to gaze at her, guileless, those liquid eyes as soft as a unicorn's.

"I'm okay with it," he says. "Come outside, though, see my garden."

"In November?" Ruby is confused.

"He wants to show you where he grows his pot," Carrie says flatly.

"We-ell, sure," Tim allows, that open smile lifting his narrow face. He lights the joint and tokes deeply. "That too. C'mon, Ru." He stands, and Ruby does, and Carrie watches them but doesn't get up.

A back door painted milky purple opens off the kitchen, and Tim leads her through it, into a sort of dooryard—dirt packed smooth, though it's mud now—and beyond that, a chicken-wire fence enclosure. Nothing there now but overturned stakes and coils of wire, the crisp brown leavings of a garden—Tim and his wife are not particularly tidy, it seems—but he points to it proudly. Tomatoes in the summer, and peppers, he tells her. And sure, the pot.

"The happy couple," Ruby rasps. She's taken a hit of the pot, which is good, skunky and mellow in flavor. She gazes out at the remains of the garden, the stalks so brittle they might have been burned. "You never told on me," she says. "About the fire. You're a loyal person, Tim." She waits for him to say something kind in return.

"I think we could be happy anywhere," Carrie says from behind them. She's at the door, hands clasped under her belly, sharp chin jutted.

"Truer words were never spoken," Tim says, turning to smile at his wife. Ruby might never have mentioned the fire at all. "We lived in a trailer for a while," he tells Ruby. "In Abbotsford. It was all these Russians, and us."

Ruby shakes her head. Was this cool, to live in a trailer? Should she be, obscurely, jealous?

"Phone's ringing," Carrie says then, and when Tim passes by her, back into the kitchen, she pats his arm, the thicker part above the elbow.

Carrie closes the door behind him and comes to stand beside Ruby. It's cold out, still spitting sleety rain, and Carrie has wrapped a sweater around herself. Avocado wool—not everyone could pull off that color—and Ruby remembers suddenly a stone she found once, years ago, in the Flambeau. It was slick with algae, the strangest green. She'd shown it to Tim and he said, "Leave it there, we'll visit it together."

Carrie stands just at Ruby's shoulder. She says something under her breath.

"What?"

"I said, we lost a baby. Buried here, see?" Carrie points to a hillock of stones in the garden enclosure, piled like a cairn.

"There?" Ruby is cold and folds her arms over her breasts. She fingers her pin, the rough metal setting and velvety pearl. So tragedy has brought these two close. Tim and Carrie are managing the ups and downs together, while Ruby is not so good at tragedy, it seems. "I'm sorry," she says sincerely. "I can't even imagine what that must have been like."

"Life." Carrie shrugs, then turns to the door, which has opened again. It's Tim.

"We gotta go," he says. "Turns out I've got the twins coming in this afternoon."

"Batten down the hatches!" Carrie says. She almost skips inside.

"Ready, Ru?" Tim is waiting at the door, but Ruby stays where she is. She steps across stones laid in the mud, through a crooked wire gate into the garden. The rocks are smooth, dark in the rain. She hadn't seen them at first but now she can't miss them, rising above the discarded brown stalks. *Good God*, she thinks. Can you bury a child in your backyard? It doesn't seem legal, but she likes Carrie a little better, for revealing this place.

One of the stones has been written upon, in black Sharpie. SNOWBALL, it says. OUR GOOD CAT.

Jesus. Ruby whirls around and there is Tim, holding the door with his hip, eyes sleepy, and through the kitchen window she can see Carrie, watching.

"Ru." Tim proffers the joint. "Finish it up."

She hates Carrie, she does. "I will at that," she snaps, snatching the joint and striding past Tim, into the warm kitchen with its smell of cardamom. Carrie has busied herself at the sink. Her shoulders are thin, pointed beneath the cobwebby green sweater. Her shoes look as though they are made of soft hide.

"Ruby saw our little grave," Carrie says in a singsong voice.

Back when, Barbara might have said: "We grant others the power to make us feel stupid." Sound advice, of course. *Mama*, Ruby thinks. *Where the hell are you now?*

"That's your cat," Ruby accuses.

"Fisher got him," Tim says.

Fishers. Like wolverines. Growing up, Ruby coexisted with a revolving cast of barn cats; though Moon nourished them, leaving out kibble and water, he never let them into the house. Sometimes they became a fisher's dinner, prey to those sharp little teeth.

Not a baby.

"This town is crap!" Ruby cries, anything to wipe that superior smile off Carrie's face.

"Whoa," Tim says. "This is our life here."

"We like it here," Carrie says, her voice triumphant, as though she has been waiting for Ruby to say exactly this, all along. "I see deer. We're going to get a house." She tosses her head, smiling at Tim. "Hey," she says. "I've got work. You've got the twins and their cavities. Can you drive me?" She seems to pirouette away from the sink, a beautiful, rounded doll.

They are both moving on from her outburst, like a fart at the table or the ignorant ramblings of a child. And what is it about the look that they exchange, which makes Ruby feel ugly and stupid and alone? She glares at them, thinking of her sere bright condo; she wants to weep in terror. She waits until Carrie leaves the room, then touches her tooth with her tongue. "You are such a copout," she says to Tim, darkly. "We were going to live in Paris." Ruby thinks of the blue paint in her mother's room.

Tim gazes at her. "I couldn't have done any better than Carrie," he says. He reaches for the joint in Ruby's hand, then thinks better of it. "Jesus. You know," he begins and then stops, shaking his head. "You may be smart, but you are heartless." He's still holding her gaze, unblinking, his face a mix of contempt and pity. When she finally looks away he says, "But then you've always been like that. You think you're so…You haven't changed a bit."

Ruby pushes past him, to the window with the view of the garden and its lonely grave, the pile of stones chocolate-black with rain. Her tooth throbs. She knows he is happy here; more than that, she knows he loves Carrie, mean as she is. "Yes, I have," she says.

When she turns around she expects to see his face, the insult in it, where it used to be kindness and sex both, but the kitchen is empty. She hears muttered conversation in the next room, then laughter barely muffled. They come into the kitchen together, Carrie wearing crepe-soled shoes; with blue elastic, she pulls her hair back into the tiniest ponytail. When she smiles at Ruby—finally, broadly—Ruby sees that her teeth are perfect. There's just the faintest light in Carrie's eyes, like a dead star.

"We gave you lunch," she says.

"I hate sandwiches," Ruby informs them both. "Have a good life." She grabs her purse and throws the blue stuffed bear onto the table, with its gentle soft face that makes her sad. "For the baby or whatever." She won't look at either of them; in her haste, she cracks her shoulder against the doorjamb and the sound it makes in the silent kitchen has the sick resonance of breaking china. It isn't until she gets outside that she realizes she still has the joint. It is damp in her hand now, no longer smoldering, and torn in the places where the paper is weak.

CARRIE

Homegrown

The toy is used, obviously, marked with a greasy thumbprint and right here on the tag it says *daKotA* in faded green marker. The name underlined with stars. Carrie tries to remember what Val ever said about her sister. Tim never talks about his old girl-friends, while the word around town is that Ruby is smart and makes good money at a good job; if there's anything negative, Carrie doesn't hear it. But Ruby's from here, and Carrie isn't. What Carrie thinks is that the woman is a joke. Rolling in like a hippo and touching all their books like she owns the place. She probably wants kids, though. Carrie rubs her belly. Of course she does.

Carrie allows herself a secret smile. Baby on the way, all the promise of that, and even six months pregnant she's better looking than most. It's always been that way. Over the years, in order to get along with other women, Carrie's learned to pretend she's not pretty, and that she enjoys the friendship of women as much as she appreciates men. But she still knows how to put another woman off balance. (Men? They've always loved her, always wanted to protect her.)

Not so different from what Ruby herself was doing though. Right out of the box you could tell she was showing off how smart she is. Just the way she put things. "You like to *read?*" Smiling and smiling, but you could see the dislike in her eyes.

Different as night and day from the sister, Val; sure, Carrie and Val were friends for a time. Val would come in for a cup of coffee at the diner first thing in the morning. She would have just dropped the girls off at school, Carrie learned, and would go on to help her mother later, stuck in some sort of generational sandwich, which Carrie respected but didn't envy. (As she sometimes told Tim, "Better her than me, god*damn*.") Val made Carrie feel good about herself, about her life, in a way some other people didn't. She had an aloofness that wasn't unkind, and which Carrie could relate to, not being from here.

Never mind that Carrie came from Iowa City, outside of Iowa City, actually, as her dad raised pigs. She was still considered *city* around here, and if no one was unfriendly, it became apparent that she belonged only because she was Tim's wife.

At first Carrie had tried to fit in. She wore running shoes with her jeans; for a short while she'd tried to organize a cooking club among the women she met in town. Like a roundabout, where every month a different person hosted, and they went so far as to call themselves The Cooking Klatch (a name Carrie hated but went along with). But Carrie found that while everyone was happy to participate, they talked amongst themselves, about people she didn't know, and at night's end they'd all be bidding affectionate goodbyes to one another and sometimes, standing apart, she'd be forgotten. It got to the point where she felt like a fifth wheel, so she told them she didn't have time for the group anymore, covering her hurt feelings by making fun of the women to Tim, how provincial they were, and how all they talked about was their kids. She told him, and believed, that without her holding things together, the group would probably fall apart. "I started that group!" she said. But one time she went into town for something, and walking by the Delta Café, which had opened recently and given the diner where she worked some competition, she saw the women eating lunch together, fond and laughing, and she was miserable.

"You hate that place," Tim said when she told him. "Aren't you glad you didn't have to eat their crappy fried chicken?" After that she threw the gym shoes away and wore her black boots with everything. She tied up Tim's giant Packers T-shirt with a rubber band so that it showed off her figure, and she wore strange, organic-looking necklaces and pins she made herself from wire and beads. The way she dressed made her stand out.

When she ran into The Cooking Klatch women, in the IGA or at the little coffee shop in town, they were polite but distant.

But Val wasn't like that. She wasn't usual. She was friendly, her smile vulnerable when she looked up from the scribbling she did in blue ballpoint on the diner napkins—poems, Carrie learned, hovering with the coffeepot—and the two struck up a friendship that flourished most of a year. Carrie got to know Val's family: the husband, Len, who was always working, but seemed decent enough, and Junie. Nice kid. When she and Val used to hang out, they'd pick Junie up at school and go to the park, the one by the little housing development that went up after the tornado blew through. Junie would hook up with whatever kids were playing and Carrie and Val would drink black coffee and talk about the problems of the world, as Val put it. And poetry, and art. Val had questions about these things, deferring to what Carrie said, because Carrie had been to college, Val said, and she *knew.*

Carrie would tell Val about her art, the abstract painting that she was trying now and instinctively knew was good. But she needed to hear someone else say it, and Val did that for a person. The day Val saw Carrie's paintings, she had come over for coffee and stayed almost until suppertime; that was perhaps when they were closest as friends, right before Carrie found out she was pregnant.

Art made Carrie feel tranquil in a way most things did not. "It lifts my heart," she said that day, uncharacteristically earnest, and Val accepted that, the way she would accept a birthmark, or a scar. The way she accepted without question that Tim grew pot, and how this bothered Carrie, just a little, although Carrie loved her husband fiercely. She thought Tim was a balance to her, and she had told Val this too. In turn, Val said something about motherhood; in those giddy months of friendship the women exchanged feelings and secrets like jewelry. Carrie promptly forgot whatever it was Val had said, though some nights now, rubbing her belly, she tries to remember. Something about the way love was parceled out, how sometimes you had to act the way you wanted to feel? In any case, for a while there had been girls' nights out, at the Rusty Nail, both of them drinking girly drinks in venomous colors and acting drunker, gigglier, than they really were.

Sure, they had some good times. But after Carrie got pregnant, she made excuses about going out. She'd return Val's calls but not as quickly as she might have done in the past, or she would make plans but then cancel at the last minute. Val was hurt. "You feel good now, but things will change again and you'll need a friend," she'd said. Val still calls sometimes, though less and less frequently, and Carrie is always the one who ends the conversation: *I have to go now*, she'll say, not troubling to disguise the boredom in her voice. Somehow Carrie manages to communicate that maybe all this time, she was just being kind to Val. As she was kind to Val today, getting her bitchy sister in to see Tim at the last minute.

Because being available to others outside her immediate circle (Tim, the baby) is tiring, and Val has her share of trouble. There is the mother, demented now, from what folks at the diner say, and that older girl, Dakota. Trouble, that one. Promiscuous, and not even in high school yet. Carrie feels protective of her life, that calm she wants to cultivate for the person growing and turning inside her. Eventually, Carrie will teach this skill to her daughter, who they'll call Lena; Carrie and Tim have already decided on the name. She will teach her daughter how to be a survivor. But all that is in the future yet.

So she doesn't regret the loss of a friend, though Val says she might, one day.

The bear is warm in Carrie's hand.

"The weather's bad, love," Tim says, walking up and reaching his arms around her from behind. "We'll have to go after her; she can't be out in this." Tim sets his chin on her shoulder, looking out at the white lines of rain. They both listen to the shushing sound it makes. "I feel sort of guilty." When Carrie doesn't say anything, he adds that he kept Ruby outside before, to look at Carrie's sculpture. "I wanted her to see what you can do," he says.

"I don't think she cares what I can do."

"Maybe she does," Tim says.

He is a good man. He warms up the car for Carrie while she waits inside. He pulls up as close to the door as he can and she hurries out to the car, the rain slanting; he has The Doors playing when she slips inside, laughing and breathless, and the music seems to go with the weather. And he's a good driver, taking it slow on the wet roads so Carrie actually sees the flash of yellow, the moment Ruby (who made remarkable time walking—she'd gotten pretty far) slides down an embankment into the grasses. Carrie glances at Tim, who's scanning the other side of the road and misses it.

"Maybe she got a ride," she tells her husband.

He drops her off at the diner, right at the front door, and she kisses him on the mouth. "Love you," she says, and happiness surges through her. When she gets inside she learns that Marnie has called in sick.

"Strep," Tony the busboy tells her glumly. His hair, worn short and close to his head like most of the boys around here, is dyed aluminum blue today. Every week it's different.

"That's all right," Carrie says, and means it. She doesn't like Marnie. "More tips for us," she says, and winks at the boy, who's still in high school and obviously smitten with her. Part of it has to do with the fact that she shares her tips fairly with him—not all the waitresses are so generous—but part of it is just who she is, what she has come to expect from men, all men. Carrie peels off her wet jacket, hangs it in back by the kitchen, ties her hair back in a fresh tiny ponytail, and grabs a rag to wipe off tables. The thought that Tony wouldn't look twice at someone like Ruby brings Carrie satisfaction. "I like your hair," she tells the kid, brushing past him.

She likes it up front, where the plate-glass windows let in the light, even on a day like today. Carrie stands, patting her belly, looking out in the direction toward Tim's office. He'll pick her up tonight; they'll go home and eat chicken à la king. The rain rushes against the glass.

One night, some weeks ago, she had awakened to the sound of rain. The cats—a scabrous black tom who'd wandered into the motel courtyard almost two years ago, and the elongated sandy cat they call Griffin—and Tim were with her, wound together, of a piece, a helix in the slippery quilts; she was loath to go back to sleep. She felt such luminous calm, such freedom from the outside world, with its demands and judgment.

"You want something to drink?" Tony asks. He's stationed himself by her elbow, ready to help.

"No, honey, I'm fine, thanks." He's sweet but by the end of shift she'll be ready for a break. His attentions can be wearing.

"Why don't you check the ketchup, Tony?" Her voice is still kind. *Tim. Lena. Carrie. Mom.* She misses her mother, though she wouldn't admit that to anyone but Tim. Sometimes Iowa seems very far away.

Tim. Lena. Carrie. Mom. The names run through her head like beads on a rosary. This is her magic circle. Carrie arches her back and rolls her shoulders, yawning. The human spirit is such a needy one, she thinks. She keeps her circle small.

JUNIE

Bug

The big yellow bus brings her from school, and she sits alone in front, by the bus driver, because Dakota, who usually sits with her, is already home. Because of the swears. Even Junie knows this. Her sometimes friend Melly said Dakota was a bad girl (friends can be mean), but Junie knows her sister isn't bad. Dakota makes brownies and lets Junie lick the spoon, for one thing. And didn't she let Junie sleep with her best Blue Bear last night when Mama had to go help Gram, and Junie was sad and wanted her mama?

"She'll be back, Junebug," Dakota said, and she climbed into bed with Junie and put her arm close until Junie fell asleep. When Junie woke, Dakota was back in her own bed, and the room was cold and filled with moon, but Blue Bear was still there with her, soft except for the bald place on the ear. That was Dakota's bear.

So Melly was wrong, and didn't even Mama say once how friends can be friends but sometimes not?

What doesn't take long in the car takes a long time on the bus, there are so many stops to make. At school Miss Manny has pinned up pictures of pumpkins, and friendly looking pilgrims. She has hung what she calls Indian corn, with its dark kernels, what Daddy calls flint corn. The classroom stays in Junie's mind the way it does not when she has Dakota to distract her. Today she thinks about the paste smell and the worn places in the floor that Miss Manny has smoothed out with gray duct tape.

School stays in her mind all the time it takes for her to walk from the bus stop home. It's raining but Junie has her rainbow bubble umbrella; the gravel walk is full of puddles. Mama is not at the window, waving and waiting with Jellybean the way she used to be. In fact, the house is so quiet when she lets herself in that Junebug is afraid. The curtains are pulled together except for a fat stripe of gray light on the living room carpet from where they don't meet. No TV on, and no smell of coffee or anything cooking. Mama doesn't cook so much right now, but Junie likes the suppers in metal trays just fine, like the meatloaf last night, in its little section, and there were hot apples, too, that burned the roof of her mouth. That hurt but she didn't cry.

"Mama!" she cries now, scared, and then she hears her sister's voice, coming from their room: "That teacher *is* a cunt! You ask anyone!" A harsh laugh then, and silence.

"Dakota?" Junie creeps down the hall. There is a smoky smell coming from their bedroom; Junie knows Dakota burns incense sometimes, though Mama asked her not to when no one else is home.

"Yeah, I told her that, like she'll listen. She's at work now." Junie cracks the door and sees Dakota lying on her bed, talking on the phone. Junie pulls away and goes back to the front room. She knows enough not to bother her sister when Dakota's talking to friends.

Mama so sad lately, and Junie just wants to make things right. She wants to make Mama laugh. Dakota in trouble again and Junie needs to fix things but she has to think how.

She goes to the front cubby to put away her backpack. Junie loves her backpack, which is printed with a happy space alien and smiling stars. She passes Dakota's bag on the couch, and it makes Junie's heart hurt, Hello Kitty all marked up like that. She hugs her own backpack—"You be good, space alien guy"—and puts it snug in its cubby, then leaves her umbrella open so that it can dry. She wanders into the kitchen. Junie can make her own snack: white bread with butter and sugar on it, and a glass of juice. The butter is hard to spread and so the sugar doesn't stick the way it's supposed to; most of it ends on the counter, but she wipes the shiny white laminate with her shirt and sits at the table by the clay lamb Mama bought. The lamb is always the same, and Junie likes it.

There's yelling now from the bedroom. "I hate that stupid school; they'd have to pay me to go back next week!" *One, two, three.* Junie counts the kitchen cabinets in her head. "They did me a favor when they kicked me out!" *Four, five, six.* Junie plugs her ears and chews her bread. Then she gets a sheet of lined paper from the kitchen desk and uses her best handwriting to write Mama a note.

I LOVE YOU, it says. THE SKY IS NICE.

XOXOXOXOXOXOX

JUNIE

She can't think of what else to say, so she draws a picture of a ladybug, which Melly showed her how to do, and Junie is proud of her ladybugs; she could draw them all day. She draws one and colors it red and black, pressing hard with the crayon, it even breaks a little. More yelling from the bedroom, so she draws a second bug next to the first and she makes it so their little black legs are together, like they're holding hands. They both have big smiles, and she colors the second bug green, 'cause that's Mama's favorite color.

"She doesn't know anything about me!"

Seven, eight, nine. There are nine kitchen cabinets. Junie makes more bread and butter and sugar and takes this piece with her to the dark little hall, chewing hard, the ladybug picture in her other hand.

"She thinks I'm stupid, but I'm not, and I told her, *I hate you!*"

"Well, sometimes I hate you too!" One time, not so long ago, Junie heard her mother say this to Dakota, and it made Junie gasp; it made her middle feel like it does when Junie stands on the diving board, the higher-up one. She knows Mama would never say that to her, Junie, and she knows, too, sliding the picture under Mama's closed bedroom door, that if Dakota sees it, the picture will make her grumpy, and she won't let Junie sleep with Blue Bear, not tonight and maybe not other nights too.

"Why can't you be more like Junie?" Mama had said to Dakota that time.

"Suck-up," Dakota will say when she sees the picture, because she's said that before, but Junie knows she's just trying to make Mama happy, with her eyes dark like a raccoon the way they are.

She's glad she's not Dakota, who makes Mama act crazy and mad, even if Dakota has Blue Bear, and prettier hair, and older friends who dance the way they do.

She goes to wait and wait in the living room. Mama will be home soon. Junie doesn't turn on the television; she pulls out her spelling paper. *Yell*, says the sheet. *Bear*. Junie forms the letters, mouthing the words, again and again. She's her mama's Junebug, isn't she?

RUBY

Nirvana

Ruby has to walk the two miles back to the dentist's office, where her car is, through a pitiless sleet that scours her face and nets the surrounding fields, obscuring them. A frustrated indignation burns in her like the low steady ember of a cigarette, leaving her breathless. How dare he judge her? A college-educated hick who lacked the courage to live in the world? She is almost to King Burger, with its painted sign. It will look as it always has. It will look like her past. Ruby walks quickly, her shoulders jacked forward. When Mom dies Ruby won't have to come back here, ever.

No doubt Tim and Carrie are looking for her when they drive by, windows down despite the weather. Their faces look blurred, and the heavy Ford moves cautiously, slow as a parade car on the icy road. But Ruby is clever, scrambling into a ditch overgrown with grasses, knee high but dead now, crisp with ice. When she clambers out of the ditch, hard grasses break and tear at her hands. Tim's taillights wink in the sleet, then disappear. Ruby brushes off her pants and continues walking. She thinks about how Carrie is smarter than Tim, but not as nice. Her feet make ticking sounds on the pavement.

Ruby's car, smelling faintly of coffee, is a comfort when she reaches it. Tim's car is parked next to it—he's back, taking care of the twins, presumably—so she lets herself in quickly and drives around the corner. She doesn't want him to see her; it's past three p.m., the lonely time of day, and she breathes through her mouth. Heat blasts, and music; she has found a radio station with country music. Ruby has always liked country, its desolation. Its astonishment at the ways people can be. Now she turns the music up, and she is safe here.

Merle Haggard's "Kern River" comes on; God, what a good song. That chorus. Ruby pushes the seat back so she can stretch her legs, and, shivering, pulls her wet sweatshirt away from her belly. Wet as sump. Something Moon used to say. She finger-combs her hair, stealing a glance in the mirror, and making a sound like wind in a bottle. The sweatshirt is ugly—but her pin! It glistens with rain.

She'll get rid of the sweatshirt, she thinks. Give it to Goodwill; maybe later she'll see it on someone else, some stick of a girl and the sweatshirt hanging on her like a fat woman's shirt. It will change hands until it ends in a landfill or the cloth wears through and then it will be gone. *Stop now, you're okay,* Ruby thinks. *That could have been worse.* Couldn't it? So they thought she was a bitch, so what? Tim had invited her. *Be careful what you ask for.* Leaning back, she closes her eyes; it might be she falls asleep but it feels like she's thinking.

What it was like, Moon and her driving down to school. Barbara and Val were going to come, too, but at the last moment Barbara said she couldn't do it. "I'll cry," she said. "Best I say goodbye here." Val had plans with friends, it turned out, and so it was just Moon and Ruby on the drive down. They didn't talk, but they had their music.

That first year Ruby was in a dorm. She was supposed to have a roommate but whoever it was never came. Moon helped carry her few things in. He said goodbye without ceremony and then he left, which was his way. At one point, girls on the hall poked their heads in; some of them liked campy Bette Davis movies and listened to Nirvana and eventually became Ruby's friends. They chose her. But at first it was just Ruby alone. She sat on her bed, which she'd made, neatly, with a brand-new quilt that her mother probably couldn't afford. It was a gift. "My college girl," Barbara had said.

Ruby gazed across the room at the other, unmade bed which never was claimed. *I'm a musician,* Ruby thought, and the loneliness seemed part of it, it seemed okay. There was joy there. It was the same when she'd go out that first year—this was later, when she'd made her friends—she'd be out there at a restaurant or a concert, but she was alone too. Ruby didn't mind. She didn't equate loneliness with failure then.

Suddenly a song she doesn't recognize is playing, and it's raining even harder. Ruby sets the wipers going (still screeching, she has to fix that) and pulls the car out, rain glassine on the windshield, the radio turned up and over the wipers' shriek. On the way, she passes the house of her favorite grammar-school teacher (two plaster deer out front, a Packers flag), and she wonders what Mrs. Schadrie is doing now. Is she alive even? She'd seemed old when Ruby was nine, but maybe Mrs. S., glasses on a chain around her neck, had really only been middle-aged—Ruby's age now, even. It bothers Ruby that the house has been painted white. It used to be green.

LEN

Roof

You don't want to dig into the sheathing below. He uses a shovel to pry off the old shingles, and it's backbreaking work, made worse by Robinstadt's little "visits," as the man calls them. Val says that's a euphemism for checking up on Len's ass. Robinstadt, with his leonine head and expensive red coat. He'll stand next to the barn and peer up at Len, barking out advice, something about the angle. Len, who lost part of the hearing in his left ear in a boating accident years ago, is never really sure. But he nods, and keeps working, and he's the one Robinstadt keeps on.

The wife Len doesn't mind. Pam Robinstadt is mousy and sad, but kind; she brings him coffee, leaving it in a scarred ceramic travel mug near the barn dooryard when he arrives at daybreak. She comes by at midday, too, and it's then Len comes down to eat his sandwich.

Take today, for instance. She calls to him and though it takes a moment—he is in his work trance, mind closed—when her high, thin voice finally registers, he swings down the ladder to where she stands bundled in her brown jacket, thin cheeks marked with spots of red.

"You move like an athlete." She always says this, and he hitches his shoulders with pride. In school, he was the awkward one—shambling, out of true. Even if he'd had time for sports, he wouldn't have excelled; the few times he tried to play football, the pigskin slipped through his hands as though greased, and the friends he had time for knew not to ask him to play. But here on the roof, the tools feel right in his hands. He likes the heft of his shovel; he likes the clean lines marked on the tarpaper he rolls out from the eaves on up. There's been a brief lull in the rain and Len makes use of it.

"How are those girls?" Pam Robinstadt asks. She doesn't wear makeup. Her eyes are huge in her face, but today she looks brighter, what with the pink of her cheeks and a cheerful yellow scarf wound thickly around her neck. Breath trails like smoke from the corner of her mouth.

Before when he's talked about his girls, he has lied a little. "Dakota's going to bake again this weekend," he says today. "She's just like her mama." Dakota probably doesn't know the ass-end of a cookie sheet, but Len senses the girl's desire to please, buried somewhere deep, and the cookies are a harmless-enough invention. He almost told Pam Robinstadt once that his Dakota made it onto the soccer team, but in a town this small, his lie would have been found out within the day. Better to keep the fibs manageable, harder to prove. "Her chocolate chip cookies—"

"You'll have to bring some in sometime." Mrs. Robinstadt gives a little chirp of delight and touches her hair, which is piled on top of her head and secured with pins.

"Hell, yes. No, pardon me, ma'am. I meant, sure I will." They both laugh. "Hard to keep 'em on the plate though," he adds. "Between me and her mama and her sister, them cookies don't last long."

If she ever knows he's lying, she doesn't let on.

Junie, now. He can tell true about the pictures she draws, how her teacher wrote "Such a fine girl" on her report card, underlining the "fine," in red pen. Junie loves cats and her Barbies and riding with him to get donuts. "She likes the ones with sprinkles," he tells Pam Robinstadt, and the woman leans forward. She actually seems to care, and that's hard to come by, Len knows. His own mother telling him when Junie was a baby, "Listen, boy. People either have children of their own, or they don't. Either way, they don't care to hear you yapping on about those girls."

Okay, then. He'd thought grandmothers were supposed to

dote, but then his mother's always been her own breed. Len packs his own lunch, and lately he's taken to making an extra sandwich, just in case Pam Robinstadt wants one, and today he has also brought two packaged snack cakes. "We ate all Dakota's cookies but I brought us something good," he says, lugging a bench from the corner of the barn into the doorway, and laying his red bandanna (clean) across it.

"I declare, I don't know where you put it!" she says, which is just Mrs. Robinstadt being nice; Len knows he has the beginnings of a spare tire. "The Mister, he'll be wanting dinner, but I expect I could have a little something now."

"Take a load off, then."

It's been raining off and on all day, but the barn is pleasant with its warmth and animal smells, and in the doorway they can look out across the road, and a field that in summer grows silage corn to the line of trees beyond. The house is to their left and just out of his line of vision if he doesn't turn his head. From his pack he pulls out the sandwiches in their wax-paper wrappings and sets them on the kerchief, next to the cakes. He owes her this much, the way she listens to his stories.

Pam Robinstadt nods and reaches for the sandwich just as the door to the house creaks.

"Early for dinner, ya?" Bill Robinstadt marches across the yard. He routinely stands with his hands on his hips and he's a big man, gusty-boned and broad in the shoulder, a good two inches taller than Len.

"It's hungry work," Len replies, easygoing enough, but he is already standing, shoving his sandwich back into the blue pack.

"I'm making some soup," Pam Robinstadt pipes up. "Dinner at one, sweetheart." Bill glowers at her, then turns on his heel.

"I don't pay a man to eat dinner," he tosses back, his strides long. "And don't go leaving your garbage. I got bears." For a man, he has a big ass.

"I have to go," Pam Robinstadt says. She leans toward him, and for a moment Len is afraid she's going to say something more, something intimate that will hang between them always.

People tell Len things, about their marriages or their children, how they are afraid of sickness or aging or debt. He doesn't know why. He doesn't know why his own wife sometimes does not.

"You enjoy that dessert now, ma'am," Len says quickly. He presses the cake into her palm, puts a hand on the ladder.

"And you give those girls a hug from me." Her voice is both apologetic and anxious.

From the rooftop Len watches her go. She is like a rabbit, something desperate and lonely in the way she moves across the muddy barnyard. Robinstadt waits for her on the front steps of the house. Len imagines the man saying, "You eat dessert like that and you'll get big as Marathon County," or some such crazy talk—the woman can't weigh more than one hundred pounds—because she gives him the cake, her head ducked. When Pam Robinstadt goes into the house her husband lingers a minute; he looks up at the barn, and seems to meet Len's eyes. Holding the stare, Robinstadt tears plastic wrap from the cake and shoves the snack into his mouth, whole. Len shakes his head, returning to work. Seen through Mrs. Robinstadt's eyes, he is rich indeed.

That thought, it has legs, making him happy enough to call Val later in the afternoon, even though they'd talked once in the morning already. "Just checking in," he says, and he can tell she's surprised. He asks about her day—she had to go into the IGA today and so he knows to ask if Mark was the manager, because he's the nice one and then Val's day will have been a little easier. He stares out across the Robinstadt yard. It's raining again, and he's taken refuge in the barn. There's plenty to do in here, but in this moment he is happy to hear Val's voice, and when he takes a swig of coffee from the travel mug, cold now, but sweet with cream, he pretends for a second that she made it for him. He tries to think what she might like to hear. That's always been a puzzle for him, something to figure out. "Your mom will be okay," he finally says.

"Maybe," she says, her voice flinty, and he sets the coffee

down. He asks what's wrong, if the doctors said something about Barbara, and she says, *No, no, nothing like that*. Was it work, then? Something with Ruby, or the girls? And then Val's voice breaks, and it comes out, little by little, until he knows at least a part of it. Dakota's been kicked out of school.

"We're lucky," Len reminds her, happy that Val is *talking* to him, even if the news is bad. At least they can share this.

"God, Lenny. Sometimes I don't feel so lucky. I don't know how to help her."

Len tries to think of what to say. He tries to hold on to the feeling of pride that being with Pam Robinstadt sets into him. Pride in himself, in the family he's made. His pride sometimes falters, but it lives next to the love, which does not. His love is a constant. He shows his love for Val even when she doesn't know it; he won't tell her what Robinstadt said about Dakota, for instance, and this Berryman. Not even in the joking way he'd planned, as though he didn't for a moment consider it true.

"We'll be okay," he starts to say, but Val's distracted—he can hear Junie in the background, something about one of the cats—and Len isn't really hurt when Val cuts him short. She offers to call him back, and that's something you don't hear every day.

He sees into his wife's heart. His Valentine. And Dakota. Mrs. Robinstadt. Misunderstood, the lot of them.

RUBY

Fisher

When she gets to Cedar Manor, it is almost suppertime. The parking lot is near empty and she parks close to the door, but even so, by the time she runs from the car and steps inside, she is wet through again. The main hall is tan and pale peach, dated colors, but the staff has tried to make the passage cheerful. Photos of the residents, wearing paper hats from last month's Halloween party, hang at intervals. Ruby finds her mother's photo. Barbara is smiling, wearing an orange sweatshirt, Junie on her lap. Val had told Ruby about the party. The little ones could trick or treat in the hallway where the more mobile residents lived, and Val said Junie, in a princess costume Val ordered online, had had a blast. "Small victories," Val said.

Ruby passes the hall television, tuned to a late-afternoon movie. Four or five residents are lined up in their wheelchairs. One of the ladies is watching the screen with bright eyes, knitting in her hands, but the others are asleep or stare blankly, mouths slack. Ruby takes a breath. This part of the hallway is always a gauntlet, though she imagines Val has an easier time of it. Val probably knows every one of these residents by name; she's probably gotten used to the stress that makes Ruby, right now, feel as though she's hauling a sled of brick. Ruby passes the wheelchairs, making herself smile and nod at the knitting lady, who gives a little wave.

Inside Room 112 the shadows sift across the walls and there is Mom's bed in its tight wrap of linen, blanket folded back neatly. The other bed is empty; perhaps Mom's roommate, a woman named Carol, is in the dining room.

"Mom?" Ruby says, as if she can summon her mother, explain her into the bed, this place.

"Mom?" She's out in the hall now, the lights green and fixed overhead. A cat wanders by; its real name is Nunner, Ruby knows, and it belonged to a resident who died last year. He'd brought the cat when the rules were different and so the cat was grandfathered into the current no-pets administration. The nurses keep it on, calling it Sailor and feeding it cream. A blocky creature, satisfied enough, it haunts the room of its former master, watching TV with the new resident late into each night.

"Ruby?" It's Sandy, one of the nurses, and Ruby's favorite.

"Hi!" Ruby starts, and the nurse smiles at her. She's a kind woman, probably in her late fifties, though she looks older, her skin webbed with wrinkles from a lifetime of smoking. Sandy had her "colors" done years ago and will wear only black, red, and white; a crimson turtleneck peeks from beneath her white uniform smock. "I'm a winter," she confided to Ruby once. "What are you doing, hon?" she asks now, and her eyes are yellow, sagging and staring like eggs beneath the lights. "Poor thing. Soaked through. I guess it's still ugly out?"

"Looking for Mom," Ruby says, suddenly afraid that she might cry. She thinks of her fight with Val to make herself bitter and strong. "Mom's sick," she says.

"Well, sure, hon, but she's in the hospital, you know. She'll come back by and by, once she's better. They have to get her— you know—stable."

Idiot. *Idiot.* Of course Mom is in the hospital. Right after the stroke or whatever it was. She wouldn't be here.

"Right," Ruby says. "I came to get her things. Her blanket, with the blue trim? She loves her blanket." Ruby touches her mouth, to keep something—telling? inappropriate?—from flying out. Her tooth might hurt, if she lets it.

"I'm sorry about your mom. Come on all of a sudden, this latest. Such a sweet lady. Nary a complaint."

Which isn't how Ruby sees Barbara, not anymore, but she nods.

"Tell your mom we're all praying for her," Sandy says. She has pulled a chocolate bar from her pocket, and, as if Ruby is a small child, she proffers it, mouth corked to the side with pity. "Here, sweetheart. You look like you could use a little sugar. When's the last time someone did something nice for you?"

I can't remember, Ruby wants to say, but she doesn't and takes the bar, clutching it to her chest.

"Don't forget her blanket," Sandy says.

"Right!" Ruby rushes back into Barbara's room and wrests the blanket from the bed, folding it into an untidy rectangle. She and Val have tried to make Barbara's room nice. Val got their mother a lamp at a garage sale and Ruby turns it on now; in its soft light the room is cozier, almost homey, the glaring blue walls less shiny and intense. A bulletin board hangs near the window, pinned with a calendar and photos of Val's girls; over Mom's dresser hangs a print of a table, a chair, a window, in clear Scandinavian colors. The picture, framed in light wood, was a gift from Ruby, who told Barbara when she opened it, "Now you have a view into another world." She gazes at the picture now and tries to imagine herself in that bright room; it is the future in that room, and she is respected there.

"I always liked that picture too." Ruby whirls to the door, where Sandy stands, an unlit cigarette in her mouth.

"I think you and I like it better than Mom does," Ruby says. The room smells like strawberry room freshener, the kind that plugs into an outlet. Ruby doesn't necessarily like the fake sweetness of it, but it is better than, and covers, the other smells.

Sandy takes the cigarette out of her mouth and tucks it into her breast pocket. "She likes that picture, honey. We talked about it once. She likes the colors. Your mom told me it was a gift from you."

"Really?" Ruby is surprised, and pleased. She hadn't thought that her mom would remember that. "I got it from a shop near my house. The woman who runs the place is from Norway. My mom used to say she wanted to go there. To Norway, I mean. I thought this was the next best thing."

"That's real thoughtful, Ruby. You and your sister are good to your mom."

Ruby remembers why she likes Sandy, who doesn't tap her watch, the way one of the other nurses did last Christmas Eve, when Ruby arrived later than she'd hoped. At least Ruby had come! From Chicago! Through the snow!

"You give me the benefit of the doubt," Ruby says.

"What's that, lovey?"

"Can I ask you something, Sandy?"

"Shoot," Sandy says. She leans against the doorframe, her turtleneck red as life's blood.

"I tell myself the good moments are worth it—even if Mom doesn't remember them the next day. Do you believe that?"

"I believe love is never wasted. I believe we carry it with us," Sandy says.

"I'll try to remember that," Ruby says. "Thanks, Sandy." Her voice trembles and the sloppy blanket spills from her arms. She clutches the chocolate bar in one hand. "Hospitals are scary, you know? I hope Mom isn't too scared."

"Oh, honey. She has your sister and you. She's got friends. That Pearl, she comes once a week. Your mom's had a good run. That's what you'll remember when she's gone." A beeping starts up from somewhere down the hall. "That's for me," Sandy says, straightening. "My ciggie will have to wait." She smiles at Ruby. "You take care now, hon." The nurse strides away, shoes squeaking on the tiles. The doorway where she stood seems to hold a muted green light.

Ruby sits down on the edge of her mother's bed and tears the wrapper from the chocolate bar. She takes a great bite but her tooth aches; she has to stop before the bar is gone.

She has always hated hospitals. She has always feared illness and death. If she got cancer, Ruby thinks now, the person she would call would be Lorna. Lorna could handle it. Lorna would go with her to the hospital if she were here now. She would tell Ruby a funny story about Jim; she would bring along the book she's been reading, about a cat in a library. She'd be unapologetic about it. "So it's not Tolstoy!" she'd laugh. "So sue me! The cat's nice; the book's nice. What can I say? I like nice!"

Lorna is nice but hours away. Val isn't necessarily nice, but she is close by. And she cares—about Mom, certainly. Ruby stands, tucking the chocolate bar in its foil wrapper into her pocket. She will return to the house, which might be blazing with light, and she will ask Val if they might go visit Mom together after all. The hospital being such a fearful place.

᷾

At Val's, the door is unlocked and ajar. The living room lights burn, as Ruby had imagined, even the overhead fixture Val rarely uses, a stern white lozenge that brings out the dirt. Ruby can see its harsh light through the front window. She pauses on the front step, the doorknob in her hand, listening. It is as though the world has taken a breath; the only sounds are the ticking of her car as it cools in the driveway, and a radio, knit with static, from somewhere deep in the house. Ruby opens the door wide. The television is on but the sound is off, and Dakota stands in the middle of the room, her hair loose and untidy. Junie shrinks against the sofa. And there is Val, face seamed like a much older woman's, hands pressed against her cheeks.

"We'll ask your father," Val says.

"What's this then?" Ruby stands in the doorway, and in the unforgiving light she can see a rash like pepper, red and thick along Val's jaw, and she understands all over again that she doesn't know her sister, if she ever did, any more than Val knows her. Dakota must be in trouble again; that much, at least, is clear. Tough, stringy Dakota, Ruby's favorite as she has admitted to no one. Always an undercurrent of melancholy to that one, which Ruby appreciates about her niece. Like Ruby was at that age: restless. Boys, weed, music—nothing helped if you were cut from that cloth. Those were the free days, the days before work took up 90 percent of life, and yet Ruby hadn't enjoyed her teenage years. Dakota doesn't look like she enjoys them either; even when she was a baby, she had a knowing look.

Junie, with her open charm, isn't like that, and Ruby almost feels guilty that she doesn't love her younger niece more. But so many people already love Junie.

"Everything okay?" Though of course it isn't, and there is a flash of irritation, even anger, across Val's fine features.

"Jellybean's *gone!*" Junie keens, breaking the queer frozen tableau of mother and daughter and daughter, faces white as lime. "And we think a fisher might have eaten her! She was my best girl!" The child starts sobbing, and Ruby moves to her niece awkwardly, sitting beside her on the sofa and hugging her against her hip the way she's seen Val do, because Val and Dakota are so strangely still. Junie's round face is mottled and streaked with tears, and Ruby pities her then; she remembers that her niece is a child, a state that in and of itself deserves pity.

Fishers. The very largest marten. That's how Moon would describe them, with their dark, dark fur, their dark natures, and mouths full of teeth like razors. You never forgot their flat, guttural screams. Fishers were essential, permanent parts of Ruby's rural childhood, invoked when the barn cats would sometimes vanish, not for a day or a week gone hunting, but forever. The girls could never find traces of these cats once they disappeared. And though Moon warned them both that the cats, which prowled the farm and rid it of mice, weren't pets, the girls sometimes persisted and thought of, say, gray, fox-faced "Elise" as a member of the family; they mourned the losses. Ruby and Val never saw the fishers, either, which made the creatures somehow more frightful, like forest-dwelling boogeymen. Moon showed them a picture once, a pen-and-ink in a book of nature he kept at his desk. The book smelled of rot, and after a while, the girls learned not to name the cats.

"I didn't let her out," Dakota mutters.

"And a good thing for you!" Val says fiercely. "As if you aren't in enough trouble!"

"Stop," Ruby says. "Tell me what's going on."

"Dakota's been kicked out of school until God knows when,

and now this. I can't take much more, I'll tell you." Val moves
to the window bay and peers past her reflection into the dark.
"I don't know where that damn cat is." Distracted, she turns
abruptly. "How's Mom?"

"Fine," Ruby lies. "The same. When did you last see Jellybean?"

"This morning," Junie whimpers. She has molded herself to
Ruby's hip. "The fishers are mean."

"I didn't let her out," Dakota says.

"Mama?" Junie pulls away from Ruby to scrub at her eyes
with the backs of her hands.

"*Someone* let her out," Val insists darkly. "Your sister's been
at school."

"Mama?"

"What, honey?" Val is just barely keeping the exasperation
from her voice.

"Do you know where Blue Bear is?"

"You've already lost him?" Dakota's voice is scornful, and
Junie starts crying again.

"Relax." Ruby holds her hands out, placating, because experience has shown that the girls will listen to her, even if Val
doesn't. "It doesn't matter," she says. "What matters is that we
find your cat. Dakota, come with me. We'll search the woods.
Junie?" Ruby catches Val's eye. "Don't you have homework or
something?"

"I have homework," Junie agrees through her tears, sounding relieved.

"Okay, stay here with your mom. Jellybean might show up
on her own, and if she does you'll be here. Val? Yes, it's cold.
We'll take the car, and Dakota can wear my sweatshirt," Ruby
says. The girl has already slouched to the door.

"Get your hair out of your eyes," Val says to Dakota.

"I hate fishers," Junie says.

"I hate," Dakota whispers, at least that's what Ruby thinks
she says.

VAL

Reader

Val stands by the front bay and watches Ruby's departing car, the red lights winking like planets in the dark.

Ruby taking Dakota out. The relief of that. Val thrills to the brief giddy sensation that for now, someone else is taking care. Dakota has surely guessed what Val does not currently have the energy to disguise: The real love she feels for her daughter—will always feel for her daughter—might sometimes be eclipsed by the fact that she doesn't like Dakota very much right now. And because she is relieved of that confusing burden, if only temporarily, Val thinks she might float to the low living room ceiling with its sparkled acoustic tiles; she might extend her arms like wings. She turns to Junie, and the child is startled, then smiling, when she sees the easy joy in her mother's face.

"I'm sorry I got mad, sweetheart," Val says. "I am not at my best today. *Definitely.* Do you really have homework?"

"No. I just said that." Junie giggles uncertainly.

"Let's do something different, then. I'll turn off that radio. You turn off the TV. Let's—let's play checkers!" And again that startled joy. Junie scuttles to the remote to turn the television off and then brings the cardboard box, flattened at the edges, that holds a checkerboard and mismatched pieces—some wood, some plastic—but enough of each color to play a game.

Val gets these bursts of relief, that feeling as when she ends a visit with her mother, who for much of the time now inhabits some strange and incomprehensible interior place. Although every now and again the vagueness clears from her hazel eyes and she'll say something like the old Barbara would, something so wise and insightful that Val grieves her losses all over again.

But when Val leaves her mom's room, there's always that lifting in her chest. "Free!" she'll think, understanding that this is hope she feels for a little while. She might get a cup of coffee at the diner, she might sit with the Bukowski book she longs to understand. She is still alive, isn't she? And at these times she loves everything: the black coffee in its thick chipped mug; the feel of a pen in her hand; both her daughters, as thwarted and promising, damaged and resilient, as they are.

No hope. Surges of hope. Again and again.

She didn't get to the hospital today. Let Ruby take a turn at sitting vigil, because Val doesn't believe, not really, that their mother will die. Not today. And the cat, not her either. Jellybean is chasing a mouse, or eating part of one, its bladder a tiny white balloon. Somewhere in the dark, she is the least of Val's worries.

Val helps Junie set up the board. "We'll do this together," she says, and she can see that Junie is relieved and happy, and she sees how her younger child adores her. "You have a good day, lovey?"

"I had a good day, Mama." Junie still talks to Val about everything, but sometimes Val worries that her daughter, young as she is, tells her mother what she thinks Val wants to hear.

"Melly nice?" Val doesn't always like Junie's best friend, who can be petty and jealous, though Val understands that's how girls can be.

"She was nice. She shared her candy at lunch. And, Mama? She invited me to her birthday party. Can I go?"

"Of course you can," Val says, watching Junie line up her pieces with chubby fingers.

"I can't wait! Melly says there will be games and maybe we'll watch a movie!"

It is a comfort to Val that her Junebug is still happy. "Should we play here?" Val asks, and Junie says that yes, they will play on the coffee table; the little girl arranges pillows for them both to sit on.

"Wait!" Junie says, disappearing into the kitchen. "Blue

Bear?" Val hears her calling. When Junie returns, she holds two Twinkies and the pottery lamb. "Mama, you need to eat more," she says, echoing something Len has said on more than one occasion. She places a Twinkie carefully on each side of the board. Then she arranges the lamb on a coaster, as if on a pedestal. "For pretty," she says. "I can't find my bear, but it's okay. *Lambie* can watch us play. Now," Junie says. "Now we can start."

Val reaches out to touch the rough sparkly lamb. *This is good*, she thinks, and in fact she will remember this moment with happiness in all the years ahead: the Twinkie, the lamb, Junie's crooked smile. Maybe she will write about it later; maybe it doesn't matter if what she writes is any good. *I'm a dabbler*, Val thinks, but there is always that hope that this time she can capture the way Junie hums when she is thinking. The way she counts when she is upset. The sticker on her hand is a smiling whale. Val wants to get it all down, even the hard things.

When Moon was devoured by cancer his eyes would wheel up, sightless. "Is it real?" he would ask, because the medications brought him pictures, as he called them, though none of them scary: tractors and whirling platinum spheres, corn that pushed through the tough flowered wallpaper covering the walls of his hospital room. This was near the end, when the dark star of cancer had grown through all the treatments.

"Mama?" Junie adjusts the lamb so that it faces Val. "It's your turn."

"Yes, it is!" Val says. "And I'm gonna beat you!" She laughs, her love thick in her throat, her chest. "But first, how about we make some mood lighting?" Val stands and turns off the harsh overhead light; she leaves on the floor lamp, with its muted glow. She moves her pillow so that she is sitting next to Junie. "There! Better, right?"

Junie squeals happily, and Val pushes a red disc forward. "You are good for me, little one," Val says. She tears open the plastic around the Twinkies, offering one of the cakes to her daughter. "Yum," she says. "But we have to bake again, don't we? It's about time we made some cookies."

"Peanut butter," Junie says. "The kind with the chocolate kisses pressed in."

When Moon was ill, Val threw herself into baking, as if by filling her uncle with sweets there might be no room for the cancer to grow. She went through Barbara's old recipe books with their penciled notes, trying to find the recipes Moon had always liked best: the no-bake cookies called "bird nests," the stained-glass cookies with their thumbprints of jam. He could not eat what she baked, and she could not stop thinking about the cancer, which she imagined choking Moon's bones in cobblestoned sheets. Mutant cells begetting cells begetting cells. She tried (and failed) to write about *that*. How death could be ugly and frightening, yet the cancer itself so elemental, so magisterial, that she respected it.

"Mama!" Junie reaches over and squeezes Val's hand. "This is fun!"

"Yes," Val agrees. "Yes, it is." No matter what has gone before, no matter what is still to come, there is tonight. She squeezes the child's small hand back, shifting on her pillow. "Hey, I ran into your teacher at the IGA yesterday."

"Miss Manny?"

"Miss Manny. She says you've been doing well with your reading. I thought we might try some chapter books, you and I. Okay?" Val sees where she might capture Junie's king, but she moves another piece instead.

"So we can still do book time, right? You and me? Even though I'm a big girl?" Junie and Val like to cuddle in Junie's bed, reading together. Val's been too tired lately, but she can imagine how it will be when they start up again, her and Junie, reading *Little House in the Big Woods*, the dinosaur blanket tucked around them both.

"Yes, lovey. There's a series about the olden days I think you'll like. I tell you what, I'll pick it up at the library and we'll start it tomorrow night."

"Oh, Mama! I love books! I love *you*!"

"That's our thing, isn't it? Our books!" Val smiles.

Ultimately, Val always came back to the books. Reading comforted her, no matter what else was going on in her life. She would read to Moon when he was failing, a stupid mystery, paperback, and bloated with water damage, abandoned in the laundromat and jubilantly discovered by Junie the week their dryer went out. The cover was torn away, and Moon was gone then too. He couldn't follow the plot. But Val was a good reader—she had always enjoyed reading to her girls—and in those last days the sound of her voice seemed to soothe Moon, when they were alone but also that one time when the room was full of visitors and the competing clatter of voices. She took pride in that. Ruby, who wasn't there, thought the reading a mad, doomed errand and told Val so when they spoke on the phone, but Val didn't care. She would drop the girls off at school (Dakota) or day care (Junie) and then drive straight to the hospital. She wanted to beg Moon not to leave. She read to him, instead; those long mornings were, she believes, a solace to them both.

"I like when you read to me, Mama," Junie says. "You do voices, and not very many people do that. Even Aunt *Ruby* doesn't do that!"

Val laughs. When they read the Babar books, she had tried to use a French accent. "Pretty soon we'll read the Harry Potter books, and then I can try a British accent," Val says. She was strong for Moon and she must be strong for Junie.

"Harry Potter! Just like Dakota!" Junie cries. Because Dakota still loves those books, even now. "I think we should watch a Harry Potter movie together. Do you remember the story Dakota tells about, where she and Grandma made butterbeer and it turned out gross?" Junie laughs and then looks wistful. "I wish Grandma could come over now."

"I know you do, sweetheart," Val says. "Me too."

It is happening again—the decline, the loss—and this time it is her mother. "You'd think I'd get better at this," she had told Carrie, but their friendship was already unmoored by then, and Carrie had smiled vaguely, stroking her vast belly.

"I can't even imagine what you must be feeling," Carrie'd

said, presumably kindly, but Val still remembered the thrill of jealousy that coursed through her. Carrie's parents were relatively young still, and certainly healthy, making visits from Iowa to help their daughter prepare for her baby. Val met them in Carrie's kitchen, one of the last times she had been invited over. At first Carrie's mom seemed remote, but it turned out she was genuinely nice. At one point she gave Val a hug and said something about how glad she was that her daughter had found such a good friend. "You're delicious," she told Val, as though Val were a cupcake, filled with cream.

"Oh, that's Val, all right," Carrie had agreed, with the confidence that comes with being loved, with being loved always, and more, and best. Val still remembers that her friend was cutting the tags off a romper patterned with lambs. Carrie's mother had brought the romper and was paying for a special crib for the baby. People like Carrie, they belonged in the world; maybe they thought they owned it. Maybe they really did.

"We're self-reliant," Val told Len when she got home. Val had seen how Carrie took her own mother for granted, and she understood that her friend couldn't imagine, or care, really, how death upended everything. Carrie had no clue what it might be like to never have a mother again.

"You and I can make butterbeer to go with the cookies," Val says now. "Let's see if we can get it right this time."

"Can Daddy help? He's a good cook."

"Yes, he is." Val thinks of Len. That mother of his, and yet he learned to parent somehow. "Of course Daddy can help," she says.

"Okay," Junie says. "I'm going to win." She jumps a chain of Val's checkers, giggling.

"I hope so," Val says. Junie is rubbing her eyes; they'll eat an easy supper, and then it will be bedtime. Val smiles at her daughter, who still believes in her. Val must do what it takes to preserve in Junie what she, and Ruby, and probably Dakota have already lost.

"Do you want to know more about the book we'll read together? There are two sisters—"

"Just like me and Dakota," Junie says.

"And one is small and dark and mischievous, and the other sister is golden and very, very good."

"I want to be like the golden sister," Junie says.

"You *are* like the golden sister," Val says. "And when we get to the fourth book, we'll read about some of the girls' friends. One of them, Nellie, is *not* very nice!"

"Sometimes Melly is mean but she's my best friend. Mama?" Junie reaches for the lamb and makes him do a little dance, there on the table. "Do grown-ups have best friends? Is Miss Carrie *your* best friend?" She sets the lamb back on the coaster and regards the board sternly.

"Mama has lots of different friends," Val says.

"Aunt Ruby?"

"Sisters love each other, yes."

"I'm your friend," Junie says.

"Yes, you are, lovey."

"So, we'll read that book tomorrow?"

"Yes. You'll like it. The author is very good."

"Everybody is good at something," Junie says. "Melly is good at math. I am good at drawing and dodgeball and cats. All done!" she cries. She has captured Val's last checker, and she lifts her arms to her mother. She is still not too big to be hugged. "Mama?" Junie says, and Val bends to lift her daughter close. "My pretty mama."

Remember tonight, Val almost says out loud. She tightens her grip on Junie, who is warm and solid. "Tomorrow we'll read," she whispers to the child. "Love you." She has that.

"I'm hungry, Mama."

"You want a potpie?"

"Yes!"

"Okay, let me start the oven. You can have an apple now to tide you over," Val says, who is hungry too, and trying, the way you do, not to be afraid.

CAT

The Hunt

She is one of two cats in the house; she'd been abandoned by another family. The first people were unkind and the cat does not think of them at all. The new people, who are a better sort, are four in number; the littlest one chose her, at the place with the metal cages. Her life has been good since then. The comfort of a blanket to sleep on, and the man scratches her cheeks with bent fingers.

The little one grows indignant when people say that cats don't love anyone. "You don't know Jelly!" she cries, and the cat, which does love her people (though no one else), thinks of the little one as her kitten, fondly.

Jellybean is the name the woman gave her, though the cat has her own name that she tells no one.

She is grateful that she has a house now, even as there is still the wild part of herself that likes it outside; when she is out, she hunts. She is hunting now. Birds and mice, the tender striped chipmunks; she slips out when she can. She has her own agenda, like today, when the woman answered the thing that rings, rushing from the house to the car, and she easily faded past, soft on her paws. The woman was agitated, with wet coming from her eyes; the cat, who never has wet from her eyes, does not know what this means. She knows that the smaller of the girls has this condition sometimes also.

The cat is in the woods, and there are the chipmunks; there are rabbits. This is the moment. Her belly scrapes grass.

DAKOTA AND RUBY

Rabbits

Dark as ink outside, and the cold is dull and still. Her aunt's sweatshirt is damp and hangs like a dress, letting the chill in. Dakota's miserable, but she won't admit it. Ruby, in a T-shirt that stretches across her breasts and butt like a second skin, has got to be more miserable still. At least it's finally stopped raining.

"Where do you think she got to?" Ruby asks.

"Jelly likes the woods." Dakota shrugs, and the two of them continue along the deer path that leads from a park in town, where Dakota used to play and Junie plays still, and into the pine woods extending along the road and clear back home. There are houses set along here, but scattered; sometimes the path skirts someone's backyard. It was Dakota's suggestion, when they couldn't find Jellybean from the car, to try this path. "Junie has found her at the park more than once," Dakota says, and Ruby sweeps the beam of a flashlight she pulled from her trunk—back and forth, back and forth—across damp earth laced with tree roots. It's easy to stumble—they have to take care—and the swinging light makes Dakota feel sick, or dizzy. If it had been anyone but Ruby, Dakota would long ago have told them to quit the fuck doing that.

"I used to love this path," Dakota says. "When I was a kid." Her breath rises before her face like a wraith.

"You don't anymore?"

"Not at night like this. It used to seem...like being free." Dakota speaks slowly; she's thinking, she wants to get this right. "Now the dark scares me. What I don't know scares me."

"But you know this place," Ruby says.

"I guess."

"You know the people here."

Dakota is silent, and Ruby flicks the flashlight back so that they can see the way they came. Pine needles are soft, layered thick on the path in patches like snow. To either side are the pines, branches dead on the lower reaches. Dakota pulls the hood from Ruby's sweatshirt up over her ears. Far away, she can hear the warbling cackle of a loon. Ruby is silent, and for a heartbeat Dakota almost feels happy. The needles underfoot are slippery, fragrant. "Here, kitty kitty," Ruby calls.

"I'd like to show you a place," Dakota says.

"Where's that?" Ruby's voice is mild, the way it almost never is with Mom or Gram. Dakota understands that in some ways, she has the privilege of seeing her aunt's best self. "Here, have some chocolate," Ruby says. From the pocket of her corduroys she produces a partly eaten chocolate bar, its torn wrapper swaddling the bit that's left. "It's got biscuit in it."

Dakota takes a square of the chocolate and eats it slowly. She hasn't really eaten much since breakfast. She knows this drives her mother crazy; there's that, and also the light feeling she has when she fasts, as though something clear and bright runs pure in her veins. "Turn here, see? Where the path branches? Just a little farther." The path is narrower here, the woods deeper. "See?" She thinks, but does not say, that this is her magic place.

They have entered a clearing no bigger than the gym at Dakota's school, carpeted in wet, matted grass. Dakota has stamped down the grass on previous visits, and perhaps the owner of this land has too, a man named Berryman, who comes here to tend to his animals. The locals say he's a half-wit, but Dakota thinks that he—wisely, in her estimation—just doesn't like people. One time she came upon him here and because she was quiet and didn't interfere, he let her stay. He let her return. Berryman is probably in his early thirties, a small man, shaved-headed; he has rabbits here, in a large wire pen with a screened top to keep out the predators, and Dakota loves how the rabbits move freely in the space that has been allotted to them. It seems as if

Berryman plays games with them, and holds them like kittens, though when she asked questions—their names, what it was they were playing at—he wouldn't say.

"It's okay," Dakota had said. "You don't have to talk to me." And that was a relief, actually, not to have to make conversation. Adults—and even her friends—ask so many questions and then don't listen to the answers. Dakota talked to the rabbits quietly that day, and she could feel in her arms and hands afterward how calm she got.

That's how it was, being with Berryman, who was gentle like the rabbits, and Dakota came to know his schedule—he worked at the local dairy and came here after his shift ended—and she liked to think that he enjoyed her company.

The rabbits are black shapes in the hutch. They have eyes like serum, liquid and dark. Dakota knows this, and holds the picture of them inside herself during the week. When her friend Mackenzie takes it into her head to blow her off, or Mom prefers Junie the way she will, Dakota can call upon the image of the rabbits, the way they are soft in the world, filled with just themselves, and then she is untroubled.

"Jelly might be around here," Dakota says. She looks around, tries to see the place as her aunt might. She has never been here at this time of night. Her mother doesn't even know she comes here, though that day will arrive soon enough, Dakota knows. Just last week, old man Slade at the minimart hinted, darkly, how it didn't do a young girl's reputation good to be sneaking around with half-wits. And in the woods, he guessed, nothing came to too much good.

They think the worst of her, or they pity her, which is worse.

"Here, kitty!" Ruby calls. Dakota slips back the loop of twine holding the pen door closed and reaches inside, lifting out a rabbit white as apricot bloom. It drapes across her arms and she strokes it, cooing. "Its ears are velvet," she tells Ruby, straining in the dark to see her aunt smile.

If Slade knew about this place, then pretty soon everyone else would. Dakota wanted to tell him that Berryman, who'd gone to Iraq back in '05 and come back like he was, a shadow man, wouldn't harm her or anyone else. "He's restful," was what she'd said, but she was wearing dark eyeliner like a Goth—she hadn't removed it yet, the way she did every day before getting home—and Slade shook his head.

So what if he disapproves? She feels old inside, and she's glad enough to be that way. It was exhausting being a child, all that pressure to "have fun," and she hadn't really known how to do that, ever. Friends like Mackenzie would come over, and they'd stare at each other: What do we do now? Junie never seemed to have that problem. She has the gift of fun, or maybe it's joy, which is why everyone loves her.

"Listen," she says to Ruby. Sometimes the rabbits make soft sounds to one another, not a purr or a moan, exactly, just what Dakota thinks of as rabbit talk. Before these particular rabbits, she'd only ever heard a rabbit scream, like when Jellybean caught a baby one once, gripping it at the back of its head. "They sound like pigeons," and then she says, "Len's not my dad."

Ruby stares. Dakota knows her aunt is shocked, but she also knows Ruby will be straight with her. Ruby is smart, smarter than anyone Dakota knows. She'll be honest, and maybe she'll tell Dakota what to do with what she suspects.

"Who owns these rabbits here?" Ruby asks. Her hands rest on the edge of the mesh roof to the rabbit den.

"Berryman. He's not my dad, either." Dakota means to be funny, though in fact sometimes she pretends that Berryman *is* her dad and that raising rabbits is something they do together.

"You talked to your mom about this?"

Dakota snorts. "I'm talking to you."

"Okay." Ruby is quiet again. "It's a complicated situation, hon." She steps closer and Dakota sees that her aunt, suddenly sharp-eyed the way she can be, is sizing her up. "You're old enough. But you should be talking to your mom about this, you know."

"I can't talk to her about anything," Dakota says, though she remembers a time not so long ago when she could. "Not right now."

And Ruby, who knows what it means to be misunderstood, to search for clues to one's true self and still come up wanting, shakes her head and says, "Len's not your, um, birth dad. He's *like* a dad to you, though. He loves you, Dakota."

The girl stares at the dark rabbit shadows. She knows Len loves her, even if he doesn't understand her. She feels sorry for him in a way she does not feel sorry for her mother. "I knew it," she says, and her voice is set.

"We have to find the cat, Dakota."

"Jelly would eat rabbits like these," Dakota says. "Chomp. These rabbits are just...they don't have a clue."

"Lucky them."

"Yeah. I guess." Dakota shivers in the big sweatshirt.

"I'm going to get you some supper," Ruby says. She puts an arm around her niece. "Listen, I met your birth dad. He was cool, but he was slick. Your mom did right by you, marrying Len." She holds Dakota close and Dakota breathes in her smell, a smell like lemons, and beneath that, something warm and oaky that makes Dakota think of the sandalwood incense she burns sometimes, when no one else is home.

"We'll find Jelly later," Ruby says. "She's okay. Hon, look at me. She's probably already home."

Dakota cries as they walk back through the woods to the car. The trees sigh. It's awkward, walking side by side with Ruby's arm around her shoulders, but Dakota doesn't want her to let go.

"The rabbit guy. Mr. Berryman. You don't think he'd put those rabbits in a stew, do you?" Suddenly Dakota is afraid, though this thought has never troubled her before.

"He may be weird, but he's harmless," Ruby says. She went to high school with Berryman's oldest brother, who was a jock, but a nice one. The whole family was nice. She's heard that the Berryman Dakota knows has been whacked for years now, fucked by the war. But perhaps he was cracked—*damaged*—even when she knew his brother back in school, a little boy with buck teeth and some sort of dark seed in there, not yet taken root. "He'll take care of those rabbits," she says.

Though really, who the fuck knows?

&

They have supper at the Dew Drop, which has a decent jukebox and booths lined in waxy red leather. It's not the real Dew Drop, which burned down when Ruby was in college. The real place is gone, she tells Dakota, but the burgers are still good here. Fat and runny. Ruby finds them a two-top and Dakota sprawls in her seat. *God, you're beautiful*, Ruby thinks, watching her niece. Usually she suspects that in a woman—in Ruby's experience, beautiful women have never wanted anything she, Ruby, has to offer—but Dakota is the exception.

Ruby sips a coffee and touches her tooth.

"Does it hurt?" Dakota asks when the plates arrive.

"Not as much as you would think. Other things hurt more," Ruby says. "But it hurts to eat." She pokes at her burger. "The guy who fixed it—Tim Baxter? He was an old flame."

Dakota's eyes widen. "Dr. Baxter? That must have been awkward!"

Ruby laughs in spite of herself. "You can say that again. I broke up with him when we were both in college. I think I was kind of mean about it, actually."

"Aunt Ruby!"

"It was a long time ago. I'm sure he hasn't thought about it for years. It was probably more awkward for his wife today."

"Carrie? She's cool," Dakota says. "She's an artist. She and Mom hang out, or they used to." She pauses, sucking the ketchup off a fry. "Poor Mom," she says. "Guess someone else got sick of her."

Across the room, a red-faced man, glasses askew, pounds the bar in time to the music; someone has cued Guns N' Roses on the juke. Ruby draws in her breath. "That Carrie person? Did it ever occur to you maybe she blew your mom off, and that says more about her than it does about your mom?" Ruby pauses. "I met that woman today," she finally says. "She seemed like a right bitch to me."

"Whoa." Dakota puts her hands up, palms out. "Whatever. I just like her because she's an artist."

"I'm sorry I swore, hon. No, don't laugh, I shouldn't do that in front of you! But Carrie's a phony. Don't let people like that take you in."

The waitress—a girl with a good figure, but when she smiles, the gums of a crone, enflamed and receding—comes to check on them and eyes Ruby's untouched burger. "That okay for you?" Her nametag says OCTAVIA.

Ruby smiles and assures Octavia that her food is fine.

The girl pats at her hair, then touches her face; Ruby doesn't know her. It used to be she'd know anyone she came across in this town. But Octavia is nice, chattering as she tops off Ruby's coffee. "I just made a fresh pot," she says.

The locals—the people she grew up with—aren't always this friendly anymore. Ruby suspects they are disappointed in what she's become; for years they were so proud of her. But Ladyford is a clubby town. You can be in, but then you can be out. Once Ruby called her mother at her room in the nursing home while Pearl had been visiting. At this stage of the Parkinson's, Barbara had started to be uncomfortable with talking on the phone; almost immediately she'd passed it over to Pearl, whose first blunt words caught at Ruby like the paired, stout thorns of a black locust tree.

"Why aren't you here?" Her dislike seeming obvious, even long-distance. Ruby listened to the woman yammer about her own daughter, a woman named Virginia, who Ruby barely remembers, and some grandchildren who were interesting only to Pearl. She'd gotten Val's kids chocolate at Easter, Pearl said. Bunnies, she added pointedly, as if this were important. Ruby wondered if the woman might like her better if she had kids.

They don't know her, not anymore. They have decided to think poorly of her, and as a consequence only latch onto things—the foibles, the mistakes—that fit that ugliest picture of her. It doesn't matter what she does; she senses their judgment. Sometimes Ruby wonders how it will be when there is no longer an older generation to be accountable to. It will be like the end of the Titans, she thinks. Quiet, maybe.

"Carrie makes sculptures," Dakota says, watching as the waitress leaves their table, takes a broom from behind the bar, and starts sweeping. Dust and straw rise from the floor in tiny clouds. "And cool jewelry. She's not like anyone around here." Ruby doesn't say anything, just laces her fingers around the coffee cup, which is thick and white. "People who are different seem to leave here," Dakota says. "Eventually. You left. You went out into the world and made a new life for yourself."

"Yeah, and what do you think about that?"

"You know what I think about that, Aunt Ruby! You're so cool. My dad left too. Dad—was he an artist?"

"You think Carrie's going to leave?"

"Oh, I don't know. She's got Dr. Baxter."

"Bryan had your mom but he still left."

"Bryan? That's dad's name? Bryan...what?"

"Len's the one who raised you. That makes him your dad in my book." Ruby is anxious, starting to feel as though she might have made a mistake, telling Dakota what she has. Now nothing will be the same in the way the girl sees the world or her place in it. School will be different. The mint-green house will. Ruby wonders whether Len will feel dismissed, and him being the one who stuck by.

"Me and Dad—Len—I love him, Aunt Ruby. But I have my real dad in my blood and I want to know what that means. Really, was he an artist?"

"I don't really want to go there. I've told you enough." But Ruby feels bad—*guilty*—about sounding snappy, so she adds, "He was a musician, okay? And God, so handsome, I'll give him that. That's why you're pretty, you know. Your mom and Bryan couldn't help but create an angel."

Dakota keeps her face still, but she's blushing. She must know she's pretty; she must get some attention from boys. Dakota told Ruby once that she didn't have so many girlfriends, that she preferred the company of guys. "They're less complicated," she said. "With them, I know where I stand. I'm one of them." Ruby wasn't sure about that last part, but she understood what Dakota was getting at.

"Your mom has always wanted you to be happy," Ruby says. When she won't spill the beans regarding Bryan's last name, her niece pouts.

"You don't understand how I feel," Dakota says.

"I think I do, actually," Ruby says. But Bryan—who knew where he was now? It is Val who has stuck by her daughter always. Val and Len. And how unkind might Bryan be to Dakota, his own child, after all this time?

"Was my dad sort of…an outsider?" Dakota asks.

Ruby stares into her coffee. Was he? He was popular, glib. He told people what they wanted to hear and then did what he wanted. "No," she decides, but when she sees Dakota's face she adds, "You're like me, baby. You're different. That's okay."

"Sometimes different isn't good," Dakota says. "Sometimes it means someone is fucked up."

"Do you think you're fucked up?" Ruby catches Dakota's eye and holds it. "Your mom told me you had some trouble at the mall." She keeps her voice gentle.

"If she knew half the things kids do," Dakota says. "There are these, like…rituals."

"Rituals?"

"I don't know; you're supposed to act a certain way. It's stupid." Dakota takes another fry, chews it slowly. "The other girls on poms," she says, and sighs. "They giggle, they shriek. They see it on TV and think that's how we're supposed to act. Everyone's so hyper. I don't do that and so I'm…weird. People think I'm being an asshole. You know? And then some kids are seriously messed up, for real. I'm different, so…they think I'm like Tavie?"

"Who's Tavie?"

"Our waitress."

"Right. Really?" Ruby had wanted that girl, who'd shown her kindness, to be undamaged. To be something like happy. "Why? Why do you say that?"

"Aunt Ruby, she's a *meth* head! Everyone knows that! So I lift some eyeliner; at least I'm not tweaking."

Damn. Ruby thinks about Sooner, what Tim said about him. Tim and his wife, a baby on the way. She thinks about the stuffed bear.

"Honey, don't shoplift. You're better than that." Ruby sighs. "What about your art?" The girl used to draw when she was little, and Ruby remembers how it would calm Dakota down when she was upset ("Go draw," Val used to tell her elder daughter when there were tears, or the threat of tears).

"I've been doing graffiti," Dakota says.

"*Really?*" Ruby raises her eyebrows. Hadn't she read somewhere, how meth labs were sometimes covered with scads of graffiti?

"Don't look at me like that. It's art. You'll see. I'm no scrawler. And—" She lowers her voice so that Ruby must lean forward to hear. "I'm like a renegade." Dakota laughs. "No, really, I have to scope places out, paint on the sly. No one's caught me yet, but everyone's wondering. I hear them talk about my stuff at school." She laughs again, but this time it's self-conscious, a bark. "The other girls...in art class? You should see what they draw. Flowers. Baby animals. So *cute*." She scoffs. "Man, I got them confused. The fuckers. I do what I like. Can I have your fries?"

Honestly, this whole day could not be more strange. Someone has put Guns N' Roses on repeat play; Axl Rose is singing about a court jester. Ruby pushes her untouched plate at Dakota. Her niece tears off a piece of hamburger bun and wipes her own plate clean of ketchup. "I love this song," she says.

"Will you show me something you've done?"

"Okay," Dakota says. And they are both pleased, Dakota eating and Ruby quiet, smart enough to recognize that it is these times that everyone wants, the being together, and the deep quiet, and both of them happy in it. At one point, Ruby nods to the pin on the sweatshirt Dakota still wears like a loose damp skin. "That pin is from Grandma."

Dakota licks her fingers clean of ketchup, and carefully undoes the clasp. "You should wear it," she says, handing it across the table. "Always."

Ruby attaches the cluster of pearls to the collar of her thin T-shirt and Dakota nods. Just like that, the meal is ended. Ruby pays Tavie, and out of solidarity, or pity, or both, leaves a big tip. The girl smiles at her from behind her hand, like a child.

It's nearing nine p.m. as they get up to leave the pretend Dew Drop, and Ruby's phone rings—Val's ringtone, a beep like an alarm. Ruby squeezes the button for mute. When they walk outside, the air is wet and fills her lungs. There is a smell to this place: the trees, the mill. To her surprise, it reassures her, even as it makes her aware of time, of the terrifying breakneck passage of it. She used to be Dakota's age, here in this place. She'll be her mother's age in no time, though she cannot imagine it, or where she might be when that time comes.

Dakota takes her hånd. "This way," the girl says. They walk south to where the storefronts end, near Tim's office. The street doesn't have a curb here, and several warehouses back up, one against another. Long ago, someone planted a line of maples along the road; sodden leaves and squashed maple keys litter the ground. When the copper mining was on, the buildings were kept for storage, but they are in disrepair now, corrugated metal walls pocked with rust, their few windows broken.

They round a corner, hand in hand, and in the yellow fan of arc light a mural glows. "See?"

"My God," Ruby breathes. She turns to her niece. "You did this?"

"Yeah." Dakota nods once, then stares down at the ground. "Like it?" Dakota's head is tucked; Ruby can barely hear her.

"My God," Ruby says again. The mural is human faces, ocher and black and yellow, painted high up so the light can touch it. There is a man in a trucker's cap, an old lady with a cloud of wispy hair. The woman's face is lined; her painted eyes are fearful.

"Is that—"

"Gram," Dakota says. "It doesn't look like her face, I know. But she told me once, she told me, 'I am in the woods.'" Dakota lifts her chin. "She was already sick then, with the…you know. That's what I tried to paint."

"You nailed it, hon."

The old woman has a neck with wattles. Glasses are suspended on a beaded chain around her neck, their lenses silver blanks. Her face has been stripped down to its essence. "I stole a ladder to paint that," Dakota says. "And there was this cracked rung. I almost broke my fucking neck!"

"It's beautiful," Ruby says. She takes her niece into her arms and sees that the girl's part is crooked.

"I walk around with my gear in a backpack," Dakota says. "That's what the boys do. I take my bike in case I need to make a quick getaway!" She laughs into Ruby's neck, but it's almost a sob. She says something that might be "I work alone."

Ruby holds her niece tight, looking over Dakota's head at the mural. The girl has painted wings on Barbara, Ruby sees, extending black from either shoulder. Hidden in those wings are secrets only Dakota can see. "It's okay," Ruby says. She wishes Dakota hadn't had to find out so soon how people get sick, or how they leave, or both. "Let's go home."

"Home!" Dakota snorts, and Ruby wonders, suddenly, how long it will be before the girl sees through her guise of wise, cool aunt. Dakota is already an adult in some ways, while she, Ruby, feels like a child. She *is* a child, going through the motions of being a grown-up.

"Keep painting," she says, thinking about the row of chairs in her condo. Ruby holds Dakota at arm's length, tries to meet her eye. "It's good you have that. It's like my music."

"You still do that?"

"I was going to have a concert."

"That's…cool. I didn't know you still… You should teach it or whatever," she says, but with a sliding away of the eyes. Dakota is already bored or impatient or both.

"Seriously, keep painting," Ruby says, holding on to the girl, not letting her go. She wants to add, but doesn't, that maybe this will save her.

PEARL

Something to Look Forward To

February 11, 2012

Dear Louise,

It's me, Pearl, and Bob and I are heading down to Florida to see Ginny and Don and the kids. Not much new here, but the snow is something awful and I'd be lying if I told you I wasn't looking forward to a little break. I hope you had a good holiday. We had the kids up at Christmas and Ginny is doing well enough although she says three kids is it. However many they have it's nice for me and Bob when we visit. That little Nathan is a hellcat but he loves his grandpa so we manage. You know I don't like Don but he's who my daughter chose and so I guess I can manage that too.

You'll be sad to hear that Barb is doing poorly. She has a tremor now and she has canceled on Circle every month since the fall. I'll tell you, we miss her kolach, but you know she hasn't been the same since Moon died. I think the house is too much for her and I have been concerned as you can imagine. I told her daughter (Valentine) as much but you know, that girl, she's proud. The older one used to be easier to talk to but honestly, when she's in town now I never know what to say to her, either. I try to reach out. I do it for Barb.

In any case the old guard at church is disappearing, what with you moved away and now this thing with Barb. I think the thing is to have something to look forward to, and I'm looking forward to seeing the grandkids. The next time I write I'll be drinking orange juice and getting a tan ha ha.

Give Norbert a hug and we will try to stop in Murfreesboro
on our way back north in April.

Yours,

Pearl

[Letter found in Louise Schadrie's effects after her death, in a
file marked "Friends."]

VAL

Gallery of Friends

Junie is in bed and long asleep, and Len has come home and gone to bed himself. He gets so tired, Len, his bowed red legs like tree trunks, aching by the end of the day. Someday he will be too old for the work he does. Some days he says so.

"Then we will figure out something else," Val tells him. "By the time that day comes, we'll have been through worse," she sometimes adds. *Now is probably worse*, she thinks but does not say.

"We always get through," is what Len says then.

Her husband and her younger daughter are sleeping, and Val should have enjoyed this quiet space of time, a rare opportunity to work on one of her own projects, the knitting she picks up and abandons again and again throughout the year (she's still working on a scarf for Dakota, hot pink, a color the girl will probably no longer wear), or her photo albums. She calls the albums her "Freundschaftsgalerie," or "friendship gallery," the way Moon taught her. (His last name was Herzog, a name Barbara stubbornly would not return to, even after it became apparent that the girls' father was not coming back.)

Val took many of the pictures herself. She's always been that way, remembering to bring a camera to family events even when she was a girl. She used to have a Kodak Ektralite; it had belonged to Ruby first. After that came a curvy Polaroid, which was a birthday gift; there might have been another camera after that, but now she uses her phone. There are photos from the trips she and Ruby used to take when Ruby first learned to drive. There are photos of the birthday suppers they had when she was a teen: both she and Ruby with bobs and bangs;

Moon looming plaid in the background; and Barbara! Barbara, her face still lively.

Val's girls like exclaiming over the clothes, the automobiles. Those were good times, Val tells them, even as she remembers the fights she and Ruby used to have, over silly things usually, prompted by jealousy; or the fact that Moon said not a word that one Christmas supper, for reasons of his own; or perhaps Barbara had been touchy about the way a meal turned out. There used to be pictures of Bryan, but Val took them out long ago. She still takes pictures obsessively, of the girls mostly, as if by logging enough film she cannot lose anyone. She can fix them in place, and in so doing understand them all.

The albums are shelved in the living room, in chronological order. Used to be it comforted her to page through them, much as counting gold reassures the rich man in the fables Junie adores. In the photos they are smiling. But now her feelings are mixed about the albums, about the way they lay out so baldly how time has passed and the changes that have occurred. Wait long enough and eventually the faces in the pictures aren't around anymore. Her own father, whom she did not know. Moon. Her mother. Dakota still smiled broadly, gap-toothed, when she was Junie's age.

Herself. Val is as old, or almost, as her mother was in many of the pictures, and this frightens her, though she doesn't understand why.

If Ruby keeps photo albums, she has never said so.

Where *are* Ruby and Dakota? Val moves to the kitchen, light and tough; she likes the feel of her body because it reminds her that she can handle anything. She stops and listens for Ruby's car and also for Jellybean, in case the cat might be lurking just outside, tail lifted insouciantly like a flag. And then they might all be reunited.

It's not so clean in here after all. Sugar dusts the counter, and the bread has been opened. Val sweeps the sugar into her hand and then into the garbage pail. She packs up the bread, tying the bag securely, though first she takes a slice and folds it over and over, into a square that will fit her mouth. The bread is soft and white, a flat lid mashed against the back of her teeth. She should eat more often. She should eat more, period. Chewing, Val paces between the kitchen and the living room, and her eyes fall on the pottery lamb next to the checkerboard. This lamb, it is just for her; she saw it at a yard sale, and it pleased her, its sparkly platter eyes so…cheerful. It has been so long since she bought anything for herself! It was only two dollars and looked as though it needed a home. At the sale it was piled onto a table of knickknacks, some of them already chipped because they were heaped together this way and that, and she had felt protective of the lamb. She carefully extracted it from under the ceramic haunch of a thick-legged horse. She had wanted to rescue it. She did.

For years, Dakota had been her little lamb.

Val thinks about eating another piece of bread. She could— she should—call the hospital, check up on her mother. She could call Ruby again, to see if they've found the cat. But then there is a pop of gravel on the drive. Muffled door slams, and the sound of steps on the porch; with a rush of cold air, Ruby and Dakota are both coming inside, strangely subdued. Val, standing in the kitchen doorway, squeezing the bag of bread, knows something is different though she doesn't understand what.

"Hi, Val," Ruby says. She makes it sound like an apology. "We didn't find Jelly." So perhaps that's it. No cat, and Junie will cry her eyes raw tomorrow.

Val sets down the bread. "Did you eat?" she asks. Dakota nods, distant, and drifts toward her room without saying good night.

"Thank your aunt!" Val says. And Dakota does, to everyone's relief, even kissing Ruby without prompting before retreating again.

"Sit down, Ru." Val gestures at the littered couch, then sits down herself, tucking one leg neatly. "I'm glad you're home." And in fact she is. "She was…okay?"

"Who—Mom?" Ruby sits down, wiping her palms on her corduroys.

"Dakota. Thank you for taking her, Ruby. Seriously."

"*Dakota*! Right. Sure thing. You know I love her, Val." Ruby stands up, then sits again. "You know, we, uh—we had a talk."

"A talk?" Val doesn't know what her sister is saying half the time. "About?"

"There's a new waitress at the Dew Drop," Ruby says. She slips off her shoes and rubs at her feet, which are damp from the grass by the rabbit pen.

"Oh! Tavie?"

"We didn't talk about Tavie. Well, we did. Tavie was our waitress. I think she thought I was cool."

"We're *not* cool, sister."

"Some people think I'm cool," Ruby says.

Our mother is dying, Val thinks. *For god's sake.* "Why are we even talking about this?" she says. "Oh, for heaven's sake, my daughters think you're cool. Tavie does, apparently. And Len. He always has good things to say about you."

"Len never says anything about anyone," Ruby says, and for a moment they are sisters, laughing together. "Where is he, anyway?"

"Asleep. It's late."

"Late," Ruby says.

They are silent then, and Val plucks a pine cone from the bowl on the coffee table. It was a centerpiece once, the gray pottery bowl filled with cones. Now it is lost in the rest of the clutter, perched atop a stack of Junie's library books. Val holds the cone up. "See this? I shall make it disappear." She waves her hand and it does. "Dark magic," she intones, and Ruby laughs, astonished.

"How did you do that?"

"Book of Junie's." Val nods at the teetering stack. "God, pretty much everything I know I learn from Junie."

"She's precocious," Ruby says.

"She'll do okay." Val gestures out the bay window, which

is black as the sea. "I hope so, anyway. She's happy. She gets along with people." Val crosses her arms over her chest. "She got invited to this birthday party? She was so excited, Ruby. She wants to go, and you know what? She'll have fun. Dakota's never liked that kind of thing, even when she was a little girl. She'd call me; she always wanted to come home early."

"Girl after my own heart."

"Ruby, I'm serious! She doesn't like the things most kids do. Pearl used to say she was a cold baby."

"Pearl's an idiot."

"I'm always apologizing for Dakota, Ruby. People are judgmental."

"I know," Ruby says.

"I want her to be happy. Junie's still happy. When I die, Junie will have other people, but Dakota—"

"They'll both be all right."

"I worry that Dakota will end up alone. She's a hard person to like sometimes." Val hugs herself. "Was she okay? You know, tonight?"

"She's an amazing artist. *I* like her, Val."

Val hugs herself harder. "I know you do," she says. "I'm glad. She likes being with you too. And tonight Junie and I had—we had such a good time. I need to do stuff like that more. With both girls." Val sighs, rubbing her eyes.

"Val, I—"

"Never mind." Val shakes her head, as if to clear it. "We still have some good times."

"I'm sure," Ruby murmurs.

"You know the manager at NorthPine? I think his name is Ron something." NorthPine is a fish fry place; when Mom is feeling good, Val takes her there on Fridays. Len comes too, when he can. Dakota's usually busy, but there was one time, when all five of them were together. It wasn't even so long ago, and after supper the manager, who always wears a bow tie, brought them a fat wedge of chocolate cake to share. "It's got to be someone's birthday, right?" he'd said, winking at Barbara, and Dakota had laughed and helped Junie with the crossword puzzle on their place mats. Ron's warmth had softened them, made them kinder to each other that night.

"That was nice," Val says, telling Ruby about the evening. "We ran into all these people we know from work, even. The Robinstadts. Mark from the IGA. How's *your* job?" she asks.

"It's okay."

"You know, I don't really know what you do. People ask me, and I'm like, 'She's really smart, so it must be something hard.' Is it hard?" Val leans forward, frowning.

"They put me in charge of the employee stock-purchase plan."

"Is that good?"

"It is."

"Pearl always asks about your job," Val says. "Then she tells me about her son-in-law's job. You know the one. Don?"

"God knows I can't compete with that!" Ruby says, and they laugh again, together.

"When I see her in the grocery store I try to walk the other way."

Ruby laughs again but then she sighs. The conversation makes her sad.

"Thanks again for taking Dakota out," Val says, breaking the silence. "That was…good for everybody, I think." And it was, it was a break. Val sometimes thinks that if she could catch a few breaks, she'd be a different, better person. "I love my kids so much. But you love a lot, then you get hurt." Val rubs her eyes. "Relationships—you know, everyone is like, 'Ohhhh, life is so unendurable without friendship' or whatever, but sometimes I think, why do we do it? Friendship. Relationships. Pets. Things can end so badly."

"Aw, well," Ruby says. "You don't think that."

"I do. Sometimes. Look at Carrie."

"Carrie."

"Tim's wife. We aren't friends anymore, you know. Not really."

"That's okay," Ruby says.

"I thought she was going to be one of those lifelong friends."

"I met her today and I didn't like her. She's not a very nice person, Val. Don't feel bad."

Val starts to laugh, but then the laugh changes into something else. "Look how things have ended with Mom," she says.

Ruby sighs. "Mom still loves us. Somewhere in there, she loves us."

"How *did* things go with Mom today?"

"Oh, well. You know." Ruby shifts on the couch. "Anyway, how about Moon? He loved you till the end."

"He loved us both. Do you remember how he used to call you Ladybird? He had names for everything. Everyone. I miss him so much, Ruby." Val scratches at the rash on her jaw. "I never got to ask him—"

"What?"

"I don't know. I guess it's endings I'm afraid of." Val searches Ruby's face. "What if we have to get used to having just one cat? What if Jelly is gone?"

"Change isn't always bad like that," Ruby says. "We just have to keep moving forward, you know?"

"I don't know. I'm afraid of losing Dakota."

"Dakota's going to be okay. You know what Mom would say? She'd say you have to be more positive."

"Maybe," Val says, but she almost smiles; yes, that was probably something their mom would say. It's hard to remember anymore. The Parkinson's, and Val's own recent experience as a mother, tell her that her cherished view of Barbara, held all through childhood and into her adult years, might be…not a falsehood, exactly, but not the whole story, if her own bewildered heart is any indication. How many times has she assured Junie, or even Dakota (at least in the old days, she could reassure Dakota then) that all was right with the world, regardless of how she, Val, actually felt? She looks back now and feels for the young Barbara, who despite her strength, or maybe because of it, might have suffered the fearsome loneliness that Val endures, day after day. "But I think I'm a realist. I want to hold on to what I have." She looks over to the Freundschaftsgalerie. Ruby looks too.

"Things change," Ruby says.

"Do you think Mom thinks—do you think she thought the world is a hard place?" Val says.

"I expect she did," Ruby says. "But she rose above it for as long as she could. Even now, you can't say she lets things get her down."

Val laughs. "She doesn't know what's going on enough to feel down."

"Well," Ruby says. "There you go."

"Did anything weird happen? When you saw Mom today?"

Ruby looks away. "I think it must be hard to be a parent," she finally says. "You are more like Mom than you know, sister."

"God, I hope so." Val smiles suddenly, reaching into her sleeve and producing the pine cone. "Hey, look," she says. Ruby claps, they both laugh, and for a moment, their eyes meet.

"Did you get my phone message?" Val asks.

"I saw you called," Ruby says.

"Okay. Good." Val rubs her eyes again and curls into the couch. "You know, I was sad about Carrie for a while, but I'm not so much anymore."

"Good," Ruby says.

"I wanted her to be like… I missed Mom."

"No one can replace Mom," Ruby says.

Val nods soberly. "Especially not Carrie." Her feet are cold and she tucks them between the sofa cushions. "Tell me again. That I'm like Mom. The real Mom, you know?"

RUBY

Cat

When Ruby was still a girl and struggling with her weight, they could never buy regular-size clothing for her; they had to travel out of town to find things that fit. This was before the internet, but Barbara made calls; mother and daughter made trips to Rice Lake, and sometimes it was a special time, just the two of them, but sometimes, Ruby, ashamed of her thighs and unhappy at how she looked in the new, broad-cut clothing, was truculent. Wouldn't eat her lunch, though she ordered a full meal, and eating out was a treat, something to be budgeted for and looked forward to. Barbara would somehow smile at the motherly waitresses, who looked disapproving, and tell Ruby that someday, someday, she'd be something special.

"I think it must be hard to be a parent," is what she said to Val.

How does she know this?

"You are more like Mom than you know, sister."

Now the other cat, Audrey, minces through the room, and Ruby stands heavily to pick her up. Her knees always ache in this weather. She slips her shoes back on, wiggling her toes against the gel insoles.

"I missed you," she tells the cat, a queenly tabby that dislikes most people but, improbably, loves Ruby. Val told her so. Ruby holds the cat against her chest and Audrey is solicitous, raising a narrow elegant paw to tap at Ruby's face, her neck. The cat smells of itself—an earthy corn smell. It purrs. Most creatures make a sound when they feel something, Ruby thinks; one longs to unburden oneself—really unburden oneself and be consoled. "Snowball, Our Good Cat," Ruby whispers into Audrey's gleaming silver fur. My *God.* She thinks about her job; there is the promotion, which should make her happy. She thinks about her concert. No one will care if she never reschedules, though her friends are kind and they will come if she invites them.

"You really think Dakota's going to be okay?" Val asks.

"I do." Ruby remembers what it was like to drive with Val, the way the road stretched out before them. She probably knew her sister best then.

"What did you guys talk about? You never said."

"You are the Gray Ghost," Ruby tells Audrey. Then she meets her sister's eye. "I think you need to talk to Dakota about Bryan," she says.

"Why?" Val has inched down the sofa and is almost lying down, her arms crossed over her chest.

"Because I think the kid knows more than she's letting on."

"Oh, Ruby." Val sits up. "What did you tell her?"

"Nothing she didn't already suspect," Ruby says. She hugs Audrey, guilt making her tone sharp. Or maybe it's that her tooth hurts again. There is the thought, sneaking, that Tim did a poor job on purpose, but she dismisses it. "She's got to know, Val. She won't trust you if she finds out on her own and you deny it."

"I'm not denying anything. Oh, God. Ruby, how dare you?" Val slips off the sofa and, not looking at Ruby, kneels and starts putting checker pieces back into a box.

"It slipped out," Ruby says quietly.

"I have to clean up," Val says. She might not have heard Ruby; it's hard to tell. She pushes the box of checkers under the couch, then uses her arm to sweep toys and stuffed animals off the recliner. She stops, staring at the pile on the floor. "What did you tell her?" she says.

"I told her Len loves her like a father. I told her Bryan's name. His first name! I told her she should talk to you." Ruby scrambles down awkwardly; still holding Audrey, she picks up a checker piece her sister missed, a dark plastic disc as shiny as blood. It's sticky in her hand. She holds it out to Val.

"Oh, God. *God.* You come in, you practically drop out of the sky, and you have all these ideas about..." Val pushes Ruby's hand away, crying now.

"You owe it to her, Val."

"So now you know how to raise a child? Funny, seeing as how you don't have any yourself."

Ruby stares at the checker piece in her hand, inexplicably gripped by a desire to laugh. "I don't know why I'm smiling," she says, setting the cat down gently.

"Neither do I."

"Mama?" It's Junie, standing at the door to the living room. Her face hovers, stricken, above a nightgown nubbled and pilled, worn almost to transparency.

"Go back to bed, sweetheart," Val says.

"Is everything okay?"

Val stands and leans toward the child, as if into a gale. "It's fine, sweet girl. Go to bed and I'll check on you in a minute. Aunt Ruby and I are talking."

"Are you fighting?"

"We're talking. Bed now."

The child turns reluctantly, then pauses. "Did you find Jelly?"

"No, honey," Ruby says.

"I'll be in to check on you in a minute," Val says. "Happy?" she says to Ruby when Junie disappears into the hallway. "Let's just step outside, okay?" She strides to the door and holds it open. Outside, black clouds obscure the moon. Ruby follows her sister through the door, arms crossed, lips pressed over her tooth. The pain is granular. It's obscene. She tries to remember something funny, or ironic; she tries to remember the way her sister used to bake, as a child, standing on a stool with her arms lit by flour. Her travel buddy, her pal.

"Now *Junie's* upset," Val says, turning to her. "*Great.* You show up and what happens? Now my girls are as miserable as Mom."

"What are you *talking* about? If they're unhappy, if *you're* unhappy, it's your own fault."

"Right! Right! Like we have a choice about anything here."
Val lowers her head and swipes at her cheeks, the angry tears
there. "Leave Mom to me—she's turning into a monster, okay?"
Val turns away, takes a breath. "No. I didn't mean that. She can't
help it, but I'm all alone here, Ruby. You go visit her today and
what? You won't even talk about it?"

"I didn't go," Ruby says, suddenly tired of lying. "I thought
we could go…together."

"You didn't *go*?"

Ruby shakes her head. Looking back at the long day just
past, what seemed to make sense from moment to moment
now doesn't seem so clear. Ruby sees herself from Val's eyes,
but she knows she's not a bad person. Barbara knew that; Barbara told her so. "I was afraid," Ruby says quietly.

"I don't care," Val says. "Who isn't? All you have to worry
about is *you*, Ruby. I'm trying to manage this and still be a good
mother. I want to keep things okay for the girls."

"The girls? The girls! Quit using the girls as an excuse, okay?
They are not the only daughters in this—this *disaster*. I know it's
hard, but I have a life too!"

"Right! Your 'life'!"

"I do the best I can! I'll go tomorrow!"

"You were supposed to go today! Hell, you were supposed
to be there yesterday! And the day before! Where have you been
when Len and I do all the work?"

"You hate Len!"

"You don't know anything about it! Len's here! He helps
me!"

"And you pay him back by being a bitch."

"I know what you think about me, I'm not stupid. But I
helped Moon die and now I'm helping Mom die. I'm trying to
make some kind of life around—around *death*! A life for me
and a life for my girls. And Len—yes, him too! He deserves
better than what I can give him right now. Did it ever occur
to you that when I get even a little bit of breathing room I *like*
that life?"

"I know you do," Ruby says. "I wish I liked mine!" And then it is silent. Even years later Ruby will not forget that, how the trees around them seemed to crouch, listening. Ruby will remember the long-sleeved T-shirt her sister wore, a thin gauzy tie-dye that clung to Val's narrow frame like a tattoo.

They've both forgotten the cold.

Ruby stares at her sister, frightened. She crouches, reaching out for the comfort of the cat, which makes no sense; the tabby is inside, and so of course her hand flaps empty air. "Mom's fine," she says stiffly. She stands and backs away from the door; when Ruby thinks of this house, she always thinks of her haste to leave it.

"I didn't call Mom today. I thought you were there." Val is tiny against the closed front door, which is heavy, its pebbled glass window too thick to let in the light. Her voice is tiny, too, and her face, in the pallid porch light, isn't angry. Just sad. One time, years ago, she'd made Ruby an entire set of paper dolls, cut from shirt cardboard. She'd cut clothes for the dolls out of stiff bright paper, and though Ruby had been too old for such things, she'd played with them all the same.

"Mom isn't a monster." Ruby fumbles in her pants for the car keys. There. Smashed tight in the back pocket. Ruby's fingertips touch metal.

"I said I didn't mean that."

Almost over. Ruby wants nothing more than to bolt. She should be ashamed, but isn't, not yet.

Feet sliding in the loose gravel of the driveway, Ruby remembers that Dakota still has her sweatshirt. But there is her purse, in the front seat where she left it. Thank God. She opens the car door, shivering.

"Where are you going?" Val says.

"I've got to meet up with Tim and Carrie." She doesn't know why she says this, it doesn't even make sense. "No, I mean Sooner. Remember him? I told Tim I'd look him up."

"The meth dealer? No, Ruby. He's trouble. He hangs out with that whack job, Berryman, the freak with the rabbits."

"We used to be friends," Ruby says, not sure if she means Sooner, or Val. She slides into the driver's seat—almost free— and adds, "Don't wait up for me. I'll be late." Hands shaking from the cold now. Her tooth aches. Her knees. If she lost weight her knees wouldn't hurt so much.

"Wait. Ruby!"

Ruby starts the car. She remembers to pull the car door shut.

Val looks so small in the doorway to her home, no bigger than Dakota. "Ruby! Don't leave! It's okay!"

Ruby can hear her, even through the closed windows of the car, but she pretends not to hear; she's in the car, it's started, she's backing down the drive, heat blasting. She does not mean to look in the rearview mirror but when she does, she sees Val, waving at her. It's not an angry wave, or a dismissive one. It is a gentle wave, and there is confusion in her sister's gesture, maybe pity, and this frightens Ruby more than anger ever could. Only when she's safely away, back in the little downtown area and cruising past the shuttered shops does Ruby think, *What just happened? Now what?*

Maybe if she swung by the hospital. She'd meant for Val to join her—she'd hoped they might go together. But the hospital and what Ruby might find there alone—what can be worse than what has just...*hell.*

"Things can't get any worse," Barbara sometimes used to say, laughing.

⁓

At Marathon County Memorial, the lot is almost empty. It is a small rural facility, clean and fairly new, equipped to handle the basics. Eleven p.m. Lamps burning in some windows, the blue halo of television light in others. In hospitals, day and night play by different rules. Where is Mom in all this? Watching a television program, a rerun, the way she used to do? She rarely followed the news, not like Moon did. It depressed her, she said.

Ruby studies the windows and imagines a lone nurse, hair

in pins, wheeling a cart filled with towels down a corridor as gray as salt. Hospitals are always awake, Ruby thinks. How many times did Val call her from this place, sobbing because Moon was slipping further away. Ruby was traveling a lot for work then. She was still buoyant in what she thought was her life. Barbara had told her not to come until it was absolutely necessary, and Ruby had listened. She loved Moon; his soldierly bearing inspired confidence, and her love grew from the fact that he'd stuck by them all. But in the end, Ruby learned that a person could be in only one place, one life, at one time. It had been hard for her to imagine what he was going through. It almost didn't seem real.

"When I'm in Chicago, I can barely imagine life in Wisconsin," Ruby told Drago once. "And when I'm up north, it's like everything in Chicago fades a little."

"What? You forget me?" Drago had teased.

"No. Not like that. But it's like, where I am, that's what's real." She did not add how this sometimes frightened her, how quickly the connections could seem to dissolve.

And Drago, who had moved frequently in his life and had family back in Zagreb, with whom he shared sporadic email exchanges, had shrugged and said, "Well, that is the way of life."

Still, she thinks about Moon's last days sometimes. Death was desperate, and as Moon himself might have said, to be embarked upon alone. Austerity ran deep within him, but how lonely might he have felt, those last days? Ruby cannot feature it. And then he died and everything changed; Ruby and probably even Val had had no idea how he'd been holding things together.

She should go see Mom now. Ruby glances at her phone. Lorna hasn't answered her text.

Outside the car it is cold, then inside the hospital doors, in the lobby, it is warm. The light is yellow and false. What if Mom *is* awake, and she tells Ruby something that she doesn't want to hear? Ruby thinks of Val in her gauzy shirt, frozen in surprise.

No. Mom won't say anything much. Ruby knows this. Standing in the hospital lobby, which is like an atrium, plant-filled and humid, Ruby wishes she could still talk to her mother, *really* talk to her. In another time, Barbara might have helped her sort through what she said tonight; she might remind Ruby why Ruby's life in Chicago was correct, and good. That's what she used to do, when Ruby would come home to the farmhouse from Madison. Moon would be watching the news; Val inevitably had a date with friends. But Ruby and Barbara would sit in the bright kitchen and Ruby would tell Barbara about her life at college. "You have found your way," Barbara would say, and in those five words all Ruby's choices were affirmed.

It's different now. When the Parkinson's started, someone—Pearl, probably—said that Barbara probably wouldn't live much longer. But Barbara is tough, and she has lived on and on, past the point when she can listen or encourage, past the point when she can be happy. Barbara isn't living anymore, not exactly; Ruby doesn't know how to describe what she is. Death is straightforward, well defined. With death, Ruby would know what to do.

She hates coming back here. She can't stop coming back here.

"Can I help you?" There is an information desk, hidden behind the plants. A woman in a white jacket stands up, frowning sleepily.

"I wish you could," Ruby says. "I just wanted…" The plants behind the woman shroud her, leaves like a scapular. "My mother's here."

The woman has a vertical crease between her eyes. "It's way past visiting hours. You can't go in, but I could call up and ask how your mother is doing," she says.

Ruby nods. She tells the woman Barbara's name, then waits, fingering her pin. Uncertain where to look, she stares at the remains of a sandwich on the desk. They are wrapped in greasy paper. There is a smell of meat.

"She's resting comfortably," the woman says then, and Ruby, who had been suddenly certain that Barbara was dead, feels wings clapping in her chest.

"Thank you!" she cries, because the woman is nicer than she first seemed. Because Barbara isn't dead. Because Ruby did the right thing, coming here to the hospital, but she doesn't have to stay—not yet.

"Thank you!" she says again. She almost-runs through the pneumatic doors, then turns to wave, but the white-jacketed woman has already sat back down and turned her face away.

It isn't until Ruby gets back to her car and starts it up that she decides she will go to the farmhouse. She hasn't been since they sold it. It's a destination. And when Ruby returns to the hospital, she'll have something to talk about with Mom.

"The house looked good," Ruby might say. "The new owners have pumpkins on the steps."

In her car is the blanket she took from Mom's room back at Cedar Manor. Ruby lays it, folded, across her lap, leaving her arms free so she can drive. The weight of it is reassuring. Blue and yellow, it smells of cat.

She should get a cat, Ruby thinks. Cats are clean. Shrewd. The future, even—something to love. Ruby would come home to her condo, and the cat would be there, its tail lifted high. She could tell the cat her plans, and it would have to listen.

VAL

Secret Heart

The cat's been eaten, of this Val is suddenly certain. Met by a fisher and torn asunder. She stands at the front window, her fingers just touching the glass that is like black ice. Ruby is gone, to meet up with that meth head. She's lived away so long she doesn't know how things are here.

Oh, Ruby is beloved by children and animals; she will eat too many cookies with her nieces and stay up late, watching Svengoolie. She doesn't talk about the things that bore a child. She talks to them like equals.

But there's more to having kids than that, Val thinks. She tries to imagine Ruby with children of her own, looking at them with the love that is born of patience and crises lived through together. Not an easy love, but real.

Ruby can rush in laughing, make her demands and indiscriminately share, then leave before Val has to tell Junie her cat is dead.

She won't understand how Val will have to deal with Dakota, and the questions about Bryan, when the girls get up and wait at the table for breakfast tomorrow. Dakota's hair, hanging tangled over eyes that smolder now. Ruby never could keep her mouth shut, could she? All through their childhood, blabbing her plans and her pain to anyone who would listen. Fine enough if it were just about her—she could make a fool of herself if she wanted—but when it came to other people's lives. That was the thing.

Because Val keeps her thoughts secret. She'd even written about this once, in a poem called "Secret Heart." If the title made it sound like something a little kid would write, the poem actually conveyed what it was Val wanted to say. It brought her solace, and she hopes there is more than this one poem in her. Because writing could be there for her now that her mother is not. If Val is lucky, writing could be a safe place to say those things no other person should know.

Like the time last month when her mother had called from the phone in her room at the senior center. "You have abandoned me here. I want to kill myself," Barbara had said.

"I know, Mama." Outside the nursing home window, there is a bird feeder, its roof slanted copper. Val tries to remember to tell Barbara about it, to draw her mother's attention to it as Val used to distract her own girls when they were small. "The birds, Mama; look out the window and tell me what you see." It grounded Barbara to look outside and find things just as Val said they would be.

"There are sparrows!" Barbara had cried.

"Sparrows. Yes."

In her own bright kitchen, Val had gotten down on her knees and scrubbed. She kept Barbara on the phone, talking, and her mother, once so perceptive, did not know that Val was weeping. There was a wicked smell of grease in the kitchen that day, lingering and insubstantial; if she scrubbed, Val thought, she could almost get it out.

"You're okay now, Mama," Val said. Fifteen minutes had passed. The floor was almost clean.

"Thank you, daughter."

That was how that one conversation had gone. Or most of it. But there were some things—worse things—that you didn't repeat, not even to yourself.

Moon would understand. He'd been to Vietnam, which he never talked about; the war was something he'd tucked away into a part of his brain that he couldn't, or wouldn't, get at, and that seemed to work for him, although her mother told Val that when he returned stateside he wouldn't go to church, not for years. And Val wonders how it struck him back then, her and Ruby with their kid problems, crying about boys or slights from girlfriends or bad hair. She forgives herself—that's what kids *should* worry about, that's what she wants her own girls to have to deal with, and nothing more—but she can see how trivial it must have seemed to him.

Val presses her face against the dark glass. What happened just now, between her and Ruby? She doesn't understand her sister.

And she is not a very good writer, she knows this. But still.

BARBARA

October

"I hate you. I hate you and I hope you remember that for the rest of your life."

She says these things. She says these things and she doesn't know why.

RUBY

Farm

That last visit had been such a disaster. Two, three months ago. Just one thing after another.

Ruby had tried to hold Junie in her lap after supper one night, but the girl twisted from her arms. "I don't like your hair," she'd said, sullen.

"Sorry." Val laughed. "Kids are so honest." Junie wasn't feeling well, she said. Or maybe she was about to not feel well, or she was tired. Val said that the little girl had been "acting up" since Val started needing to spend more time with Barbara.

Ruby, who wondered why Len couldn't just step in to help— he was the kid's father, wasn't he?—said she didn't care. She liked her hair shorter; it was easy to take care of. But then she'd snapped, "I don't like yours either," to Junie, and the little girl's lip had trembled.

"Jesus, Ruby, she's six, okay?"

Dakota, in a corner with some sort of handheld electronic game, raised her head long enough to roll her eyes. "She's six!" she said, lifting her voice on the last word, mocking.

That was the same weekend Ruby took Dakota shopping. They had made a day of it, driving to a tourist town more than an hour away. Dakota liked the shops there. They smelled like cedar, and in one, the owner had a cello concerto playing that Dakota said made her feel relaxed. The place was full of knick-knacks: ceramic vessels for jam; a wooden wall hanging for keys, shaped like a pine tree. The kind of thing Ruby used to love, to treat herself to, and which in the face of her mother's decline now seems foolish. But she had wanted to buy something. Maybe she thought it would occupy the dangerous blank places that, increasingly, Ruby has filled with chocolate, or pasta, or white bread and salt.

"Look at these earrings!" she had cried, holding up a pair of dangling droplets, red glass wound with copper wire. She ended up buying them for Dakota, and the girl had put them on immediately, pleased, though when they returned home Val had asked, "Where did you get *those*?" Worried, almost angry. Ruby had jumped in to explain that they were a gift, but not before Dakota stormed off to her room. At the time, Ruby thought maybe the problem was that she hadn't bought something for Junie too.

Ruby, driving with her hands ungloved, shivers in the dark of her car, remembering how Moon used to say, when they drove anywhere at night, that they drove the Night Car. She remembers the bear she gave to Tim. Junie's bear. She'll have to buy the kid something; children love presents and it will make Ruby feel better about what she's done. There was a gas station ahead. It used to be family owned, but now it's an anonymous BP, which means it's open, and has coffee, which Ruby needs, and maybe candy. Candy for the kid.

Inside, Ruby is improbably cheered. The woman behind the counter is stolid and red-cheeked, impassive. Probably one of the Brolins, with that mass of dark hair, but it's hard to keep track. This one is younger than Ruby; she might have gone to school with Val. Ruby pours herself a coffee at the kiosk and picks up a bag of M&Ms for Junie, but then she sees a turning rack of cheap stuffed animals and chooses a stuffed cat for her niece instead. She keeps the M&Ms to eat herself, when her tooth feels better. And nothing for Dakota this time, as if to make a point.

"Do you have wiper blades?" Ruby asks the woman at the counter. No harm in asking.

The Brolin woman is reading a magazine but looks up with a mild expression. "None to speak of," she says. "You take a cookie though, honey. Happy Thanksgiving." She gestures at a paper plate next to the register, loaded with cookies in the shape of pumpkins, and frosted orange. They look homemade.

"I could hang out in this BP forever," Ruby says, and the woman laughs then, her cheeks rosy and rounding right up against her small, bright eyes. Holy—no, *homely*—in here, Ruby thinks. God she's tired. Long day. She selects a cookie, its tilted smiling pumpkin face painted in thick frosting. Whoever made it was lonely, maybe lonelier than Ruby herself.

"Better you than me," the woman says.

Back in the car, Ruby tucks the stuffed animal into her purse, along with the candy and the cookie, wrapped in a napkin. The cat is a strange glittery purple but has a sweet face, with huge plastic eyes like buttons. (Years from now she will think of Junie every time she comes across a certain type of toy like this, big-eyed, sparkly. Ruby will always prefer Dakota, this will never change, but Junie will never know, and Ruby will always be proud of that.) Ruby starts the car and takes a mouthful of coffee, focusing on the nutty bitter heat in her mouth. Maybe Jelly's alive, she thinks. Maybe her tooth will be okay. Ruby drives out of town and the dark trees melt by. She realizes she's going too fast; she'll get to the farm too soon. And then she'll have to see what's there.

The old property lies off county Y, in a stand of pines that have grown tall in sandy soil. The farmland itself spreads out from the house like ripples in a glass of water; it never did well but hung in there enough to keep them all going. A city family bought the place and now, Ruby knows, the fields are fallow. She thinks she'll pull up just close enough to see the lights in the windows.

There's the farmhouse, old and tall, and it's dark. The pines rise black around it and Ruby can tell right away from some instinct that no one lives here now; the house isn't derelict but there is an indifference at work, its painted sides a ghastly white, and the barn leans. How can this be? That house has always been vital, it had to last beyond their years there. But wait! There is a car parked in the darkness on the far side, and one muted light moves between windows in the living room. Ruby stops the car and gets out. The air is wet and chill, lapping at her ear (still sensitive from the tooth) and her face. It's a lantern moving in there. Ruby steps forward. She'd forgotten how impenetrable the nights can be here, cloudy nights without moon or stars, and she imagines skunks and fishers creeping just beyond her car, patrolling this lonely place with claws and teeth.

Standing here, Ruby can hear the river. The light in the window is a yellow thumbprint, bobbing.

"Hello?" Ruby calls. She does it to chase the fishers away. Whoever is in the house doesn't belong any more than she does. "Hello?" She's up to the glass of the picture window— *pitcher window*, Moon used to say—and she surprises herself by tapping at the glass. Well, tapping at first, and then pounding so that the glass booms. She stops pounding only to catch her breath, and that's when she hears the sound of the side kitchen door opening. Ruby peeks around the corner of the house. A wedge of dusty light spills into the darkness.

"Who's out there?" A male voice, not angry or scared. "Who are you?"

"Who are *you?*" Ruby cries.

The door swings wider and god*damn* it's Sooner stepping out, his square face lit from beneath. He always looked like the character Clutch Cargo, but with a dome of hair and not quite so much chin.

"Ruby!" he says, and how he knows her—by her shape in the dark, or the sound of her voice—Ruby cannot imagine. "Come home?" he asks. "Welcome home!" he says, and Ruby edges closer, finally mounting the steps into the kitchen, and the kindness in his voice is enough to make her weep.

SOONER AND RUBY

The Way a House Smells

Tim's old girlfriend. In high school Sooner had always seen in Ruby a shyness, a humility, even though she was smart. And he remembers Ruby being nicer than her sister. Val is the kind of person who keeps her distance, though Sooner has never cared; he guesses people will like him or not.

"I'm taking care of the house while they try to sell it." He knows it's weird he's here so late, but he doesn't care about that either. He keeps his own hours; he's not doing anything wrong. Just checking the house every week or so for critters, and in September he mowed when the grass got rough.

"They're gone?" Ruby looks cold, hesitating in the doorway. Girl isn't even wearing a coat.

"Come in," Sooner says, though it's not much warmer inside. The couple that owned this place—white-collar types who lost their way when they both got laid off—has him keep the heat just high enough so the pipes won't freeze. The lights have been off for weeks, though. They can't sell the place; word is it might go to developers.

"You live here now?" Ruby looks so confused. No secret that her mom is really sick; that news is all over town and he feels for her. Sooner has always known the lack of a mother; he reckons it's even worse if once you've had it and then you don't.

"No, no." He explains about the job, and the couple. "I think I got the work instead of Len, matter of fact. Your brother-in-law," he adds. "Your sister's probably some pissed at me."

Ruby shrugs. "I guess you knew these people better."

"I guess I did."

They stand silently in the kitchen, looking away from one

another. The walls are bare. Just a nest of cracks in one corner, and the window's blank glittering canvas.

"So they didn't stay," Ruby says.

"They didn't really fit in," Sooner says. "That's probably why they liked me. A kindred spirit," he adds without bitterness. He knows that some people see him as a loser. And yet after high school he'd gone away for years, making good money with the salmon fishing off Alaska, and still been drawn back home eventually. The first time he'd walked into the Dew Drop after returning there'd been a clamor: "My God! Sooner! Sit over here!" His mom long dead but people still knew him, and he understood that he'd missed being *recognized* all that time he was gone. "They had some trouble with money," he says to Ruby about the couple. "I think they moved back to Eau Claire."

"The big city," Ruby says, deadpan.

"Ha! Yeah!"

Ruby is observing him; he can see her watchful face in the half-light from the lantern.

"So you do this kind of thing now?"

"This and that," Sooner says. "You come to see the old place?"

"Yeah." Ruby sighs. "You want to show me around?"

"They ran out of money," Sooner says, and holds up the lantern to guide her into the living room. The new people, the city people, had started some sort of renovation; the wall between the living room and the dining room has been knocked out, and the room is painted soft gray-brown.

"River stone," Ruby says.

"Pardon?"

"The wall color," Ruby says. "It's supposed to be the new thing. Whatever that means," she adds. It seems bigger in here now. The missing wall, probably, and during the time they lived here Barbara had accumulated so much furniture. Moon's chair, covered in brown corduroy, had always stood by the window. To catch the light, he'd say. One time, when Ruby was in her teens, Pearl had taken a decorating class at the community center, and she'd tried to get Barbara to clear out her rooms. "Make it spacious," Pearl kept repeating. It became something of an issue between the friends: Pearl's insistence on improvements, Barbara's refusal to make changes.

"I like my things," Barbara had said stoutly, and at the time, Ruby was chagrined. Why wouldn't her mother move on to something new, perhaps better? One time she'd even sat her mother down, lecturing her about how *things* can't pin the past in place. "The past keeps receding," she'd said, probably repeating something she'd heard at school; now most everything that used to be in the house is gone. And Ruby wonders. At least Barbara knew what she wanted. At least she knew what she liked.

Ruby stands by the picture window (pitcher window) and all she sees is her image in the glossy black glass. She can't see past it outside, and the room behind her is empty. Turning away, she tries to remember if she was thinner the last time she and Sooner crossed paths. "I'd like to see upstairs," Ruby says. "My old room? I was just—I don't know, I thought I'd tell Mom about the place."

"She'll like that," Sooner says.

"I thought we could talk about, you know, what it was like to live here."

She doesn't know what she expects but she feels nothing when she climbs the stairs, nothing when she stands at the entrance to what used to be her room, still a flat pink. The money must have run out before the couple got upstairs.

She steps into the room. There is the window seat, there is the tiny closet. If she opened the door, she would see one rod for clothing, one shelf; there would probably be the same cedar-y, fecal smell. Had she been happy here? Dakota used to ask what it was like for Ruby as a girl, and Ruby, at a loss for specifics, would make things up: a night she sat in the window seat and watched the moon; that she read mysteries under the covers, using a flashlight—the things girls in books do. What Ruby remembers is that she always wanted to get out of this place. Her belief that real independence lay just beyond these rooms. But the room is neither comforting nor suffocating; it is like visiting the girlhood room of a stranger.

"Want me to step out?" Sooner asks politely. Perhaps he has seen something in her face, but Ruby shakes her head abruptly. No.

"I'm not sentimental," Ruby says.

"I always liked this house," Sooner says.

"What do you remember about it?" she asks him. She really wants to know.

"Your mom was always so nice to me. I was afraid of your uncle. Stern." Sooner sets the lantern down and the light flows up like a fan, not making it to the corners of the room. He steeples his fingers under his jaw, thinking. "It smelled a certain way, your house."

"What?" Ruby might be offended.

"You know, people's houses have different smells? Not a bad thing. It smelled like bread. Old hymn books."

"Hymnals?"

"No, don't laugh. It did. I always wanted to stay over here. You and your mom, you had a nice…you had a nice relationship."

"You think so?"

Sooner laughs. "Yeah."

"Why? What was it like?"

"You want me to tell you about your relationship with your mother."

"What did it seem like to you?"

"Well, just that the sun rose and set on you." Sooner looks at Ruby and adds, "Seriously. She made you that dress your senior year, for the concert? Blue shiny stuff."

"I can't believe you remember that." Ruby wore the dress to play piano at a recital; this was before Barbara gave her the pin, but she had lent it to Ruby that night, to fasten against the dark silk.

"She was proud of you. Proud that you were smart, that

you were going places. She was too big of a person to brag, but everyone knew how she felt. Her face had a shine to it when she talked about you. No kidding! And that dress; she made it special, because you were special."

"Sometimes I think she wanted to be alone," Ruby says, remembering the road trips.

Sooner shrugs. "Everyone wants to be alone sometimes. Everyone needs to...I don't know. Some people need it more than others."

Ruby shakes her head. "And now everything's...my mom, Moon. Everyone's gone," she says.

Sooner picks up the lantern again.

"I'll tell her the upstairs is just how she left it, anyway." Ruby steps closer to Sooner in his ring of light. "Is your house the same?"

"I'm still living there. I've been working on it, though. Come see," he says.

Ruby thinks about what Val said, and Tim, how Sooner is a meth head now, or at least a cook. What would happen when she saw his lab? She read about meth houses once, in Rolling Stone. This would have been years ago; the article said how small rural towns were going to be where the meth got made. You needed privacy to cook it in your stripped-down kitchen. You needed to be out in the woods. At the time it had been hard to imagine anything like that around here, but there were busts in Marathon County all the time now.

Ruby examines Sooner's face, which is impossible to read in the half-light. In the article, they showed before and after pictures. First some ordinary-looking person, they could be anyone, and then the way they got meth mouth, teeth rotted right out of their heads. Ruby thinks about Tavie, the waitress, and how she hid her mouth with her hand.

"Smile," she commands Sooner, and it's just random enough, her saying this, that he does. Well, he's probably not an addict, anyway; his teeth look sound.

"Sure," Ruby decides. "I'd love to see your house." She'll

take her chances. It's better than returning to Val's, in any case. "It's funny. I told my sister I was looking for you."

"How *is* Val?"

"She's kind of a bitch," Ruby says. She thinks for a moment. "But I guess I can sort of see why."

RUBY

Worm Farm

The thing is, she can't remember exactly who she was to him. To Sooner, who was Tim's friend in high school; improbably, Sooner and Tim were on the wrestling team together, both of them frail as sparrows and lanky, so that it was something of a joke. The team always lost. Afterward, there would be pizza.

"You make do," Ruby's mom used to say in the face of Ruby's incredulity. "That coach has got what he's got."

In high school, Sooner was an amiable pothead, and he liked Ruby because she didn't judge. "You're a good person," he told her once, but what did that mean, exactly? Ruby cannot imagine what he thinks now. Remembering her lunch at Tim's, she flushes and wonders how often Tim and Sooner talk, and what they talk about—*God*. It seems weeks ago that she was safe in the river-stone walls of her condo.

At least there wouldn't be a Carrie to contend with at Sooner's place.

But. "Married?" She has to know.

"Nope. You?"

"Naw." She laughs, and something is settled between them, and they can go about the business of being friends without awkwardness. Or not. She doesn't remember him being this serious.

So, Sooner lives in what used to be his mother's house, which now might or might not be a meth lab. It was little more than a summer cabin when he grew up in it. His mom was always a nice woman, but despairing. Sooner's father died in a hunting accident when Sooner was barely nine, and when his mom drank, which was often, she said she blamed herself for his death. She claimed to have had a dream in which Ronnie, her husband, had walked into a lake that swallowed him whole, and that she never should have let him go out on the morning his gun malfunctioned. Her alcoholism was an open secret in town, and that, plus Sooner's agreeableness, made other kids' mothers take him under their wings. In high school he was always bringing home tins of cookies or loaves of bread ("we just had some extra") that his classmates were made to pass on to him.

Even Barbara, worn through with worries about the farm and always just managing, with Moon, to make ends meet, used to insist he join them for supper. She might be picking up Ruby at school and there would be Sooner, without a hat, ears raw from cold. "My mom'll be along," he always said, to which Barbara would retort, "She can pick you up at our house, after supper." She was an excellent, inventive cook, configuring filling, one-dish meals out of whatever she found in the cabinets. Canned corn in everything from stew to potpie, and the spaghetti sauce she made! For special, she'd make meringues, their strange stiff sponginess melting into sugar in your mouth.

Sooner's mom never cooked, she just kept drinking, and then she died, years ago, when Sooner was still in his twenties. There is the story about a worm farm now, and it's just crazy enough to be true. But this business about the meth lab? Ruby wonders what she'll see when they get inside.

"I'm working on things," Sooner says. "Tearing it apart from the inside out."

He gives her the keys to the farmhouse, allowing her to walk around inside one more time; she wants to see what it is like to be there alone. "Just lock up when you leave," Sooner says. "I'll meet you at my place." She steps into the living room, looks to the corner where the television once stood. She and Moon used to watch old episodes of *Monty Python's Flying Circus* here. Val would be out with friends, of course; Barbara, who claimed not to understand the show, used to work in the kitchen, her domain. Ruby and Moon, though, they laughed and laughed. They never talked about the show afterward.

Ruby crosses the room; the noise of her shoes on the uncarpeted floors makes her anxious and so she steps out of them, walking carefully in sock feet to the kitchen. "Goodbye," she tells the room, so changed by renovation that only the cloudy window over the sink is really familiar. "Goodbye," she tells the living room; slipping on her shoes again, she closes the front door softly behind her. The yard is dark, uneven. In the car she glances at her cell phone. There is the message from Val, from earlier this evening, when she is ready to receive it.

She doesn't check the message (though she will days later and it's funny then, to hear what Val had to say). She wonders if Drago ever listened to the last frantic messages she left him, messy diatribes in which she told him that her heart was broken, that he was a son-of-a-bitch and that they could make it work, of course they could make it work. "What am I supposed to do now?" she had said.

Ruby puts the phone away and repeats to herself the directions that Sooner gave to his house, in case she has forgotten the way.

જ

When she pulls into the rutted lane, her lights pick him out in the side yard. He's hunched over, shovel in hand, tossing something into a hole. A mug and a plate, it looks like; as she drives closer he straightens from his work and comes to the side of her car, smiling. Ruby smiles back, studying the house that looms behind him. It has always stood high, as if on stilts. Right now the front door is several feet above the gravel walk. No front steps.

"We can go in the back," Sooner says. "I've got some beer, if you like."

"Yep. What were you doing, man?"

"Cleaning up." He gestures behind him, to the shovel he leaned carefully against a tree.

"Were you burying...*dishes*?"

"I'm sick of doing them," he says, shrugging, and she laughs in spite of herself. He's always been weird, Sooner has.

The house is a modified A-frame, with a loft for sleeping upstairs, and a living room and kitchen and bathroom downstairs. Sooner has also added what seems to be a bedroom on the main floor; Ruby glimpses it as she moves into the primary living space. Everything is raw wood, splintery; the place smells of mice. She wouldn't want to live here but she is relieved to see that the kitchen looks clean. No meth lab here, no weird red stains, no propane bottles littering the floor. And what would she have done if the kitchen counter had been a mess of Drano and lithium batteries? Would she have jumped up, run into the woods? The thought makes her smile.

"Happy girl," Sooner says. "You want a joint? I got some weed from Tim."

Who thinks you're a meth head, Ruby wants to say. It's all so complicated: who really cares about whom. Are he and Tim friends after all? "Naw," she says, but she nods when Sooner extends a bottle of beer. She sits down on a shabby couch and folds her arms across her chest; the wall behind her is just studs, and it's cold.

"You need to eat?" Seen up close, in the bright overhead lights he has installed, Sooner looks unwell. Dark pockets sag beneath his eyes. Middle age, Ruby supposes, though it shocks her. She wonders what she looks like to him and instinctively sucks in her belly.

"I could eat," she says, thinking of the food she barely touched at the Dew Drop.

"I'll make us burgers," Sooner says. He sweeps a pile of books off a tubular metal kitchen chair, the only other seat in the room, its torn plastic seat mended neatly with duct tape. "You still eat meat?"

"I never stopped," Ruby says.

While Sooner cooks, he tells her about the worm farm. It's in the spare room, he says, gesturing to the space that might have been a bedroom. "They live inside when it's cold out," he says, probably because of the look on her face. "I use a bed system."

"A bed system," she repeats. "What the hell, Sooner?"

He laughs, and Ruby remembers, suddenly, how she could always make him crack up. "People use them for night crawlers," he says. "Or fertilizer."

"So this is working out okay for you?" It's a sincere question; Sooner would know she wasn't being sarcastic. She's never had to walk on eggshells around him.

"I get by." Sooner shapes hamburger meat into thick patties. He asks her who she's stayed in touch with. "Weren't you friends with Jackie?" He starts warming a griddle and chops an onion, sprinkling it into the pan. Ruby stares past him, suddenly bored. Talk about old times, old ties—it has nothing to do with her.

"What's she doing these days?" she asks, not caring.

"She got in a car accident, out by Green Bay," he says. He places the patties on the griddle and they make a crisp sound. "Tim told me she's in a wheelchair."

"God." Ruby doesn't know what else to say. Jackie had been an uncomplicated girl with weary toughness in her face; in high school, she looked up to Ruby because Ruby was smart, and a grade older. She was a reliable shopping companion once Charlene left town. But it's been so long; it's like hearing about a stranger in the news. "I'm sorry," she says. "I guess we're all living long enough for bad things to have happened to us."

"Mmhmmm," Sooner says. He turns the patties. "I'm reading Frankl," he finally says. "About suffering. Everyone over the age of forty should read it."

He puts the burgers on paper plates. Red juice from the meat runs in rivulets, and the plates sag a little. Sooner has heated up gluey mashed potatoes in the microwave too, and there's a scoop for each of them, round as ice cream.

"No buns," he says, and hands her a plastic fork. On the table is a thick candle that looks like melted frosting. He lights it and smiles. "Candlelight, though."

"I think I read Frankl in college. You're reading him now because...?" Ruby forks up a bite of her burger; though the outside is black, the meat is almost raw. *Christ*, she thinks, and concentrates on not gagging. She sets the plate aside and watches Sooner eat slowly, chewing carefully and putting his fork down in between bites.

"Why do you think?" Sooner licks his fingers and regards her. He is sitting opposite, and Ruby gazes at his sloped shoulders, the hollows in his cheeks; she sees the complicated sadness in his eyes.

"You're sick," she says suddenly. And then she is afraid.

"I am," he says, and shrugs. "I am alone, and I'll probably die alone." His voice is easy. "I've had some time to get used to the idea." He shrugs again, and his eyes are very big in his face, like the eyes of the rabbits in their pen.

Ruby won't ask him what he's sick with, but it's cancer, of course. She is almost sure of it.

"Cancer sucks," he confirms calmly. "I know you know that."

Val knows more, Ruby thinks, but she nods.

"I'm sorry," she says. "What are you doing for it?"

"Not enough." He grins. "It's beyond surgery. It's burrowed through my body like Grant through Richmond. Let's talk about something else," he says. "Tell me about your mom."

"That won't cheer us up any," Ruby says, and then they both laugh. Sooner always had the gallows humor. "I don't know about Mom," she admits. "I'm afraid to go see her." She feels that she owes him the truth somehow, because of what he has told her. And it's a relief to say it in any case. She tells him that Barbara's dementia has made her someone else. "My mom is dead," she says. "My real mom."

"What's Parkinson's like?" Sooner asks. How funny, Ruby thinks. No one has ever asked her this, not so directly.

"She's stiff," Ruby says slowly. "And she writes so tiny now. Or she did, when she was still writing." Ruby moves the hamburger around on her plate, breaking the red meat into clumps with her fork. "It's so weird. I guess she doesn't write anymore. I hate Parkinson's," she declares. "Parkinson's can kiss my ass!"

"You tell 'em," Sooner says affectionately, but then he says, "I'm sorry, Ruby." They stay where they're at; it would be weird to get up and let him hug her, but what Ruby remembers later is how comforting this moment is.

"It's humbling," Sooner says, almost marveling, and whether he means the Parkinson's, or cancer, or all of it—decline and death—it doesn't matter. Ruby is ashamed that she ever thought he might have a meth lab.

"I'm glad I'm here," she says, thinking of Val's house, where she has never belonged. Even the hideous burger is a comfort; he made it for *her*.

"Nice pin," he says, nodding at the collar of her shirt. She runs her fingers lightly over the pearls, nodding, and then he stands and makes for the kitchen. "I'm gonna have one more beer," he says. "You?"

The second beer is colder than the first. Sooner has also brought out a package of cookies, the soft doughy kind with frosting so thick it stands in peaks. Ruby takes one and stares past him into the worm room. A soft light mutters in there, and she can see a cot covered with a blue blanket, a box of dominoes, a glass half-filled with something clear and viscous. Sooner's guitar leans against the doorframe.

Sooner follows her glance and smiles. "You used to play better than me," he says.

"I still do." She eats the cookie in one bite; her gait as she makes for the guitar is wobbly. She's so tired, and she hasn't eaten much, and now the beer, which is heavy and dark. But Ruby gets the guitar and plops back on the sofa.

"I adore music," she giggles, licking blue frosting from her fingers. "Did you know that?"

"I think you were something of a prodigy, madam," Sooner says gravely.

His sincerity makes her grateful and then sad. "Big fish in a small pond," she says. "I do HR now." When she gets home, the rows of chairs will still be standing in her condo. Ruby strums, dismayed by the sudden tears on her cheeks; she knows that when she cries, her mouth twists in an ugly way. "That's the rumor." Ruby plays the opening chords to "Blackbird."

"Val's proud of you, you know," Sooner says. "Your mom used to talk you up, but now Val boasts on you." He sips his beer, thoughtful. "I always knew you'd do something big," and it's nice the way he says it. She can't put her finger on it, but it's better than Tim's nice.

Ruby sets the guitar across her knees. "Most people my age, doing what I do, want to become an HR director."

"You want to do that?"

"No."

"Then don't." Outside, there is a weird sawing yowl, and the hairs raise on the back of Ruby's neck. She thinks of Jellybean, alone in the woods. Once upon a time, the tips of her fingers were tough from playing.

"I used to have a professor," she tells Sooner. "He played the guitar and he'd show up sometimes at this coffeehouse. He wrote songs and they were good; in the 1970s he had been this sort of It Guy and we felt sorry for him because we thought he hadn't gone anywhere. But I bet he just liked what he did. I'll bet he was comfortable with that. I hope so, anyway." Ruby pauses. "What happened to us?" she finally asks. "I live at the edge of winter now." She and Tim used to talk this way, as if to keep everyone else at a distance. At the time it was an affectation, born of pride. Now that she means it, the emptiness of the place it comes from scares her.

"Naw," he protests in a low voice.

"Are you afraid?" she whispers.

Sooner has never made a spectacle of his troubles. "We're okay, honey," he finally says. "We do the best we can."

MOON

1995

Babs didn't miss Eddie anymore. Moon could tell. There had been a hole for a long time, but she missed him less and less with each passing year; eventually she and Moon had been raising the girls longer than Eddie had been in her life. And Moon was always there; he was steady. Both of them knew that Eddie had not been a dependable man; feckless, inconstant, he came home from out-of-town jobs having spent the money not on groceries, but on a new suit for himself. A sharper, both Moon and Barbara knew, though never mentioned.

Moon never married, which he understood people thought was curious—there were rumors, some thought he might run "that way"—but the truth was that he was taciturn and shy, and it was Barbara's good luck, and good luck for the girls, that he stuck by them. This, too, remained unsaid between the sister and brother; it was like them that they did not remark on it.

Ruby almost done with college now, and changed more each time she returned home. He used to call her Ladybird, after Lyndon Johnson's wife. She had a goofy elegance to her, and though she was a big girl, she moved with grace. She wouldn't be coming back, not to stay; Babs had already warned him. This surprised him, but he didn't know Ruby, not really. He didn't know either of his nieces well, though he'd lived with them for years and loved them with singular duty.

He could see that Val had the quiet toughness of his sister—her mother—and he respected that. He'd even told Val once—and meant it—that she had good instincts. She'd do all right. His own sister he knew. He knew she was strong, and he liked her better than most women, because she said only what needed to be said. He didn't think he could have lived with her all these years if she'd been another way.

Babs had friends who liked to talk, who "spilled their guts," as they would frequently remark. When they came over for Nescafé and biscuits, Moon went out to the barn or he got in his truck and drove out across the river. One time, escaping out the back, he heard one, Pearl, say, "Are you happy, Barb?" That one was always in everyone's lunch.

"What's happy?" Barbara had shrugged. "If you don't expect something, you won't be disappointed." His younger sister. He didn't know how she came to this way of thinking, because their own parents—not cruel, exactly, but nevertheless severe, unknowable—never gave their children any clue to their own way of seeing the world.

When Babs and Eddie were engaged, and at the wedding— to which Moon wore a new shirt with a blue stripe—and even for a while into the marriage, there was a sweetness between them. One time, Moon remembers, his sister and Eddie must have just gotten this house. It was too big for them; they didn't have enough furniture to fill it. But Babs was so *proud*. She and Eddie would have Moon over for supper sometimes, and one evening as he walked up the drive—it was late April or May, the air plush with spring—he saw them through the pitcher window. His sister was spinning, giddy and laughing. They must have been listening to music (Eddie loved music), and Babs twirled and twirled until she fell into her husband's arms. Moon never regretted not marrying except for possibly that one night. When Babs answered the door, her cheeks pink, she was laughing.

She toughened, though, as he did. After Eddie left for good, the siblings grew together and became set in their ways, and part of how he saw the world he took on from Babs, as he might have, in another life, learned from a wife. Sometimes he thought he should thank her for that. He made her a bread-board, awkwardly shaped but from a beautiful piece of heart-wood maple, colored darkish red, with a fine even texture to the grain. The bread she made was the best in the county.

So much between them can go unsaid.

RUBY

Funeral

"A lot of people came to my uncle's funeral," Ruby tells Sooner, because he'd still been up to Alaska when Moon died. "I didn't know he *knew* so many people." She plucks the guitar strings, extends her hand for another beer. Sooner is stretched on the floor, which is subflooring, but covered neatly by a patchwork of wool blankets.

Ruby had driven up for Moon's funeral in the blustery days after Halloween, and the wind had polished new snow into a glaze as hard as bone. For the service she'd packed a black wool dress, which exposed her chunky calves, but this time she bought the right size, understanding that there would be no time to lose weight—or *try* to lose weight—before the funeral. It had happened so fast, Moon's decline, and Ruby was ashamed of how relieved she was when it was all over. The routines of her own life remained reassuring, and when they drove to the church, wind beating against the car, Ruby tried to summon them in her head: espresso from the cunning silver pot; her yellow cup; the rock of the L as she commuted to work. Every Friday night, then as now, she and Lorna would meet for drinks and supper.

Val had insisted they all drive together. "We have a big car!" she'd said, adamant even when Ruby suggested meeting at the church, and how she could bring other passengers in her little Honda. "We're a family, for god's sake," Val said, almost in tears, and so Ruby relented. Len drove, and Val, tiny as she was, shared the front passenger seat with her mother. Ruby pretended not to hear Junie's complaining sigh when the girl's car seat was smashed into the middle, in back. Ruby's hip pressed against it. Len cranked the heat, and outside the snow spit against the windows like grit; in the light, fast failing, it was the color of lead. "We're a family," Val repeated. But Barbara, already in the throes of the Parkinson's, had been a little distant. A little strange.

"My dress itched like billy hell," Ruby says. She takes a swallow of beer. That hideous black dress. Someone, Pearl probably, or that daughter of hers, Virginia, had asked her if she was pregnant. Ruby was standing at the buffet table, methodically eating the lemon squares. The front of her dress was powdered with sugar. "No. Just fat," she'd said, shaking her head, and Pearl or Ginny, whoever it was, had at least had the decency to blush.

"Moon dying changed a lot of things," she tells Sooner. "Mom was doing okay, at least we thought she was, and then it all just sort of fell apart." She sets the guitar aside and regards Sooner, chin propped in her hands. "I know it's been harder on Val than me, but it's still been hard."

Sooner nods.

"I used to get mad at Moon, for dying and leaving us with... For leaving us."

"That seems like a pretty understandable response," Sooner says, and this finally propels her to get up and hug him. You know when someone likes you—live long enough and that at least is clear. He isn't just being polite. As she gets older, Ruby has a greater appreciation for what a goddamn relief it is to be with someone who doesn't think she's sub-par.

She smiles bleakly into Sooner's neck. "I don't miss Moon the way I thought I would," she says. "He was never a part of my life in Chicago and so when I'm there, I don't think about him much. But when I come back here, then I miss him, a lot." Ruby pulls back to look at Sooner, letting her arms slide down and around his waist. "And I think if he walked into this room right now, I'd remember what I've learned to live without. Why being with him made me feel safe and good. Is that weird?"

"No," Sooner says.

Ruby continues gazing at Sooner. "I thought you had a meth lab," she says. "I thought you were sub-par."

Sooner's face is expressionless. "That's the rumor," he says. "Does it bother you?"

"Not at this stage of the game."

"We come to the point where things don't get to us?"

"Or they get to us even more," Sooner says. "Don't let that happen, Ruby. You start thinking that way and it's your funeral."

"Okay," she says. "You're nice." What a stupid thing to say, and she knows she's a little drunk, but she also knows she'll still mean it when she's sober.

She would have slept with him—in fact she would have liked to—but Sooner smiles at her wistfully and removes her arms from his waist. "Not so many working parts, anymore," he says. "I think you'd be disappointed."

It's almost too late to go to bed. "Do you want to go swimming?" she asks.

RUBY

Swim

Wooden with cold, the tarp has been secured with a border of rocks and folds back on itself like the lid on a sardine can. When they pull it back, they see that the motel pool is half full of water. Ruby stands near the raised platform where a diving board goes in the summer, and the pool reminds her of Val's birdbath. "My sister used to look up to me," she tells Sooner, though he is fussing with the tarp and she's not certain he hears. Ruby has borrowed some of his clothing—a turtleneck that chafes her neck, a windbreaker lined with fleece. When she told him about the pool, he'd laughed out loud. "That would be just random enough," he'd said, when she described how she wanted to strip and jump into the pool naked. He said it would be like the Polar Plunge, a fundraiser they had up Phillips way. "People jump into Long Lake in the middle of January, you know? I might not get another chance to do something like that." But now they're here, in the dark and the cold.

"It feels good when someone admires us," Sooner says, straightening up. So he heard her after all. Ruby pokes at the folded tarp with the toe of her sneaker.

"We aren't really going to swim, are we?" Sooner asks. He peers at the dark, sludgy water. Behind them, lights from the motel twinkle; the house where Carrie and Tim live is lit like a stage. On the drive over, Ruby imagined that she and Sooner were married, that they shared a life in his A-frame. If things were different, and she'd cast her lot here; he has such a fine mind, and he likes her. But he's dying. There's that.

"Naw, I was just funnin'," Ruby says. If the water had been

clear, she might still have done it. "Are you and Tim friends?" she asks, looking at the house.

"In a way," Sooner says.

"I had a really weird experience there yesterday. I behaved badly." Ruby pushes her hands deep into the pockets of her pants. "You like his wife?"

"She's hot," Sooner says, then giggles, so Ruby knows he's just trying to provoke her.

"I don't care for her," Ruby declares, and without thinking she pushes one of the smaller rocks with her foot until it rolls into the pool. "There!" she whispers.

"What you doing, girl?"

"I think Tim takes advantage of your friendship," Ruby says.

"It's not a big deal. We're not exactly close."

"Human beings can suck."

Sooner squats and sits back on his heels, regarding her. "But you gotta respect humans. We're sort of like cancer. We do what it takes to survive. Down to their molecular core, cancer cells are hardwired for the same."

"That isn't exactly noble."

"Depends on how you look at it," Sooner says.

"Help me with this." Ruby has chosen another rock—bigger, spangly with quartz in the lights from the house. "This rock should be in the pool."

"What the hell?" But Sooner stands and moves closer; together they are able to pitch the rock into the pool. It slurps going in.

Ruby peers into the slushy, black water. She can't see where the rock went. "It's like rocks in a river. The Flambeau, right? My mom used to tell me that Ladyford is the only town on the main Flambeau." She giggles. "Big fuckin' deal, right? But that was Mom—she just liked knowing that. She found that interesting. And that's okay. Some people, though. Some people are *full* of themselves."

Ruby grunts, her fingers wrapped around another rock. "Some people think they are hot shit." She wonders if ten years from now she will remember this night. She is shocked sometimes, at the things she forgets. A light sleet has started up again, and her hands are numb.

"Ruby, you can't let people get to you," Sooner says.

"Easy for you to say; you'll be dead next year and then you won't have to worry about them." She means it to come out in the joking way they have between them, but she's shocked by how mean it sounds. "I'm sorry!" she says quickly.

Sooner doesn't answer. He has his head wrapped in a scarf, with a hood pulled over; in the dark, she can't make out his eyes, or the shape of his mouth. Hands jammed into the pockets of his hoodie, he could be the Unabomber. He could be Jesus. "Just because I'm helping you with—whatever this is—doesn't mean I think you're right," he says finally, and she is relieved that his tone is light. "I can still tote that barge," he says. "I can still lift that bale." He starts moving around the pool, nudging the smaller rocks in with his feet. They disappear into the water, making their sucking sound.

"Whooo!" he cries. Maybe they are both a little drunk. After a while, they are hurling the rocks in; it warms them. "You know what else Mom told me?" Ruby says at one point. "Flambeau. That's French for 'torch.' And it leads to the Mississippi, or part of the way, the Flambeau does. It's like a highway. 'Our little river,' she used to say. 'It connects us to the world.' I just like the way she used to look at things. *She* was a whole world, my mom." The sleet comes down harder; Ruby is soaked to the skin. "That's what I want to be, you know?" They work together to get the last rock in, and Ruby whoops.

"Who's there?" someone cries; it might be Tim.

"Whooo!" Ruby shrieks again, stumbling as she grabs Sooner's hand and pulls him toward where they left the car. The door to the house opens, and there's Tim's long silhouette. He's holding something—a pot, a dish towel—and he calls out again, "Who's there?" before turning back into the room. His voice uncertain, and Ruby is glad he'll have extra work tomorrow, or in the spring. Getting those rocks out will be a chore.

In one of the motel rooms they pass, a curtain is pulled aside; within the bright-lit room a naked man gapes, and his woman, with her smeared and painted face.

JUNIE

World

Everyone's asleep and Junie creeps out of the house, past Dakota in her bed and then Mama on the couch. The glow clock by her bed—it's shaped like a teddy—said four-seventeen, but she's going to look for Jellybean. The cat has always liked her best and she'll come if Junie calls. So cold outside but she found Aunt Ruby's sweatshirt draped across the desk where Dakota does her homework. The sweatshirt, soft, is big and sloppy and a little damp, just like Aunt Ruby can be.

She likes her aunt but she loves Mama. Mama came in and checked on her after Junie got up the first time tonight. Mama held her until she calmed down, because Jelly hadn't been found yet and the grown-ups were fighting, which is scary and gives Junie the twisty feeling in her stomach. Mama's arms felt good. Junie snuggled into Mama and pretended to sleep then because she knew that was what Mama wanted her to do.

Junie is a big girl and she's not afraid of the dark. Sometimes she'll close her eyes and walk around the house, to see how hard it is to get somewhere. Dakota told her about Helen Keller and how she was blind and deaf and couldn't talk. Junie likes to see how that might be, eyes squeezed tight, then she opens her eyes again: Ta da! She can't undo this, though, how black everything is, and the little bit of rain. There are so many trees! *One, two, three.* Junie counts the trees in her head. *Four, five, six.* But Junie knows the path behind the house pretty well; it's how she and Mama get to the park, and that's where Jelly will be, she is positive. The cat is so fat and always sleeps mashed against her.

Twenty-one. Twenty-two. "Jellybeeeeeean!" she yells. She's sleepy and grumpy and she just wants her cat back. Audrey the cat is okay but Jelly really loves *her*, Junie. Everything is different now, how Grandma forgets things, and then how Mama cries. Junie knows about the sad even though Mama thinks she hides it.

"Jel-ly!" Dakota and Mama yell at each other the way they do; Daddy says leave them be and once he just took Junie with him and they went for an ice cream. "Let's let them work themselves out," Daddy said. He waggled his eyebrows to make her laugh, but Junie isn't dumb. She knows that something's gone wrong. On the phone, Mama reminds Grandma of things in a funny, different voice like she's trying not to be mad, or scared. Grandma used to live in the big house, the one with the barn that smelled like hay and warm things. Junie can barely remember it, though she remembers not liking it when Grandma moved, but then the senior center was nice, with its peach-colored wallpaper and the ladies Gram called her girlfriends. Junie keeps getting used to things, and then things change.

Grandma, Mama, Daddy, Dakota. "I am me," Junie thinks. Walk-running along the trail, which is dark and almost like a tunnel in the pines, she understands suddenly how she is alone. Not just on this path, but in the world. Everyone has to walk their own way. No one can do it for them. She stops, breathing hard, no longer counting trees; she even forgets Jellybean for the moment. "I am *me.*" Junie tries to keep her panic at bay, but it is there, in the shadows under the pines.

If the cat came back, things would be better.

"Jelly!" she screams, and begins to run again. *Forty-five. Forty-six.*

Her cat has yellow eyes, and paws like paddles. A butt as big as the world.

VAL

Night

Val can't sleep. She rests on the couch in the living room because her rule is this: you lie in bed for fifteen minutes and if you're still awake then you get up. Sometimes she reads. During her friendship with Carrie she began to read poets and writers that she knows are considered "good"; there was one long essay from which she pretty much figured out that mankind was doomed, for example. She and Carrie talked about it, and Val kept up. She did okay, she didn't come across as weak, or silly. She wasn't born smart, not like Ruby—but now, thanks to Carrie, she is that much smarter.

You would think that would be a comfort, but in the bleak, black hours before dawn she returns to the writers she and her mother enjoyed, when Ruby was in college and they would stay up reading after Moon had gone to bed. There's a series that Barbara always liked, about a little town called Millburg; she would say that the books made her feel cheery. Sometimes she'd ask Val to read out loud to her while she finished what was in the mending basket. Although Millburg's citizens faced real problems—divorce, job loss, an angry child—there was something appealing, even reassuring, about their challenges. Nothing that a warm batch of cookies and a sit-down with the new, befuddled-but-handsome vicar couldn't fix. If you met an orphan on the first page, chances are he'd have a home by the last.

Val is still comforted by these books, which she and Barbara drowsed over until it was time to properly go to bed, even as she doesn't believe them. They lay out clearly what is Good, or Bad, a perspective so much more manageable than, say, the ideas Val gets in the middle of the night. *When Mom is gone*

I might feel better. I might get in the car and just drive. Sometimes Val wonders if that's how Ruby felt, all those years ago with the tiresome road trips. At the time, Val didn't really want to leave home. She'd pretended for a while to like their trips, even as a part of her understood how fleeting it all was and feared what she was missing back home. Life at the farmhouse already seemed to be slipping away, though only she seemed to see it. Val used to get carsick, but it would be different now; she'd be the one behind the wheel.

Tonight she is too distracted to read anything—she can't even follow what's going on with Millburg's new (and only) sweet-shop owner, who may or may not have set her sights on the vicar's brother—so she turns off the lamp and lays the book on the floor. Staring dry-eyed into the darkness, Val rehearses what she might say to Dakota about Bryan. She replays what it was exactly Ruby said, not yet ready to go back to the room and the bed where Len sleeps and dreams. About barns, possibly, about doing the right thing.

She eventually must have slept a little, because she has a dream of her own and at first she thinks that Moon has come to comfort her. She's been waiting for that, because people ask her, even now, *Have you felt your uncle's presence?*

It's gotten to the point where she lies and says she has, because it is a disappointment to her that she has not. All the stories you hear! "My mother came to me in a dream." "I can still hear his voice in my ear, advising me." "I feel her presence." Val thinks of Moon and feels nothing except for the loss of him, which fills every empty space within her, sand in a Mason jar of rocks. She misses him more now than she did even just after his death. Because wouldn't he have experienced the long slow loss of Barbara the way she herself does? Wouldn't it be something they shared?

Val always tells Junie, who barely remembers him, "Your great-uncle Moon is watching over you; I can feel him enjoying what we're doing. He's happy because you're happy." She says this to make him come alive for her younger child and hopes it's true. She says this to keep him alive for herself. Because honestly? A part of her fears the day when she has learned to live without him; she fears the distance from him that that will have taken her, when he already feels so…*gone*.

Some nights she tries to convince herself into a dream. *Give me a sign!* she thinks, almost begging, trying to fix in her mind the way Moon looked at supper, single-mindedly eating his ham, or leaning against Horehound, his snap-brim cap pushed back. *Make me feel a part of something larger, something magical! I miss you so much.* She knows that part of what she misses is her younger self. Barbara can't validate her anymore, and though it was never in her uncle's nature to lavish praise on anyone, she tells herself that a spectral Moon might understand who she has become. He might ratify the way she cares for his sister, for example. The way she parents the two little girls who since his death have continued to change and grow. Would he recognize them now? At the time of his death, Dakota was sweeter. Easier to understand. That boy Kevin who comes over has piercings in his cheek, and Moon has been spared that. Still, Val tries to guess what he might say to his great-nieces. And to her. Val.

Many people, as they age, talk more about the past. Moon was never this way, his thinking being, no point in regretting it now.

Of course he did say something, once. Long after her father had left, and Moon had moved in. Val was ironing his handkerchiefs in the living room, the ironing board set up so she could watch television. Andy Griffith, Dick Van Dyke—she liked the old shows. Moon had come in the way he did—purposefully, not saying a word—and carefully set out a brush and a tin of shoe black, neat on a towel. He polished his shoes with severe circular strokes until they shone like glass, and then he suddenly made the closest thing to a personal comment that Val ever heard him make—then or since. "You are a comfort to your mother, Valentine," he'd said, standing to leave, and too shy or surprised to answer, she'd lowered her head over the ironing and nodded.

He'd said more, she thinks, and though she cannot recall the rest of it, the smell of ironed cotton can still bring that day back to her. Val thought of it recently, while ironing one of Len's shirts, and she stopped what she was doing and carefully ran through what she does remember. At least she has that.

And at first tonight, when the back of her head got that odd buzzing, falling-back sensation that meant she was drifting to sleep, almost there, she thought it was finally happening. That Moon had come to tell her whether she was still a comfort after all. To fill in the parts she no longer remembers. To fill her up. There was the creak of a floorboard—Val could have sworn it—and she felt a presence leaning over her, as if to give a kiss. Her eyes were closed but then it became absurd and a little creepy, the way the figure said, "Za za *zor* zee," in a monotone. She woke staring into blackness, except there was the little plastic nightlight in the hallway, shaped like a Christmas wreath.

A dream. Of course. She swings her legs off the couch. Is Ruby home? She must not be; the house is so quiet, the kitchen dark, and where would she sleep, with Val on the couch? In the girls' room? Val creeps down the hallway, trying to remember exactly what the dream-spirit said. "Za za *zum*," she thinks, drifting past the empty pink cavern of the bathroom, pushing the girls' door open. The room is lit by another wreath nightlight—Val bought a box of them on sale after Christmas last year—and there is Dakota, sprawled in her bed, face calm in a way it is not during the day. The covers are bunched under her slim, white arms. She won't wear the flannel nightgowns Val buys her; she laughs at them, her mouth twisted. Perhaps Dakota is dreaming of Bryan, her head filled with whatever rubbish Ruby put there tonight. *Thank God for Len*, Val thinks suddenly. Dakota needs a father, and Bryan, for all his charm, could never be that.

Back in high school, all the girls had wanted Bryan. He sported a thick mane of hair that he combed straight back and fixed with gel; he knew what to say. No one had wanted Len. Barely anyone knew Len existed. But Bryan's hair might be thinning these days; he might have actually ended up with one of those girls, both of them thickened by middle age. What else had Moon said that afternoon? The ironing. Andy Griffith. Something about instincts. Val watches her older daughter sleep and understands that all those long-ago rivals for Bryan's attentions probably wish they had someone like Len now. *But I got Len.*

Val's eyes swing to the other bed, which is empty. The pillow in its red dinosaur pillowcase has been shoved against the headboard, a stuffed elephant in place of the missing Blue Bear, tucked carefully against it. "Junie," Val whispers. "Junie!" she screams.

RUBY

Day

Ruby, tooth throbbing in time to the beat of her blood, wakes thinking of her mother's milk soup. The soup has three ingredients—milk, butter, noodles—and Barbara used to make it to console her daughters. When Bryan periodically broke up with Val; when Ruby didn't, after all, make it into Juilliard.

The walls of Sooner's house are imperfect, veined with minute cracks—between the window frame and the wallboard, for example—through which light breaks. No wonder it's cold, though a space heater beside the couch clucks reassuringly. Someone, Sooner, covered Ruby with an assortment of the blankets from the floor. Teddy bears on bald fleece; a ragged wool blanket striped in red. But one quilt is beautiful, green and yellow and white sprigged cloth worked together into a pattern of diamonds. It's perfect except for one square, which has been marked with brown coffee rings that intersect like a Venn diagram.

"Sooner?" The house is filled with morning. Ruby, holding the damaged quilt close, smells coffee and, faintly, manure. Though her head is thick from the drinking last night, though she can see her breath and her tooth feels a little bit strange, she likes it here. Last night she and Sooner returned home after four a.m.; they slept on the couch together, head to toe, keeping each other chastely warm. My God, the feeling of a warm body next to hers! He gave her the inside of the couch—"So you won't fall off in the middle of the night!" he said, chivalrous— and his long lean back, bony against hers, guarded her, radiating heat. It was a comfort, the way Sooner's helping her with the rocks was a comfort. She hopes it meant as much to him as it did to her. Ruby badly wants to give him that gift.

"Sooner!"

She's still wearing Sooner's sweater and coat, and her shoes; she slept in them, wet as they were. Pushing aside the weight of blankets, Ruby goes to the window. Outside is a yard of packed earth, then dried grasses brown as crackling, then the forest. Concentric rings, with the house an epicenter. Sooner stands near a row of plastic bins in the grass, holding a shovel loosely in his hand. He is bundled in a parka, a ski cap perched on his head but sliding up because it's too small. His hair pokes out in greasy whorls. He stops and stretches, looking at the sky.

Past Sooner are the trees, and a brown stream choked with branches; this part of the woods is scrubby and uneven, thick with undergrowth. The nearest neighbor might be two miles away. No one comes here save the deer and Sooner, and it is a secret place. "I'm afraid," she tells the thick, wavy glass of the window. Sooner cannot hear her but she pretends that he can. Tim thinks she is heartless; Val thinks she is self-absorbed. Moon has died and soon enough her mother will die too. "I'm afraid that I've made the wrong choices, I'm afraid of what has come of my life." Admitting this is like a knife, slitting deep into the flesh of a peach and finally hitting the stone.

Sooner looks back at the house then. When he waves, her heart lifts. Ruby glances into the mirror next to the door—her face warped and strange in the spotted glass—then hurries outside. The light is sharp. On the trees, a few remaining leaves quiver.

"I'm working," he calls to her, pointing behind him to the bins. They look like little pagodas made of stacked trays. "This was like a worm condo this summer. I'm just packing it up for winter."

"Worms live there?"

"When it's warm," he says. "Remember what I told you last night? I move them inside when it gets cold out. I gotta leave the lights on for them. Figuratively speaking."

"I don't have a clue what you're talking about," she says. She feels such affection for him! Over their heads Canada geese labor, honking, and behind that is the static of crows.

"Four and twenty blackbirds, baked in a pie," she calls to the birds. She moves closer to him but is afraid of the tall grass, what might lurk there, and she plants her feet just outside that ring. The packed dirt of the yard is smooth and rounded beneath her shoes.

"I don't have a clue what you're talking about," he says, smiling.

Ruby, hand against her mouth, smiles back and thinks about the milk soup again. "Do you remember how my mom used to cook?"

"Beef stew," he says, using the spade of the shovel to tamp down the top of one of the bins. "Spaghetti."

"She doesn't cook anymore," Ruby says. "It's almost as though that never happened."

"But it did happen, so long as we remember it," Sooner says. He tries to stab the shovel into the ground and the cold earth rings. "You know what the Buddhists say: The glass is already broken. Everything ends. It's gravy when we have it; come on, girl. C'mon. Let's have some coffee."

"Buddhists talk about gravy?"

"C'mon, you." Sooner leans the spade against a tree. He takes her arm and it's reassuring to walk with him into the bright house. Once inside, he sheds his coat but leaves the hat on; his movements careful, he pours her a cup of thick dark coffee and she wonders how much pain, physical pain, he feels each day. They stand in the kitchen, and he listens to her tell about the part of her life that was Drago, and Tim. Carrie, and the way she makes Ruby feel. "Tim loved me," she says. "Now he doesn't."

"You left him," Sooner reminds her, not unkindly. "Besides, did you have fun?" He's pulled bread for toast out of a battered tin breadbox. Tim used to make toast. The first morning after the first night they were together—his parents were out of town, for a funeral? a family reunion?—he made her breakfast, and the tenderness with which he did so left her weak with gratitude. He had placed slices of orange all around the plate, a bright corona.

Ruby pokes in a drawer until she finds a knife that looks clean. Sooner hands her the first two pieces of toast and she butters them, scraping her knife across the brown ribs of bread. "I did, but it ended up that neither relationship was real," she says.

"They were. They brought you pleasure once. It's different now, that's all." He busies himself with a pan, cracking two brown eggs into it.

"Sooner, you're happy here, aren't you?"

He pauses, stirring the eggs. "I try to play the hand I'm dealt. But if you mean here, Wisconsin, yeah. This is where I belong." He looks up at her. "But that's me."

"You're the kind of person who could be happy wherever, Sooner," Ruby says. Her face colors; Carrie had said that, about her life with Tim. "I always thought no one could be happy here. But people are. I think even Val is happy here, in her way."

"Everyone's different. And things change. Like I was saying." He shrugs and in his face is the cancer, gray on yellow on white.

"Why can't things last?"

"Them not lasting doesn't make them untrue." For the first time, Sooner looks impatient. "Listen, girl. I don't have any-thing to lose. I'm almost done. But you?" He peels a strip of microwave bacon from a thick pink loaf and lays it on a plate. "I won't need dishes a year from now. You will."

"This isn't the best time for me, right now." Ruby is imme-diately embarrassed, saying this to a dying man. But Sooner's face is calm. No judgment. "I was going to do this…thing. A concert. I had it all planned. Even an encore! Do you know *Jesu Joy of Man's Desiring?*"

Sooner nods.

"Everyone loves that, right? That's why I picked it. But Mom got sick. I don't know—what if I never do the concert?"

Sooner sets the microwave to high and turns to look at her.

He slips one of the leathery-looking eggs onto her plate. "Then you'll figure out what you *are* going to do."

"People judge me here," Ruby says. She tells Sooner about the last time she saw old Pearl. How the woman was polite but chilly. Ruby had brought her mother to church and Pearl made a fuss over Barbara even as she fixed Ruby with a stern eye. Afterward, there was coffee in the church basement, and when the ladies filed into seats at the long, paper-topped tables, Ruby's pretty sure Pearl stepped aside so as not to have to sit next to her. "I mean, what is she, five?"

"Welcome to the human race."

It's so cold in the house. Their breath is silver, lifting to the ceiling in clouds. Somewhere else living things are coupling and fighting and making up. People are singing and eating cereal. Someone is knocking at a neighbor's door. But it's so perfectly still here.

Ruby takes a bite of toast, ignoring the ghastly egg. "Things didn't turn out...*I* didn't turn out the way I thought I would."

"Aw, Ruby. We're all of us changing. Always. You, me, your mom. Val and Tim and whatever guy sold you gas on the way up here. When our bodies change, when our circumstances change. How we feel about it. That's just the way it is." Sooner shrugs. "And then it ends. No one gets out of this world alive, right? And me so handsome." He laughs. "But that doesn't mean we can't own the time we've got."

"Where have you been the last twenty years?" Ruby says.

"Ruby."

"Val is surrounded by people who have known her all her life." Ruby thinks about the manager at NorthPine, his bow tie and the cake. "Newer friends...death is the hard stop. You get to a point where there's no more time to know someone well. For them to know you."

Sooner smiles, his face gentle. "I don't think you're there yet."

Ruby pauses. "Thanks for helping with the rocks. I've known you for a long time."

"I like you, Ruby."

"Thank God." She sets the plate with its untouched egg on the counter, then steps to him and kisses him, calmly. "Is there anything I can do? For you?"

"I'm good," Sooner says.

"You are," she says. "I have to go see Mom," she says, looking out at the trees, which are bright and bare. Then she says something strange. "This is my home."

"I know. Take some more toast. Take a piece of bacon. And I fixed your wipers this morning. They were for shit." The sun at this time of day: his hat, ribbed pink wool, is lit around the edges. The hat isn't greasy, or unraveled. Not in this light, which softens the ruined planes of his face. She won't see him ever again, but it's a good image to take with her into the world.

&

Ruby drives quickly, the M&Ms she bought rattling in her purse like a castanet. Woods stream past—the broadleaf hardwoods of white ash, soft maple, basswood—and the sky is high, a polished blue. All the steps to get through this next day, and the days after that. It is easy to imagine that she might lose heart. But she got a text from Lorna—*You're beautiful! I miss you!*—and she has coffee in the car. Sooner filled a red thermos for her, its silver insides scaly from use—and he put milk in it, lots of it, as if he knew.

He told her to keep the turtleneck, and though it's scratchy, it makes her feel brave. She's fastened Mom's pin to the thick folded neckline, and when she glances in the rearview mirror she can see it, how light reflects softly from the pearls like a glory.

Now she's at Marathon County Memorial, which is cheerful in the daylight. As cheerful as a hospital can be expected to be, anyway. Some of the plants banked against the glass in the front atrium bear waxy blooms.

"I've come to see my mom," Ruby tells the woman at the information desk, and smiles. There was the kindness behind that coffee, thick as motor oil, and a delicate light flooding her car. The way the tree trunks gleamed. It all gives her a feeling that might be hope if she doesn't examine it too closely.

The woman is a different one from last night, weathered and sensible, and she looks up Barbara's name and tells Ruby in a pleasant country voice how to get to the room. She is probably a local, and it pleases Ruby when the woman smiles back at her and writes Barbara's room number on a little paper. There is the business of the elevator, crowded with young people carrying stuffed toys and an IT'S A BOY Mylar balloon. They get off first, a laughing, jostling mob, and then Ruby rides alone to the third floor, which is quiet, as if snow has fallen there.

She pauses, having suddenly lost her momentum. The hallway is wide, with a nurse's station at the end, and closed doors all along it. She wonders if she should have brought a gift— magazines, a clutch of flowers, a balloon like the one she saw in the elevator. But there is no balloon for what she wants to say. *Don't Die. Please Be My Mom Again.* Ruby starts walking briskly down the hallway, looking at the room numbers. She hears a buzzing, but maybe it's the overhead lights. Ruby's hands are empty.

Here it is.

In Barbara's room, the blinds are pulled and her mother lies still. Her hair is a drift of down across her pillow; she grips a stuffed animal in her hand. A lobster. Hand foxed like the pages of a book. The room smells faintly of urine, though the linoleum floor is clean, and the bed, small in that great expanse of tile, seems rooted to the floor by a tangle of tubes.

"Hi, Mama," Ruby says. Her mother's eyes are open, and glitter; as they regard each other it is as though Ruby's whole life has come rushing, heedless, to this place. She fumbles in her purse. "I brought you a cookie. From the gas station. See?" Ruby stops. She won't talk to her mother the way she might talk to Junie, to a child. She won't do that to her, she won't do it to herself.

"Eddie?"

Ruby reaches up and touches her own hair—how many days has it been, now, since she took a shower? It clings to her skull like a cap. "No, this is Ruby, Mom," she says, and stands perfectly still.

"Ruby!" Barbara says. Her voice slurs with effort, and this is something new. In the past year, her voice has become soft and whispery, as dry as paper. It is still soft—Ruby has to lean in to hear—but it is also thick, all the words seeming joined. Probably the stroke. Or whatever it was. Ruby hugs herself and decides that her mother sounds pleased. "Ruby, do I know you?" (*Ruy-eedoahknawya.*) Ruby can see her mother squinting earnestly, her face naked and shiny across the cheekbones, which are broad, like Val's, and look burnished.

On the nightstand are Barbara's glasses. The frames, large plastic rounds, are tinted pink, like the inside of a mouth. Ruby bends to arrange them on her mother's face and sees the copse of bristly hairs on her mother's chin. She takes a seat on the edge of the bed and stares out at the bright hallway. "Well, I think you know me." The hallway walls are clinical yellow, cracked from years of extremes: the heat, the cold. "Better than most people." There is a space in Ruby's chest, growing, as film burns, from the inside out; if she isn't careful, all the good feelings from this morning might leak out. She thinks of Sooner, and that makes her brave. She leans to turn on the bedside lamp.

"I broke my tooth," she says. Her mother's glasses wink like a signal Ruby cannot know.

"If you have your. Teeth. When you die," Barbara mutters. "They last. In the grave. Bones," she says.

Ruby moves her shoulders. Her mother's words slur together, but Ruby can understand. "Let's not talk about dying. Okay?"

"Dying," Barbara agrees. Somewhere down the hall, someone is humming. Humming like a purr, low and contented, but in a minor key.

"Damn tooth still hurts," Ruby says. She knows she would be comforted if her mother cared, the way she used to.

"Mmmmmmpf," Barbara grunts. "You look. You look like my...hmmmmm." She plucks at the lobster. "My girls."

Ruby shifts her weight and tries to move so she can feel her mother, who is hidden, it seems, in the high narrow bed. "Mama, tell me, do you think I'm a good person?" She has to ask it, after all. "I threw rocks in a pool," she adds, idiotically. "It wasn't a very nice thing to do, but still, I was glad." Ruby gently slips the stuffed lobster from Barbara's grasp. Her mother's room at the senior center is full of stuffed animals won at Bingo, their faces pouched and dusty. Someone—Val probably—has brought this one, their mother's favorite, to the hospital; Ruby takes the creature into her hands, cradling it.

"That...on my pillow," Barbara whispers. "One side. Cat— my cat. Other one. Side."

When Ruby was a child, the limit was three stuffed animals per bed. If she or Val got a new one, they had to figure out which creature in the existing animal family had to go. There would be tears, saying goodbye to Herm the elephant, or Poppy, a stuffed dog with a torn ear. But that was the rule; Barbara, a frazzled single mother saddled with a dying farm, had no time for beds loaded with plush. "It takes you too long to make your bed as it is," she said once, standing at the door of ten-year-old Ruby's room, arms folded across her chest. She was daunting but almost elegant, the way she stared down Ruby's tiny stuffed animals. She wasn't being mean; that was just how it was. Even then Ruby knew how tired she was.

Ruby moves the tiny plush claws so that it looks like the lobster is waving. "Because, Mama, I don't want to be one of those people, those people who never know the meaning of what has happened to them."

Ruby sets the lobster carefully back on her mother's pillow. There is so little left, after all: Barbara's life pared down again and again. First the house was streamlined and sold, Barbara's possessions made to fit into a single room in the nursing wing. When she got a roommate, Ruby helped Val edit the blouses and pants in Barbara's closet by half. And now here they are. It is impossible to predict what things, in the end, will stay with us. Ruby tucks the lobster against her mother's cheek. Parents and children, she thinks. The way they take turns protecting one another.

Barbara's eyes glisten. "Ruby! I have two...girls," she says. A long moment passes. The humming from the hallway comes closer, so close Ruby thinks she might have to say hello. The humming stops and someone walks quickly away.

"You think I make good choices?" Ruby's throat makes a clicking sound. "Remember how I went away?"

"Did you see my lobster?" Barbara asks. *Didjaseemylobstah?* Ruby bends closer, and her mother's head jerks on the pillow. "Listen. You comin' to take me? Out of here?"

"Oh, Mama." Ruby sighs. "I like your lobster. It's sweet."

"Val? Sweet Valentine," Barbara whispers.

"No, Mama. I'm Ruby."

"Oh." Barbara gazes upward.

It has been years, but Ruby feels a pull like stitches. She misses her father, or at least the idea of him. Ed might understand, she thinks, and perhaps he could have warned her, years ago, what it's like to get away, to go away and still be disappointed.

"I went back to the old house," Ruby says. "It looks...well, I don't know. It's hard to know what I want things to be." She is quiet for a moment. "I don't know if I belong anywhere, Mom."

"No," Barbara agrees, her voice pleasant. Then her face straightens. She peers at Ruby. "You played guitar," she says, perfectly clearly.

"Mama?"

"You could...play to me. My. House. I could sleep, and you'd be. Singing."

Ruby starts to cry then. The things we expect from the dead, the dying. She crosses her arms over her chest, grabbing fistfuls of Sooner's sweater. The pearl pin rocks in her hand, edges sharp but the pearls cool.

The things we expect. After the Parkinson's descended,

Ruby wasn't jealous anymore of how motherhood brought Val and Barbara together. But once, Ruby can remember coming to town, and she and her mother were standing in the kitchen. Ruby wanted more, and she wanted it to be something special just between the two of them. She asked Barbara about Ed, what he was really like, and where he lived, and if she, Ruby, was like him. She kept asking about her father until Barbara cried, until Moon came in and told her to stop.

"Mom," she says. The shadows in the room are the blue of snow at night. Blue like the print in Barbara's room, the view into another world. "I'm glad you like the picture I gave you," she says.

"Ruby?" Barbara turns toward the lamplight, her eyes glossy as a doll's. "My...girls," she sighs. "Mystery."

The sun ticks against the blinded window. Barbara covers her eyes with her hand, peering through her fingers. "Okay," she says. "Okay." Her face becomes crafty, conspiratorial. "You know...Ruby? My Val?"

"A little," Ruby manages to say.

Barbara closes her eyes. She pats the blanket, reaches up to the pillow, her hand closing around the stuffed lobster. "Mine," she mumbles. "Swim." She almost seems to sleep. "I hope my girls are...happy." *Ihopemygurlarehap.* Ruby leans close. "Don't you?"

It all comes together then: the smell in the kitchen, of coffee and cornmeal; drizzly spring afternoons spent studying, studying, to get out of this place, rain tapping staccato against the metal sheeting Moon had used as a back porch roof, plump floret of meringue melting on Ruby's tongue as she wrestled through another equation. The touch of Barbara's rough hand, very light, against Ruby's neck, when she thought Ruby might not notice.

"I was," Ruby whispers. "I can be." She cups Barbara's chin and her hand brushes the stubble, hairs gray and stiff as wire. "Mama," she says. "We have to do something about your chin."

Ruby rummages through her purse and withdraws a pair of

tweezers. She tries to carry everything in her purse. Sometimes she has what she needs, after all. She turns the lamp so she can see Barbara's face clearly, and Barbara lifts her chin, closing her eyes like a cat in the sun. Ruby works slowly and carefully, gently holding her mother's chin in her hands. Barbara grunts with pleasure, though the last few hairs are softer and harder to grip. "There you go," Ruby says finally.

"Mystery," Barbara says. The room is dim save for the circle of lamplight. But later, when Ruby thinks back to this moment, it is as though she and her mother were bathed in sunlight. Years later, that's how she'll remember it. How for a moment she saw Barbara in all her incarnations. Ruby has known them or heard about them so many times that it is as though she has witnessed them all: the girl with knobby knees who worshipped her brother; the young bride who loved dancing; the mother who had to accept that she would raise her children with a different man; the old woman who clung to life even in its diminished state.

Ruby turns out the light. Wasn't this what she and Val have both always lobbied for, these moments with Barbara?

She is a solitary, sitting in darkness.

BARBARA

Magic Lantern

She works her mouth around the teeth remaining to her.

For a moment the nurse seems to be saying it is time to check her blood pressure. No. Ruby. Ruby's voice coming to Barbara while she is sleeping. But she isn't asleep, and here is her lobster.

Ruby.

Sometimes images appear just behind her eyes, like slides from a magic lantern show: holding her child. The smart one. Ruby, but younger, smaller, her hair plain brown but soft like corn silk, lit by late-day sun. Face wet with tears, because there was something about the other girls, girls in the same grade but they didn't understand the books Ruby loved. They were jealous. They made fun. Barbara, holding Ruby, knew her oldest would have to look elsewhere.

Valentine always had friends. She fit in, and then Valentine was telling her, *Mama, I'm having a baby*, her young, beautiful face a balance of fear and pride. They'd been standing outside the house, in the dooryard, and through the bare branches of the trees you could see the river. The river was brown and strong and Barbara thought about how it would still be there long after she'd died, and Valentine, and even the baby. All these things she couldn't explain, how a baby would take them all just that little bit further, and she had cried out with real joy. She was glad her younger daughter had seen that. "When your kids are happy, you're happy," she'd said to Valentine.

For years she wrote letters, even after that had gone out of fashion, to her friends and family. After a while some of her friends took sick. Some died. There were fewer people to remember with and so she wrote to their children. She wrote to Ruby, who lived in a city with a skyline like blocks. Memory makes us who we are, she wanted to tell her daughter.

Almost everyone is gone. Though there's Pearl, and her own body, which she has lived in for so long. It sometimes feels unfamiliar now.

One time, Barbara had swum across the lake, her sturdy brown legs pumping. Water streamed off her when she stepped up on the mucky opposite shore.

My God, she had been splendid.

CHOIR

Roundelay

The woods are black, and Val runs in her thin shoes, not registering the frozen ground; Dakota, who woke when her mother cried out, runs behind her. They are both afraid, because they heard the steady *buvve buvve buvve* sound, and although they do not yet understand that it is the sound of a semi-automatic rifle, the noise is frightening in its unfamiliarity. Even as she runs Dakota imagines how she might paint this scene: the trees, the red she might use, the dark slashes of cobalt. Darkness holds many colors. She cannot help herself; it is how she sees it. She follows her mother, feet pounding, and the earth chimes like an iron bell.

They arrive in the little clearing out of breath; Junie stands beside the rabbit pens, and there is no cat, there will never be Jellybean again, but the strange man, Berryman, is there, patting the crying child sternly, and the rabbits mill and grunt.

"Damn cat tried to eat my rabbits," the man growls, pointing at a break in the wire pen. "I chased it out and then I shot at it." His face is stone; he won't apologize for this. Only Dakota sees the gun leaning against the fence. She doesn't know that it is a Kalashnikov, Russian made and from the war; that's Berryman's souvenir, taken from the hands of a dead mujahid. But she guesses that it killed Jelly, that it probably blew Jelly to pieces. In the dark she can't see the blood, but she takes her sister's hand.

"Never mind," Val says, and Dakota understands that her mother has seen the gun too. Val, crouching on her knees in the damp path, holds both girls to her coat, the top buttons as shiny and black as berries. Later they will both be grounded, their television privileges revoked because of everything that has happened, but for this moment they are blameless; she knows something about loss, Val does, but to lose a child. "Dakota," she whispers. "Junebug." Her relief is without limit.

"I'm here," she tells her girls and looks around the clearing, eyes fierce.

The girls murmur that they love her, and Val says, "I know." Mothers always know.

The three walk home, to the messy green house that is a good place, Val understands, because her daughters are growing up there. Someday they will leave that house, and her and Len, too, but not yet. Not yet. It will be Val and Len who teach their girls how to endure. Len is steady. She's always known that. Others will help as they can. Ruby, in her way. Val thinks of Bryan, driving the Great Plains with his guitar sliding across the back seat. She will have to decide if he is worth the risk. Sometimes you have to guess.

                        ॐ

And Tim and Carrie, twined in the big bed in their own home with the clock and the sculpture, naked and eating jam on bread. Morning. Yesterday such a strange day, and Tim knows from what Carrie doesn't say that she hates Ruby and is intimidated by her.

"Those pants!" Carrie says drowsily, her pretty face hungry.

"What did you say to her?" Tim asks. "She got so upset." In the end, Ruby and Carrie had a keen intelligence in common, and him, and that combination had filled the rooms. Tim rolls over, stroking Carrie's back. He loves his dark angry wife, a prettier version of the woman he loved first; closing his eyes, he remembers what he felt when he understood that Ruby's life could no longer contain their relationship. That maybe it never had.

"Oh God," Carrie says. "I can't even remember. Do you know she gave us a used stuffed animal? What are we supposed to do with that?"

They laugh, and Tim puts the plates on the floor, just crusts left over, with smears of the red jam. He turns off the light.

They left a lot of lights on last night. It's still dark out, too early to get up. He lays his hand on Carrie's belly; he imagines how their child will grow. There will be that luminous indefinite time before she has to confront her own limitations; he expects to extend that as long as he can, for her sake, or perhaps because it is gratifying to him. He wants his daughter to know her own inner light.

Sighing, he scratches at the cat extending heavy beside him, and he is happy in spite of it all—his in-laws, who meddle; the vandalism of the motel pool, which he hasn't yet discovered. The fact of his own average gifts.

ॐ

Len springs out of bed the moment Val wakes him. Thinking it is Barbara at first, his hearing such as it is and the way Val says, *She's gone; she's gone.* He has to sit down on the edge of the bed then, to understand, and Val puts her arm around him.

Later, he is the one who goes back for Jelly's body, and there are only pieces, really. He pulls on gloves and puts what is left of the cat in a plastic bag, and then a shoebox; he tapes the box shut so the girls won't see.

On Sunday they will stand in the backyard together. Five of them—him, the girls, his Val, Ruby—by a rock Junie has painted with jellybeans in thick, glossy acrylic. Junie will cry, clutching the new stuffed cat; she holds it out in front of her as though she is blind. Len will dig a hole for Jellybean. He will remove his cap. Modest heroics. This is what he can give them, especially Val with the burdens she carries. He will take her elbow, pointed as a shard.

ॐ

Dakota knows she can paint the way it felt, the dark night opening up and the way Mama held them both. Buttons pressed against her cheek so they left marks. Closing her eyes weeks after the fact, Dakota sees blacks and yellows and smiles at their intensity. She could show Bryan her painting, if she ever meets him. Maybe he would understand her. Most boys do.

And women? Dakota thinks of Aunt Ruby, who liked her mural. Her grandma's kindness. Her mother is strong and fierce—there is a safety about her—though Dakota is not ready to admit that to anyone, not even herself. She is not ready to wonder about her mother as a person. Junie. It is hard to dislike Junie.

❧

Mice trace paths through the construction dust, leaving careless tiny turds in the kitchen, and Sooner lies in his bed downstairs, the room he prefers to the loft on nights when his bones hurt as if their very marrows are ground glass. When he cannot sleep he plays the guitar, not as well as Ruby but the music is still satisfying. He thinks of the woods that go from here nearly up to Superior. Worms turning the earth there, but indoors, too, in bins he has built himself; he can almost hear this and he pauses for a moment, joyful.

He is grateful for every sunrise. For the fact that Ruby will remember him. He doesn't, after all this time, expect too much.

❧

A machine that powers her mother clicks and buzzes. Barbara is sleeping. Ruby watches her face, soft with sleep and with the dementia. She digs in her purse and finds the pumpkin cookie, still of a piece in its napkin; she lays it on the tray table beside the bed.

Her mother can't tell Ruby who she is, not anymore. And who are we when we can no longer tell any version of the story of our lives?

Sometimes there is someone left to tell it for us. Someone who loves us, the way Ruby and Val love Barbara. Someone who admires us, the way Ruby hopes Sooner admires her. Everyone gone soon enough, but still. Ruby thinks about what Sooner might be doing even now, and it comforts her that she can still imagine it, for a little longer.

And sometimes we are left to tell the story for ourselves.

Ruby closes her eyes and concentrates on her breathing,

which she times to her mother's. In this way time passes; eventually, she sleeps. She dreams. In the dream she is her mother, before Ed left, and as Barbara, she exults in her handsome husband and two perfect girls. Strange, to see herself from her mother's eyes; Ruby in the dream might be seven years old or so, swimming in the river, thick arms arcing into the water, pale but strong. She learned to swim in that water. "Be careful!" she calls to her childhood self. "Take care!" Her voice urgent, loving.

It is late when Ruby wakes and stands in the dark room, shaking off her dream like sheets of green water. A concerto is supposed to be for an orchestra, Ruby thinks. And yet one musician, on one instrument, can play Bach's work. Ruby stretches. Her mother sleeps. *I'm lonely here*, Ruby thinks, even as she understands that if she were home, it would probably be the same. She rubs her mouth. Some things you just have to get through.

It is later still when she swings her heavy purse over her shoulder, when she decides that she is ready, after all, to move forward. To see what happens next, as fearfully and wonderfully as it might.

Moon

Goodbye

He had hoped to die at home and Val arranged for hospice, but in the end he died before they could get him there. In the hospital Moon's days passed. Mid-afternoon, the autumn sky pasted a square of blue light across his bed.

He slept and when he woke he told Babs—he was the only one who could call her that—that he had been dreaming of the yellow birch, which grew in the dooryard at home. *Again*, she said, smiling. That tree was his favorite, the way black scored the bark. Moon liked that about the tree, its scarring and imperfection. He had seen what perfection—or trying for it—could do. He had seen it destroy strong men, and he didn't want any of it. He told Barbara, again, that he would like to sit under that tree, that he would like to die there. One time, long ago, his niece Ruby had come home for a visit and taught him tai chi there. Moon closed his eyes and imagined the movements of his hands and body.

It's all right to go now, Babs said. She was to one side of him, then the other; it was impossible to tell how much time had passed. Though she wasn't religious, she wore a cross around her neck, flat and gold, luminous as the birch. People wanted Barbara there when they died. She held them. She had been present when their own father had died from cancer too. From a young age she had been a comfort and had somehow understood the secrets of dying; she had known what to say. Though she herself was failing, she rallied when Moon got sick. She held him against her sweater and he could hear her heart beating beneath the red wool. He sat up when he could, and told Babs that things had been worse, and they had been; Vietnam was much worse. He'd seen there how little regard life could be given—how poor it could be. His desperate prayers were never answered in that place. Perhaps it had been watched over by different gods. When he returned home, he'd even lost faith in life for a while; now he didn't want it to end.

Persistence had gotten him through before. He wanted to see how things went for his nieces, whom he'd loved as if they were his own. They came and ranged around his bed—the littles, too, one named after a month and the other after a state. Was it April? Montana? Ridiculous, their names, but they were good girls. He opened his mouth to tell them so. The night-blooming cereus, he wanted to say, is cream and ivory. It blooms for one night only. Babs took his hand and told him, hush, it's all right. In the next moment, he had forgotten what he meant to say. Something about staying power. There were always black days, but you got through.

He drifted, and when he woke Babs was alone; the girls had gone. (That was as it should be, he knew.) Don't cry, he told her. He would not make it to the tree. Hush, Babs said, let go, and he drew the last breath in.

RUBY

Be Here Now

It is storming again. In the parking lot, the sky is black water; ice rains down. When did the day change into night? When did the rains begin? Ruby stands at the glass entrance doors, watching the sky open. A nurse runs in past her, holding a magazine over her head to shield it. Her hair is protected by a plastic hood. "Some weather!" the woman cries and Ruby says what weather indeed. The nurse stands in the vestibule, shaking out her wet coat. "You know someone here?" Her voice is kind.

"My mom," Ruby says. "Barb Kopecky?"

"Nice lady," the nurse says, offering Ruby the magazine.

The time she and her mother have had is a happiness. Their relationship all its own. "Yes," Ruby says. She nods and takes the magazine, holding it over her head as she runs outside, the soggy pages collapsing against her palms and wrists, her feet slapping through a crust of ice.

Inside her car, Ruby sets the wipers going, and they are perfect, working as they should so that the glass is clear. She sees her sister run through the storm then, into the harsh light of the entryway. Val's headscarf is dark with sleet; her blouse billows beneath the hem of a coat that looks rough as blanket. Her prettiness is striking, even in neglect, and she is flanked by her daughters; inside the front doors, Val puts her arms around each child, and the three with their heads down, together, are their own world. The girls look like their mother, Ruby realizes, and in that moment she knows that she will never have children of her own. She thinks about Tim and Carrie, their gift of ease in the world.

Sleet batters the car and Ruby gropes in her pocket for Tim's joint, which she finds and lights. The summer before college, she and Tim used to take his truck to the patchwork of farmer's fields outside of town. One night, naked under a blanket, they smoked and talked about the nature of love. "It shapes a person," he'd said. Tim's face was alert, inward-looking—as earnest as his lovemaking, she'd thought then, disparaging. Love had nothing to do with what a person can become, she'd retorted. She'd felt love as an obligation. She'd felt her own life opening out then, love and Ladyford and her childhood in its slipstream. Now she wonders if Tim actually pitied her.

Ruby smokes the joint down, the seeds popping and bits of ash blowing red. She pokes at her tooth with her tongue. Tim had said she would need a root canal once she got home, but that the tooth would ultimately survive, thrive even, despite its unseemly state. We're called upon to reinvent ourselves, again and again, as long as we can, Ruby thinks. And what secret part exists within each of us that resists decay? Wasn't that what Sooner was trying to say? And there was Moon, fighting the cancer. Becoming and dying at the same time.

In moments or hours Val will come back out this door, this lighted entryway. "I know you hate being here," she said to Ruby once, in earshot of their mother, after a fight between the sisters. This was years ago, before Moon took sick, or Barbara. Ruby herself had not understood that it wasn't Val, or Tim, or even this place she renounced, that in fact she had spent a lifetime trying to escape the little girl in the big body, the Ladybird who needed to be better at everything and didn't grow up—not really—until she wasn't anywhere near best anymore.

We love one another as best we can, Ruby thinks suddenly, watching the door. She sucks at the last of the joint. The fight she and Val had yesterday will fade. The appointment with Tim. But here was the secret that no one could tell you, that you had to learn for yourself: What she and Val have is better than nothing. If Ruby is smart, she will accept that. Sooner or later all this will end—first for Barbara, then for one of them, then for the other. Death lives within them. This is what they have to work with.

Something kindles within her; she might wait here and call out to her sister when Val returns. Ruby straightens in her seat. She will.

ॐ

Val never hears about the promotion, which Ruby ultimately doesn't accept. Sooner will already be dead when Ruby starts teaching piano, but when she returns to Ladyford for his memorial she will tell Val about that, how she posted notices at Book Cellar and at a coffeehouse Ruby likes, called Kopi. Kopi is where she stayed for hours the morning Val called her to say that Sooner was gone. She wore her red sweatpants that day, the sparkly ones; they were snug, but she'd wanted them for a long time. She wore Sooner's sweater.

And Kopi is where she will meet up with Shelly, one of Lorna's friends. Lorna organizes the date and the three of them get together, dipping flat biscuits into coffee and searching for common ground. Ruby doesn't really connect with Shelly, a harried mother who seems stressed and uninterested in friendship. Shelly talks mostly to Lorna, but the woman has three children; the oldest is named Ellen, and Ellen will become Ruby's first student. Perhaps that is what Lorna had in mind the entire time. Bespectacled, pale, the girl has the long fingers of a musician.

The women meet on a Tuesday morning. Ruby will always remember that she brought along *Man's Search for Meaning* to read. She arrived early and read the book at a table near the door. When Lorna and Shelly arrived, she laid it in her lap, and when Lorna asked about it, Ruby tried to explain.

"I learned about this book from Sooner," Ruby will tell Lorna. She will say the same to Val at Sooner's service, which takes place weeks later, in March, a crust of snow like iron still laid against the ground. "Frankl talks about how, you know, when you can't change a situation? But you can change how you look at it."

Val will listen intently, her face still. Ruby doesn't know what her sister is thinking. She never asks what she'd like to: if she ever was the sister Val wanted.

"I think he's basically talking about knowing what to accept," is what Ruby says. God, Ruby misses Sooner. But there is Lorna's kindness. There is the warmth Ruby feels when she suggests to Val how Dakota might like Kopi, how maybe her niece should come for a visit.

"She'd like that," Val says, looking happy herself.

Ruby, who sees her sister's smile, will not guess what Val thinks, which is, *It has always been so.*

Sooner will have asked that Ruby play something by Bob Dylan at his memorial. She chooses "Forever Young," which she thinks she can manage and practices at home on the walnut Kimball. During the service there is a time for testimonials, and Ruby will stand at the front of the church, twisting her pin with its shining pearls, and say that Sooner was kind. Wise and perceptive. She is awkward but happy, or happier, at least, and the happiness makes her feel beautiful, even when Pearl corners her downstairs.

"Tell me about your grandkids," Ruby says, summoning kindness because the woman is good to her mother. The reception is right after the service, in the church basement, and church women ladle dumplings and stew onto every plate. At the end of the line is an enormous sheet cake, iced white and decorated with frosting rosettes colored yellow and blue. "Sooner would like this," Ruby tells Pearl, and takes two pieces of the cake. She eats it all, and marvels that Sooner is dead while her own mother has attended the memorial. Confined to a wheelchair, but still. "Ellen, the kid I'm teaching?" Ruby will say to Val, reaching over to take Barbara's hand. Barbara stares past her, smiling though she says nothing. "Ellen reminds me of a young Dakota. Yeah. Sure, I still have my day job. It pays the bills, right?"

But all this—Kopi, the way Ruby looks forward to seeing Ellen each week, and the grace of Sooner's service—is still ahead. All the years yet to pass, after the farm is sold to developers, after Barbara dies in her sleep and when Ruby herself will grow old. She will try her best to act in the way she thinks her mother would have wanted her to. She will persist, because Barbara's tenacity, her toughness and lack of false sentiment, live within her. And Moon's resolve: these things are part of her, even as her own body changes, again and again.

ॐ

Ruby finishes her joint, liking the way sleet glazes the windshield. It is beautiful in its way. The fields and meadows had been so lush that last summer with Tim. They had been beautiful too: At the end of the day deer grazed unafraid in the tall grasses, their heads dipping in and out of sight as they fed. This was before the fire, which leveled everything, clearing the decks for something new. She had had her plans. But this is where she came from, and as such, it is worthy of love or at least respect.

If Ruby listens, she can probably hear the river, constant, unseen, sighing but tireless in the gathering darkness.